CW01279070

Lost and Found

A house recalled to life

Chloë Rayban

For David Johnston
- who loved this house as much as I do.

Published by Ours et Ourson
March 2015

'Ours et Ourson' is an independent publisher of novels, poetry and non-fiction
(biography, travel, art). For more information, go to www.oursetourson.com

ISBN 978-1-326-19004-0

March 2015

Lost and Found

To hold something and turn it round in your hand, knowing that someone else, long ago, has run their fingers along these same curves and edges. It makes you wonder who they were, what their lives were like and what became of them. When Julia found objects lost or hidden or buried in her French manoir, they set her on a quest to learn their stories. The facts she uncovered changed her own life in a way she could hardly have envisaged.

Chapter One

Julia 2009

I'd spotted the tower from the road, catching tantalising glimpses of its roof, a gleaming pyramid of slate, through the trees. Coming to the crest of a rise, I slowed down to get my first decent sighting of the place. It was vast, much bigger than the photos had suggested. Not just one but several buildings. It looked more like a village than a house. The mad man. Typical of Dad to leave us in a mess like this. God how I missed him.

Another bend revealed a better view. The whole roof, a wide sweep of mossy slate with the tower beyond. Straining my eyes through the trees I nearly missed the turning and took it wide, skidding on the gravel.

'La Mulatière' - a scrawled hand-painted sign leaned against a plinthe of weathered stone. There was an avenue of sorts, the trees overgrown with something thorned and spiky that reached half way up their trunks. Now nosing my way between them I got a view of the house full on. I caught my breath. The 'chateau' they'd called it in the village. And it was certainly built on a grand scale. Dad had been vague when quizzed about its size. Now I could see why.

I drew to a halt, climbed out and stretched. My legs were stiff from driving so long. The slam of the car door echoed with a hollow sound through the building. I stared assessingly at the façade.

The house had a blind abandoned look with all its shutters closed like that. And they'd stay closed by the look of it - a thick tangle of wisteria had grown up over them, caging them in. The roof wasn't in bad nick. Some of the zinc needed renewing, it had rusted to holes and come loose in places. And there was an ugly stain where a gutter had been overflowing for god knows how long. At that height it would be expensive to repair.

'Mad *totally* mad,' I thought. The sooner we got shot of the place the better.

I glanced at my watch. It was seven already. The agent had been vague about the lighting situation. I wanted to get settled inside before sunset. I tried the heavy iron doorknob, it turned but the door didn't give, evidently locked from the inside.

The agent had said that the '*femme de menage*' would leave the key for me in something called the '*chateau d'eau*' which was to be found at the rear of the building. I left the car where it was and started to force a path through the lush tangle of weeds along the side of the house. Plants sticky with burrs clung to my ankles and I felt the angry prickle of nettle-rash spread up my shins.

There was a courtyard behind, enclosed by two wings. These were not so grand, looked more like old farm buildings than the rest of the manoir. The courtyard was bordered on the fourth side by a sagging oak-beamed barn. I recognised the '*chateau d'eau*' from the agent's description. It had another pyramidal tower but this time roofed in rosy terracotta tiles. I'd thought this must be a '*pigeonniere*' in Dad's photos. The little building had a neglected charm, its crumbling coating of lime revealing creamy stonework around the doorway and window, its conical roof of faded tiles tipped up at the edges in a way I'd noticed on buildings en route - peculiar to the region.

The door was secured by a heavy hand-forged hook. As I forced it open there was a scuffle inside and a cat shot out of the darkness and came mewing towards me. It tried to rub its body against my legs. I shooed it off. It was one-eyed, looked feral, flea-ridden at any rate. The house was probably infested with heaven knows what.

As my eyes grew accustomed to the gloom, I spotted the key left as promised, hanging in a thicket of spider webs. It was a monster of a thing, a stage jailor's key of blistered iron.

I turned back to the house. The late evening sun was reflecting back off warm stone. The tower loomed above, hard-edged against a forget-me-not sky. This courtyard was a sun trap in the evening. Cleared of weeds and brambles and with a few chairs out - it would be a place to sip an evening drink or two and watch the sun dip down, as it was doing now behind the chateau d'eau. I wondered if Dad had sat out here. I could picture him now, glass in hand, head tipped at an angle over some book or other. And it would have been more than a couple of drinks I thought wryly. I pulled myself up at this. No need to get maudlin. I'd better get on with finding a way inside.

The mammoth key turned easily in the back door lock. My first impression was the overpowering smell. Of what? Goat's cheese perhaps? Once inside I was dwarfed by the dimensions of the room. A massive chimney-piece dominated one side, rough-plastered and rimmed round with a garishly yellow painted shelf. Underneath stood an old farm sink of scratched stone with a single tap. The tiles around the sink were of the turkish style popular in the 50's and that inevitable cream and brown.

But the room was warm. I tracked the warmth down to the old range. A heavy iron casserole had been left simmering on the hob. As promised, the *femme de menage* had provided my supper. I lifted the lid. Some kind of stew. It smelt OK, I just prayed it wasn't rabbit.

Another door led to a further room. A welcoming wood fire burned in the hearth and the table was set with a plate, knife and fork and a single wine glass. A fresh baguette was wrapped in a napkin and a bottle of St Pourçain was open beside it. Under a tea towel there was a further bowl filled with salad topped with chopped parsley, a jug of vinaigrette. Some salad servers were placed next to the bowl ready to toss it. Nice of her.

I tore off a knob of bread. I hadn't wanted to stop on the drive down from Calais, afraid I might not arrive before nightfall. It would've been a nightmare trying to locate the house in the dark. I slopped some wine into the glass. If I wanted to see the rest of the house in daylight, I'd better get a move on. Taking my glass, I started on a tour of inspection.

Beyond the doorway a further room was in darkness. My groping hand located the light switch. A single bulb illuminated a high room, empty except for a dilapidated piano. The room had massive beams, whitened, limed perhaps. The walls were covered in some hideous orange fabric, torn in places revealing the rough chalk and stones beneath. But the thickness of them! I could see by the depth of the windows - the walls were a good metre thick. Whoever had built this house had built it to last. I lifted the lid of the piano and it yielded a discordant strum of broken bass notes that echoed eerily in the emptiness.

Two sets of double doors led into a further room. This was in darkness. I tried the light switch - nothing. Locating my torch at the bottom of my bag, I swung an arc of light around the room. A broken candelabra hung in a Miss Havishamesque fashion, skeined in spider webs. My footsteps made a hollow sound in the empty space. In turning, my eye caught a chilling vision in the torch beam, a wraithlike figure standing staring at me. My gasp turned to a laugh as I recognised my own reflection distorted in the fly-spotted overmantel mirror. I pulled myself together. Running my torch over the room I noted that although the paintwork was peeling, the panelling was still intact. Highlighting details, I marvelled at the decorative woodwork, lovingly fashioned, somehow feminine. The floors were in parquet, now dulled by time but only in need of a good waxing. This room ran the full depth of the house front to back and there were four sets of tall French windows. Shuttered, as it was now, the room was in deep gloom but once they were opened it must be like a winter garden - bathed in light. My heart was beating hard in my chest now. My initial nerves had gone, eclipsed by another emotion. This house was *a gem.*

'You old devil,' I whispered to Dad. 'You clever old devil.'

Another set of double doors led into the entry hall. This was a great barn of a place, lined in faux stonework with an armoire of massive proportions standing against one wall. A giant curve of oak stairs led the eye up to a beamed ceiling far above. I climbed the staircase with mounting excitement. My torch was failing. Why hadn't I thought to bring spare batteries?

At the top of the stairs I took the first doorway. This room was pitch black and the light switch didn't work. I felt my way to the window and swung open the catch. With a tug the window came open and I turned my attention to the shutters. These were harder to shift and when they actually gave, it was with a suddenness that caught me off balance.

The low evening sunlight flooded in, lighting up a room which had been lined with wood panelling ceiling to floor, carved eccentrically in the Art Nouveau style. The bed was framed in its sinuous curves and hung with faded silk.

'I think you'll like it,' Dad's voice echoed in my head. It was from that last phone call he'd made, from the bar in the village. 'There's one room in particular. Chap said it's panelled in lemon wood. Art Nouveau, or trying to be. Bit O.T.T. if you ask me.'

A bit O.T.T!

The bed had been made up for me with big soft pillows leaning on a bolster. The coarse white linen smelt faintly of lavendar. In the half light the lemon wood gleamed dully, carved into forms that were sensuous... satiny... This house was *sheer magic*.

Suddenly, I had to see everything while the light lasted. Doorways gave on room after room, bedrooms hung with spider webs and carpetted in dead flies but all high and beautifully proportioned, each with its fireplace and overmantel mirror. The rooms were en enfilade, leading one into another. No corridors. Confusing actually. A couple of times I doubled back and found myself in a room I'd been in before. There was one with three canvases painted with flowers above the doorways - by whom I wondered? I peered into the gloom. The were 19th Century in style, but unsentimentally executed.

Once I'd exhausted the first floor. At a first count, eight bedrooms in all and a single bathroom with a gargantuan roll top bath on lion's feet, I traced my way back to the stairway. Hang on. There was a door I hadn't noticed on my way up, leading from a half-landing midway down the staircase. A small oak door, elaborately panelled, fastened by two ornate bolts. These gave under pressure and I caught my breath - on the other side - a spiral of creamy stone steps led upwards - a castle staircase, hardly worn. I climbed, tense with anticipation. It must lead to the attic. Dad had said this was a showpiece.

It was. A cathedral space. Built of beams thick as ship's timbers, hewn and rivetted together with great wooden bolts, high as a church and somehow similarly awe-inspiring.

There were three shuttered dormers. I chose the central one and after a couple of tugs managed to wrench the shutters open. Unglazed and open to the elements this gave a staggering view of the countryside. The shape of the oval 'lawn' as Dad had described it, was still discernible. To the left was the decaying rim of an ancient fish pond. Beyond that, a maple tree flamed russet in the sunset. At the far end of the garden, dominating it all, was a vast tree - some kind of conifer, its dark foliage set in high relief against the smudgy contours of the countryside beyond. A Sequoia – its name came back to me now. Dad had said it was a good two hundred and fifty years old, that it had been planted to commemorate the founding of the house.

There was not a building in sight, nothing but rolling fields, close cropped by slow white cattle or ploughed in rutted terracotta, leading the eye away to a soft ridge of mauve-blue hills on the horizon. The whole lot of it right now was turning a persuasive peachy golden in the hazy lowlight.

Not a breath of wind disturbed the trees, not a car moved in the lanes. After the bustle of London, the traffic, the rumble and screech of the Tube, the taxis, car horns, police sirens, voices, phones, the endless phones ringing - the absence of noise was somehow unnerving. I leaned out. There was a shrill cry as some bird rose and flew across the lawn. *Phones*...that reminded me, I'd promised to ring Jane as soon as I got here. She wanted the lowdown. How much we could ask for the place? How soon could we put it on the market? 'As soon as', she said. 'We need the money for the loft extension. The twins and Miranda can't stay crammed in that one bedroom any longer.'

But still I lingered, resting on the lintel sipping my wine. The sunset was putting on a show, turning the maple to a ball of flame. A pair of swallows swept into the garden. Accustomed to having the place to themselves, they were dipping and swinging in arcs almost within my reach, their whistling cries sharp-tuned in the stillness. I leaned against the warm stone. It had stored the heat of the day and now it radiated it back - body temperature. The air was soft on my skin. It smelt of animals and leaf mould, wholesome and earthy. Pure heaven.

It was a conspiracy. Everything had conspired to bring me to this moment. That spell in hospital. Losing Dad. And then walking out on work like that. I breathed in a long draught of the freshness. This is what I needed. A break.

-------- -- -------

'So what's it like, *really* rundown?' Jane's voice was demanding at the other end of the line. I'd managed to get a decent signal at the far end of the garden.

'No... yes. I mean, it's terribly dilapidated. But what would you expect? Dad wasn't exactly loaded.'

'But is it *saleable*?'

'Dad bought it.'

'So?'

'Oh, I know but...'

'But what's it *like*?'

Gazing back at the house, I tried to be objective. The powdery grey of the shutters looked blue-mauve in the evening light and I noticed now that the wisteria, almost the same shade, was just coming into bloom.

'Vast. Much grander than it looked in the photos. Those long windows are massive. It must be incredibly light when the shutters are open.'

'*Freezing* in winter.'

'Umm, probably.' I realised she was waiting for negatives. 'All the rooms interconnect with double doors. No corridors - bedrooms all opening into each other...'

'Sounds like the set of a French farce.'

'Umm, could be fun.'

'What about the land? Dad said there were *hectares*.'

'The garden must've been lovely once. And there's a pond. But it's covered in weed.'

'But what sort of *condition* is the house in?'

'Well the roof looks OK, sort-of... And the walls are incredibly thick so it's not going to fall down or anything. There are parquet floors everywhere. So it won't need carpetting. Echoes like mad of course because it's empty.'

'Spooky. Don't you *mind*. Staying there on your own?'

I hesitated and then I suddenly realised I didn't. Even when I'd caught that fleeting glimpse of myself in the mirror, I'd only been scared for a moment. La Mulatière had a warmth to it you didn't usually associate with old houses. In fact, I felt safer here than I'd felt in ages. After everything that had happened recently, I guess sleeping in a deserted house was pretty tame stuff.

'No... No oddly enough, I don't mind at all. There's an incredible bedroom with a huge hung bed. Gloriously gothic. All made up for me. That woman from the village Dad found, she must be a gem. She's left me a hot meal and a proper salad... And there's a cat here. But it's only got one eye.'

'Ghastly! Rather you than me. You better get on to that notaire chappie right away.'

'I'll have to phone first for an appointment.'

'Ring him now. Sooner we get it settled the better.'

'Too late today. I'll get on to him tomorrow.'

'Listen, the twins are screaming. Better go before I'm one kid down. Keep me posted, OK? Lots of love. Ring me soon as you've seen him, won't you? Have a good night. Oh and Jules.. ?'

'Umm?'

'...mind the ghosties don't bite.'

She hung up.

'Ghosts?' I gazed back at the house now lying in deep shadow at the far end of the twilit garden. As a child, Dad had taught us never to be afraid of ghosts. Ghosts were people after all - only in a different time - that's what he'd said. Turn off time and we'd all be here at once. Imagine us crammed in together. Elbowing each other out of the way. Stepping aside to let people pass on the stairs. Sleeping in the same bed...

I walked slowly back across the grass, lumpy with generations of molehills. Frogs at the muddy base of the fish pond had set up a noisy repetetive chant. They paused as I passed and then started up again.

As I pushed the door open, the last rays of sunset entered the hallway illuminating the space with a rosy glow. I stood for a moment caught by a sense of wonder. All this was mine. Well ours if you like, it was Jane and Sarah's as well. This is how Dad must've felt. Fancy *owning* a house as grand as this. He must've been happy. But for so little time. This brought a hard lump into my throat. I went back into the kitchen and poured myself another glass of wine. I took a gulp and realised I was ravenous. The scent of the casserole lured me to the cooker.

I woke with a start in the night. What had woken me? It was the bright piping and warbling of some bird outside my window. Phrase after phrase was belted out as the little fellow went through his repertoire. It could only be a nightingale, I'd never heard one before and thought accounts of them must be over-rated. Untrue.

The long windows stood open and uncurtained against the sky. After the struggle to get the shutters open, I hadn't wanted to close them. Whoever had slept in this room before me must have seen those same stars framed by that simple curve of stone, etched as now, bright as fireworks against a night sky unpolluted by city lights. This window must be exactly as it was two and a half centuries ago when the house was first built.

Sleep had deserted me. I was wide awake now. I climbed out of bed and dragging a blanket around me, perched on the windowsill. The moonlight outside was so bright it cast shadows. So many lives had been lived in this house. Had someone else sat like me watching the silent garden in the night? They would have heard the same sounds. The cocks crowing way out of order long before dawn. The same owls hunting in the wood or these owls ancestors at any rate. I could see why Dad had fallen for the place. I suddenly felt very close to him. Under all that bravado and bluster he was such a softy. We were two of a kind - incurable romantics. I still felt a hard pain in my chest at the thought of him.

Tears smarted in my eyes. I brushed them away. 'Tears are always self-pity Jules.' That's what he used to say. It was just the fact that he was *nowhere*. That's what I couldn't bear

------- -- -------

Next morning, I sat at the kitchen table feeling a rather helpless. If we were going to put the house on the market, we needed to smarten it up a bit. But where on earth would I start?

My eyes wandered over the cracked ceiling. There were probably beams up there behind all that plaster. And that chimney piece over the cooker could be stripped back to the stone. In my mind's eye, I was chipping off the hideous tiles, laying a floor of faded terracotta, transforming

13

the room into a an authentic farmhouse kitchen. I'd have a heavy
workbench in the middle and a butcher's block, nothing built in, just big
wooden country cupboards with a nice distressed finish like you see in ads in
House and Garden.

With my mind in a whirl of fantasy projects, I wandered from room to
room cradling my bowl of coffee in my hand. I was drawn back to the one
I'd slept in - the Art Nouveau room which was now bathed in the warmth of
the early sun. By daylight I could now see the panelling in more detail. It
was pretty rough in places. Looked as if some local carpenter had been
given a brief to produce Art Nouveau and come up with his own version.
Casting an eye across the long silky panels, I noticed two of them were in
fact doors. And they weren't locked. Risking my nails, I managed to prise
them open.

Hanging inside were what I recognised with a wrench as Dad's
clothes. I hadn't given them a thought, but of course, they would still be
here, no-one would have felt they had the right to clear them out. I pulled
out a hanger and hugged his jacket. Suddenly I was a child again. I was
being picked up and held close, feeling the roughness and the muggy smell
of the wool of his tweed jacket.

I started in a half-hearted way to take the clothes out and sort them
into piles. There was a newish mac that might do for Charles. I soon had a
pile for charity and a load of stuff that only deserved to be burnt. I got down
to the shoes, the lump in my throat coming back as I found his favourite
miss-shapen pair with its perfect negative image of his feet, lying in the dust.
But there was something else in the cupboard. A couple of boxes pushed
towards the back.

The first, a wooden wine crate, chinked promisingly. The second was
wrapped in the kind of cheap paper and curled ribbon shops use in France
when they wrap a purchase as a gift.

The wine crate held a dozen bottles of chateau bottled Beaujolais.
Carefully peeling back the end of the other one, I found a boxed set of Baby
Dior - baby clothes.

Chapter Two

Julia 2008

'Someone's been busy.'

I passed on with the plate of nibbles and smiled dutifully. All Dad's friends were there. And the family, apart from Mummy of course. No doubt she'd ring me later to get the lowdown.

Sarah passed with a warning glance in the direction of the drinks' table. Dad was topping up his glass again.

'Oh for godsake, it's *his* party,' I hissed.

'A toast,' called out Dad to no-one in particular.

Sarah tapped her glass and Charles thumped on the table. The room fell haltingly silent. 'To a new life!'

'To the Peugeot and all who sail in her,' bawled Uncle Henry from the terrace.

'To France,' said Sarah.

'May you find your dream retreat.'

'Make it the South,' said Jane.

'And near a decent beach,' said Sarah.

And then the children roared in from the garden again and Jane made a lunge for the peanuts.

'You never know,' she shouted over the screams: 'One of them might be allergic.'

I knelt down and started feeding Miranda consolatory Kettle Crisps.

The conversation welled up again and the children's voices were drowned in the general hubub.

I caught Dad's eye across the room. He had flushed an angry colour. I left Miranda happily in possession of the bowl of crisps and pushed across to him.

'You all right?'

'Hot in here that's all.'

'Let's go outside then.'

In the garden, Sarah was trying to organise the children into a game of

Grandmother's Footsteps. The smaller two couldn't grasp the rules and kept complaining when they were sent back to the starting line. Tom was more interested in tearing the heads off the dahlia's.

'Don't do that darling. Or Mummy'll be ever so cross,' Jane was saying in a tired sort of voice.

Dad and I sought a peaceful corner, selecting the old oak bench at the far end of the lawn. He lowered himself with a sigh. I noted silently, he really should do something about his weight .

'I'm going to bring you all something back. Couldn't face birthdays this year. Your mother used to deal with all that. So a nice present from La Belle France. What's it to be, eh?'

'Oh I don't know.'

'Not like your sisters. Jane's already specified a nice crate of Beaujolais. Chateau bottled for Charles to lay down. I'm instructed that they are not to be fobbed off with something bought from Cité Europe at the last minute. And Sarah wants a load of something called *Baby Dior* for the one on the way. How a newborn can tell the difference between one label and another beats me.'

'Well, you know Sarah. Nothing but the best.'

'Don't be in a hurry to follow suit.'

'A baby? Qui moi?' I said lightly. It was almost as if he'd read my mind. I was late this month. But it probably didn't mean anything. I'd been late before. Nothing to get excited about.

'Not that I mind, you know, there not being a bloke around, it's her affair...'

'...to coin a phrase. And anyway, there is someone. But he's married.'

'Women these days.'

'Oh we're a mystery, aren't we?'

'Daughter's are. I should know. I've got three of them. So what would you like from France?'

'Honestly, I really don't want anything.'

'I have to bring you something or 'it won't be fair', as Sarah would say.'

'Oh all right, bring me... Bring me photos of the house. The houses. All the ones you find. That way I can help you choose.'

'Help choose eh? It's the house you've got your eye on is it?'

'Of course. I want to spend my holidays there.'

'And bring all your blokes down to be vetted.'

'All what blokes?'

'Well that Oliver fellow if you like.'

'But you can't stand him.'

'If he makes you happy...?' The question hung on the air.

I changed the subject. 'I'll probably bring my laptop.'

'How's it going - that book of yours...?'

'It's not. It's only a few chapters and it isn't getting any longer.'

'Put it first. Don't leave it too late like me.'

'You'll have loads of time to write in France.'

'If I'd had something to say I would have said it by now. And as for time in France, I'll be too busy entertaining you and your laptop. Come on, your glass is empty, let's get another drink.'

'Ernest, what are you doing hiding Julia away in the garden? There's someone I want her to meet.' Merryl had discovered us. She had one of her lost bachelors in tow. He was balding and verging on the overweight.

'Just going to check the sausage rolls and I'll be back,' I said.

That's when the pain hit me like a kick in the stomach and I doubled up.

-------- -- -------

The scanner worked its way downwards reading section by section, its red light zipping industriously back and forth as it recorded all my most intimate functions. A CAT scan. An expensive process I thought bleakly, and one they didn't involve themselves in unless they thought they were 'on to something'.

The white-coated radioligist came briskly out of her glass booth. 'You can have a pee now', she said.

'Everything look all right in there?'

She smiled kindly but non-committally: 'I only take the pictures.'

Relieved of a couple of litres of iodised water, I was wheeled back up to the ward while they processed the findings. Two storeys below they were putting me back together on cellulose, stacking me back up like the rings of a tree. In my imagination, whatever was in there had grown to massive proportions and I was naturally curious to know whether I would live or die. I made a few tentative enquiries but was told firmly that I had to wait for the verdict of the doctor.

Curiously enough, maybe from shock or maybe from the effects of all the morphine, I felt detached from it all. The pain had eased off and while in this limbo I lay drowsily wondering how they would manage at work without me and whether anyone would be able to fathom out which was the latest version of the Premo body copy. And whether someone would put my tax return in the post for me. The tax return lay heavily on my mind like indigestion until the dinner trolley came round and they hung a 'Nil by Mouth' sign over my bed. Not a good sign. Clearly, I was for the knife.

It focussed the mind. That's when I started thinking about what I'd done with my life and more importantly, what I hadn't done. There were the children I hadn't had for a start. And then there was the husband I hadn't had, who should really take the blame as much as me, for the lack of children. And the decent job with company car and company share option I should have had. And of course there was novel I hadn't finished, in fact had hardly started, which was lying in a terribly clichéd way at the bottom of the right hand drawer of my desk. I wondered bleakly if someone would find it and even finish it and whether it would become a best seller after I was dead and how terribly poignant that would be.

And then I felt really sorry for myself until Sarah bustled in with a great big bunch of funereal-looking lillies. God she was a size. And still *months* to go.

She nodded at the sign: 'Aren't they giving you anything to eat?'

'Doesn't look like it.'

'How are you feeling?'

'Much better. In fact, ready to go home.'

She frowned at me. 'I'll just go and find a vase for these.'

She sailed off. I could see her in a mirror, leaning over the nurses' desk having a 'confidential word' with them.

'What's the verdict?' I asked.

'What verdict?'

'Will I live or die?'

'It's probably appendicitus.'

'Not on. It's the wrong side.'

'But it could be thingummy. Referred pain. It travels you know. Like people trying to scratch their toes when they've had a leg off.'

'You're not helping.'

'Sorry.'

'What happened to the party?'

'True to form Dad got absolutely paralytic after they wheeled you off. We've told him it's appendicitus and now all he's worried about is whether you'll mind if he leaves anyway.'

''Course not. He should go.'

'He's booked some sort of special offer on the Shuttle so he won't get his money back if he cancels. Anyway he might as well, you know how hopeless he is with anyone who's...' Sarah caught sight of my face. 'Look, you're going to be all right. I know you are.'

'If I'm not, the leftover canapés will come in handy for the wake.'

'Oh honestly.'

'I can't help being a hypochondriac.'

'You're going to be *fine*. You'll see.

'Have you told Mummy?'

'Not yet.'

'You'll have to tell her something. She's already left six frantic messages on my voice mail. You know how she hates missing out on anything. Specially if it's something gruesomely medical.'

-------- -- -------

Two days later it was all over. They'd opened me up, dealt with it, as Mummy put it, and sewn me back up again.

I woke to find Oliver standing by the bed holding an apologetic bunch of red roses.

'Have you been here long?'

'I came earlier but you were asleep.'

'Sorry.'

'How are you feeling?'

'I don't know. Sore. Glad to be alive.'

He patted my hand. 'I'm glad you're alive too.'

'Thank you.'

'Where shall I put these?'

'Leave them. The nurse will find a vase.'

'They've moved you into the Private Wing.'

'I was on Bupa through work. Seemed a waste not to.'

'Nice room.'

'Umm.'

There was a silence.

'So...' said Oliver.

'It would have been a baby. But it was in the wrong place...' I started feeling really helpless, I didn't want to cry.

He nodded. 'Perhaps it's just as well.'

(Just as well!)

The tears welled in spite of myself.

'No I don't mean that. But Jules honestly. You don't want a baby right now, you know you don't.'

('You,' he'd said. 'You.' Not 'We.')

'When am I meant to want a baby?' I'm thirty-eight for god's sake.'

'People have babies well into their 'forties these days. There was that Italian woman who had one at sixty-something.'

'It's you. It isn't 'We' that doesn't want a baby'.

'I'm not sure that's grammatical.'

'Don't be flippant.'

'Well no, I don't quite honestly. Not right now.'

I was silent. He stroked my hand.

'A baby would spoil everything. You know it would.'

It would spoil everything for Oliver. It would spoil his evenings. Those nice dinners I cooked for him at my flat or his. And the nights of course. A baby would spoil those all right.

'Anyway,' I said pulling myself together with an effort. 'It doesn't look as if a baby will be spoiling anything. This just about ends my chances of having one. Seems my uterus is up the creek too.'

'Poor Jules.'

(Poor me. Not poor *us*).

-------- -- -------

Poor me, I sighed as I folded the baby clothes and tucked them back inside the gift wrap. And then I shrugged. No not poor me, lucky me. Oliver could go to hell. I remembered the look of total amazement on his face when I told him I wanted to break it off. 'But why, Julia, why now?' Where to begin? That cliché of his lack of commitment? Or perhaps his total selfishness? Or his blind egotism? Or maybe just his total lack of interest in what I felt or wanted out of life? He was right. Why now? Why not years ago?

Anyway, Dad would have been glad. He'd seen through Oliver from the start. I stared down at the piles of his clothes. On second thoughts I couldn't see Charles in that mac since it wasn't a Burberry. I'd better take the whole lot to charity, they might be of use to someone. I started to fold the jacket. There was something in the pocket. A paperback. A copy of Alain Fournier's 'Le Grand Meaulnes'. As I drew it out a memory stick flew out with it and went skittering across the parquet.
I retrieved it. What had Dad been writing?

I hurried to my laptop and slid the stick into a USB port. I clicked on the icon, my heart racing in the vain hope there might be some message for me - some common thought - anything to bridge the gulf that separated us. The usual things came up – stuff for his accountant, a couple of draft articles for the Oldie, a load of letters. Then the title of a document caught my eye: 'La Mulatière'. It was dated the day before he died. It must have been the last thing he'd written. I double clicked and opened it.

Chapter Three

Ernest Lefarge 2008

I took out the paperback I'd bought that morning in the gift shop in Meaulne and propped it up beside my plate. I'd stopped for despondent lunch having given up the search for yet another trip. I'd simply run out of properties to view. Like most people I'd read 'Le Grand Meaulnes' as part of a school French course and perhaps it was more than a little responsible for the unconditional love I've held for this country ever since. And why I was here now on this wild goose chase in search of my dream retreat in France.

I'd come originally to see a miniature white stone chateau in the Loire. A magical place suggested the photos, with a couple of hectares of land running down to a river frontage. Not too far for the girls to come and visit and plenty for the kids to do. In reality, it was all crumbling white stucco and statues of the Virgin. Must've belonged to some religious fanatic who'd put more faith in divine intervention than in decent roofers. Rain had been coming into the place for god knows how long. And there was a quarry less than a kilometre off, from which lorries rumbled by, regular as clockwork, at twenty minute intervals.

After that I'd driven West across the Berry where another potential find was tempting me. An oddly tall building with double towers. Renovated, so the blurb claimed, to 'an exceptionally high standard'. I rapidly came to the conclusion that the owner, who was showing me round with such obsequious attentiveness, must've done the place up himself. It had a kind of seating area, all low settees and draperies - like a Turkish brothel - where he said he gave 'soirées'. He was in the process of putting a jacuzzi in the cellar. Hi jinx in Berry eh? It was more than slightly seedy.

We ended our tour in the garden. Berry is an area of marshland, relieved by the occasional stubby oak forest or shallow lake. The haunt of huntsmen. A damp place at the best of times. In summer, I imagined it would be humid and buzzing with mosquitoes. Now at the end of an autumnal day, a clammy mist was rolling in from the scrub.

The fellow was trying to sell the place as a 'going concern'. He had a shop of sorts in the barn, selling 'Gentleman Farmer' goods: oiled jackets, hunting boots, guns and fishing tackle. He opened it up for me. Absent-mindedly sweeping the dust from a glass case full of lethal looking knives, he said it brought in 'a fair amount'. It didn't look to me as if he did much trade.

We ended our tour with darkness drawing in fast, beside what he called his 'plan d'eau'. A marshy pool with an island in the centre where a matted flock of sickly sheep stood marooned in the mist.

I decided to relieve the chap of any illusions he might be harbouring. I was sorry, I told him, but his house, charming as it was, wasn't quite what I had in mind. What was it in particular that put you off? he enquired. To be kind, I blamed the region.

'Oh you're so right,' he said, turning to me, tears of frankness in his eyes. 'As soon as I can, I'm going South. The winters here, the endless winters with nothing happening. No-one comes here. You try to sell them stuff but they'd rather drive fifty kilometers to the nearest Carrefour. I tell you, it's sheer hell.' We had a Cognac together after that and I wished him 'Bonne Courage'. As I drove off I could hear the hollow sound of a sheep coughing through the fog. Miasma. That was the word it brought to mind.

I'd driven on, not sure which direction to take. I'd no more properties to view and the weather had turned foul. Time to head back to England. I'd wait a month or two till more came on the market. And then I'd make another trip.

I'd headed East hoping to pick up the Autoroute North to Orléans, but had somehow missed the turning. In the inky black of night , I found myself in a deserted village where I chanced on a one-star hotel open for business. It was a travelling salesman's stop-over, all 'fifties linoleum and creaking bedsprings with a menu supplied entirely from the deep freeze. But it fitted the bill. I'd woken early next morning keen to be off. There was a display of tourist leaflets in reception and lacking a newspaper, I selected a handful to keep me company over breakfast.

It seemed I'd landed up in the forest of Tronçais, described in full-blown tourest-eze as 'A great living breathing swathe of green.' 'A forest planted by Colbert, the finance minister of Louis X1Vth to provide the oak to build a fleet to fight the British. It remains a managed forest today and the oak is used to make the barrels that are exported wordwide for maturing fine wines.'

I turned to the map on the back and found I was in the North Auvergne. I'd somehow veered miles off course and ended up in the foothills of the Massif Central.

The blurb continued with a glowing description of the area and the boast that up until the Eighteenth Century this region, known as the Bourbonnais, was the most prosperous part of what we now call France with numerous chateaux to prove it. But the description that spoke to me so persuasively that morning was: 'La France Profonde' - deepest France. Surely this is what I was looking for.

Later, when I'd explored the region for myself, the title came back to me, communicating in such an immediate way, its remoteness, its sleeping villages unchanged through centuries, its countless small farms with their conical roofs of crumbling terracotta, its shaded lanes winding beween traditional hedged fields where time-honoured farming methods are the rule rather than the exception.

Idly letting my eye wander over the map, I'd spotted the village of Meaulne. I was in Alain Fournier country. This knowledge brought a frisson - hardly detectable, a frail echo of the deeply embedded emotion the book had instilled in me. I tried to analyse the feeling. What was it? Optimism? Idealism? Merely the mindless euphoria of youth? And I remembered a long-forgotten promise I'd made to myself, that one day, like Meaulnes, I too would search out the Lost Domain. I'd had an idle fancy at the time - that it would still have its romanticised occupants dressed in Eighteenth Century costume. A thought that was naturally ridiculous. But still the notion inherent in the book, of peering through some chink in time, back into a seductive yet indeterminate past, drew me irresistibly. Why not? I had no real schedule to keep to.

So that day, focussed suddenly in a way I could barely rationalise, I'd driven to Mealne. I'd spent the morning, as hommage to Fournier and my farewell to France, visiting the schoolhouse in neighbouring Epernay-le-Floriel. The school where Fournier's father had taught was now a museum with its own audio-guided tour. I'd listened to the voice-over delivered in those awed tones the French reserve for their artistic 'icons'. I'd turned the pages of the copybooks filled with children's handwriting, all its perfect loops and curves hanging like notes on a stave. I'd admired the authenticity of the school's restoration right down to its deep chocolate brown paint.

But it was in the playground, on seeing the school capes hanging under the old slate roof, as if their owners would at any point come running out in a rowdy bunch to claim them, that I experienced an overwhelming wave of that sentiment Fournier had evoked. Buried under years of indifference, careless lust and disillusionment, something had stirred. The blurb on my paperback described it as 'le regard fievreux de l'adolescence'. The feverish vision of adolescence? Maybe. Yet, for a split second, it was as if a slit in time had fallen open and I'd been allowed back into my own lost youth.

Here I stood in 'Deepest France', this forgotten corner, hidden in the centre of the country. Here the mad race of what we call in the business the 'pace of change' had been retarded somehow, like an old spring alarm clock that had lost its tension and was ticking at a slower rate. This glimpse had reminded me of what I'd come for, revived my flagging spirits and renewed my determination. I wouldn't turn tail and head back to London. I would persevere. The house I was looking for was out there somewhere, finding it was just a matter of time.

Later that day, in a village not far from Meaulne, after a lunch in an overheated 'Routier' where I'd drunk rather too liberally from the 'pot' of vinegarry St Pourçain, I took a stroll through the main square and found among the habitual selection of languishing village shops, an estate agent's office. It was a run-down looking place with no lights on, but when I pushed the door, it opened.

The chap inside answered an agent's description right down to his clipped used-car salesman moustache. He got up from his desk in surprise, as if a client was a rare sight in these parts. And maybe it was. We stood for a moment facing each other. He quickly came to his senses and asked if he could help me, pulling out a chair. After displaying the standard dossiers of potential holiday homes for the unwary British: tumbledown barns, dilapidated farmhouses and those 'picturesque' crumbling cottages way past any hope of restoration, I caught sight of a single photo that made my heart miss a beat.

'What's that?'

'Not at all what you're looking for Monsieur. A large property... An old manoir.' He was about to put the photo back in his file when I laid a hand on it. It was an Eighteenth Century manoir with a single tower.

'I think it has rather more accomodation than you need,' he said with a laugh. 'You are on your own, no?'

'Not necessarily...' With difficulty, I controlled my voice. I had taken possession of the photo. My hands were shaking.

'Forgive me, is anything wrong?'

'No please go on... Tell me more about it.' My heart was beating uncomfortably in my chest.

He'd registered my interest. He changed his tone and delving deep into the filing cabinet, he unearthed a further couple of shots, two of them aerial, must've been taken from a light aircraft.

He's sales pitch revved up a gear: 'It's surrounded by unspoilt countryside. But not isolated. The nearest village is a mere two kilometres away with a doctor, pharmacy, bakery, a butcher and several restaurants...'

I wasn't listening. I was gazing down at the photos he was casting carelessly before me. The experience of the morning was still vivid in my mind. And we weren't so far from Meaulne. Certainly a possible morning's carriage-ride. At a fair pace of course.

'Some forsaken old manor... Some deserted pigeon-house...' I murmured.

'On the contrary, this place is of some importance,' he corrected me.

'How soon can I see it?'

He lifted his car keys off the desk. The movement was too slick, rehearsed almost. 'Right now, if you've got a moment.'

-------- -- -------

As his car swept up to the turning on the hill I caught my first sight of La

Mulatière.

'Stop,' I said. He drew to a halt and, unbidden, the words of Fournier, which always brought with them a frisson that ran down my spine, went through my head:

'...he was brought to a halt by surprise and stood there, stirred by an emotion he could not have defined...' 'now sustained by an extraordinary sense of well-being, an almost intoxicating serenity, by the certitude that the goal was in sight...' 'that he had nothing but happiness to look forward to...'

'Shall we go on?'

'Please.'

We crunched up a driveway entering the domain between two vast and mossy gateposts.

The agent kept up a non-stop commentary on the size and number of windows, the Southern aspect, the park and its environs. Suddenly, I loathed the man for his insistent patter. All I wanted was to be alone. To walk through the neglected gardens and take my time. La Mulatière lay behind its tangled creepers, peering through into the watery sunlight, like a lovely woman, veiled. I wanted to approach the house softly so as not to break the spell.

But the fellow was persistent. You could tell I wasn't the first potential client he'd shown around the place. He had his sales pitch off pat and wasn't going to let me miss a word. It wasn't till later I learned why - the rogue had bought the place himself and was out to make a killing.

'And if you look up, there! Just above that central dormer. You should be able to make out the inscription. 'Fait pour le Duc de Bourbon'.

'Fait?' Surely it should be construit?'

He brushed my comment aside. 'Old French. The house was built in 1758, do you see the inscription? The wings at the rear are even earlier.'

'Yes...' I could make out numbers above the dormer. 1758, carved in the seamed oak.

'Thirty or so years before the Revolution,' I commented. 'But the house looks hardly grand enough for a duke.'

From what I knew of French history the Bourbon dukes were important fellows. Surely they had proper castles with witches' hat towers, moats and battlements. This place looked more as if it belonged to some kind of flat-cap nobleman. What kind of proprietor, I mused? Was he Florent the Flogger or Clement the Just? Was this house built on wealth dredged from the exploited poor or was the Enlightenment already dawning?

The fellow was anxious to continue the tour inside the house. He put out an arm, almost in a mock bow 'Let me escort you around.'

I suppose he was a likeable enough chap. He had a roguish look in his eye and a way of putting things that made you wonder if he was serious or not. At any rate he made no concessions to my French - or lack of it. For all his amusing manner, he was most definitely not to be trusted.

He took me on a whistle-stop tour, glossing over the hideous attempts at modernisation and pointing out the finer points of the interior. Shifting my attention from the worm-eaten parquet to the massive beams, brushing over the unfortunate smell and lamentable choice of tiling, he pointed out the bread oven, the original stone sink, the chateau d'eau, the old pump still functioning.

But I had no time for tedious details. I followed him with my heart pounding in my ears. A manoir with a single tower. A courtyard behind large enough to hold quite a number of carriages. My head swam in disbelief as one beautifully proportioned room opened on to another, all 'en enfilade' intercommunicating through pair after pair of double doors. All it lacked was the ghostly rustle of silk, the phantom string quartet, the dancing shadows of its Eighteenth Century inhabitants.

Finally, he flung wide a small door that opened on to a creamy curve of stone steps leading upwards - a castle staircase, seemingly untouched. He went ahead, I followed panting, losing him at each turn, drawing level at last at the top where I found him standing in the darkness beyond a low door.

'And this, of course, is where the Duc stored the tithe...'

In the gloom I could sense a great cavern of a place. I could almost feel the weight of the timbers above. As my eyes grew accustomed to the darkness I could see the massive charpente that towered over us. Beams which must've been hewn from single tree trunks, rivetted together with giant hand carved pegs. We stood there in silence for a moment. Then he thrust open the shutters and as he did so the evening sun entered in a single band of amber. Dust motes hung on the breeze dancing in the blackness. I watched, spellbound.

He was waxing lyrical about the view. But he didn't need to go on. As far as I was concerned there could be a nuclear power station in the neighbouring field. I was totally bewitched. I was going to have La Mulatière no matter what. The search was over. I'd found my goal. At last I had come home.

Chapter Four

Julia 2009

I read Dad's last words with tears pricking in my eyes, marvelling as ever
that our feelings were so perfectly in step, as if his genes had somehow been
passed on to me as a total package, without Mummy's intervention. So he'd
found his dream house. This was a comfort in a way.

It was with a sense of seeing things through Dad's eyes that I spent the rest
of that day exploring every inch of the house. A low spring sun had come
out, sending slender bands of light through the cracks in the shutters giving
the place that mysterious Vermeer-like quality Dad had described. I
wandered from room to room savouring the sense of emptiness, the stillness,
the strangely intoxicating sense of discovery. As my footsteps echoed
across the parquet, it was all too easy to imagine the earlier inhabitants of the
house just a room or so away . I pushed doors open warily feeling as if I
might come across them at any moment, practising the spinette,
embroidering in a corner or writing in a ledger with a scratching quill. It
wasn't a creepy feeling but oddly companiable as if these past residents
accepted my presence and even welcomed it.

My exploration took me beyond the grander rooms and into what
must once have been the servants' quarters - dusty attics seemingly
undisturbed in their 18th Century gloom. Pulling at a particularly obstinate
door, which came off its hinges showering me with dust, I woke a family of
bats, who solemnly circled my head before hanging themselves back up on
the rafters.

Venturing below, into the bowels of the house, I found a dark and
slippery stone stairway which led me down into a vaulted wine cellar
furnished with racks to house a few thousand bottles, now empty apart from
a newish looking row of Chateau Margaux. Standing guard over them was a
strange slow black and yellow lizard that I later discovered was a fire
salamander. Under his unblinking gaze I helped myself to a bottle. Nice

one - thanks Dad.

Once I'd exhausted the main house, I tackled the outbuildings, making daring forays into crumbling lean-tos stacked with debris, some of which looked only fit to be demolished before they fell down.

At last, as the sun started to decline, and I'd satisfied myself that there was nowhere else to discover, no hidden room or eery passageway, no door that was spookily locked or dark stairway that was threatening in any way, I treated myself to a long slow bath in the roll-top tub.

I lay luxuriating in hot water up to my neck. Everything in this bathroom was ridiculously oversized, even the taps which gushed a seemingly endless supply of hot water that I guessed must come from some antiquated system linked somehow to the wood burning stove.

Feeling like a new person I made my way downstairs and uncorked the bottle of Margaux. I took my glass out into the courtyard. Settling a kitchen chair in the last rays of sunlight I could picture Dad beside me tipping his glass to chink against mine. 'Cheers Julia. I knew you'd love it – the house.'

I waited until the afterglow of the setting sun had faded from the sky then realising how chilly it had become, I went in and lit a fire. I'd bought myself a take-home supper from the delicatessen counter in the supermarket. A range of little plastic boxes filled with those typically esoteric French concoctions:- brawn with a thick caper and gherkin sauce, shredded celeriac in remoulade and a soft boiled egg wrapped in ham and set in a madeira jelly. I lit the candles in an old iron candelabra that sat on the mantelpiece and enjoyed my feast with more of Dad's wine.

Sitting here in a room lit by flickering flames it was all too easy to imagine the house had slipped back in time. I might well be back in the Eighteenth Century. I could imagine figures in their cumbersome clothing gathered round the fire in the adjoining room. The soft breathing of children, asleep in the bedrooms above. The distant sound of pots being scoured and laughter from the kitchens. I suddenly felt an intense curiosity about these people who I could sense all around me

At a ridiculously early hour I made my way upstairs carrying the candelabra. It cast giant shadows swinging around the stairwell, stretching to the rafters as it must have done for my predecessors. Their feet had worn those shallow curves into the stairs. Their hands had glided up the handrail, polishing it to its silky smoothness. And they had most probably tripped like me on that unexpectedly steep step at the top.

The Art Nouveau bedroom had stored the warmth of the day. The candlelight gleamed on the silky panelling. The bed looked soft and welcoming with its fat pillows. I threw open the window and let the freshness of the night air in. Then I stripped off my clothes and slid into the bed naked, enjoying the slight roughness of the starched linen against my freshly bathed skin.

I could hear some farm vehicle, a tractor probably, making its way to and fro, to a fro, in the darkness. It was reassuring hearing someone still at work out there. I had a sense of being far from all the threats and anxieties of city life, surrounded by a landscape that was ordered and productive and safe,

I reached for Dad's book and read a few pages and then realising I was dead beat, I snuffed out the candles and promptly fell asleep.

-------- -- -------

I woke next morning to find sunlight streaming into the room. Some sound had woken me? There it was again. An insistent snip, snip, snip. Not in the house, the sound was coming in through the open window. I reached for my watch. It was 7.00 am. Snip, snip, snip. What could it be? Sleepy and reluctant to leave my warm bed, my mind contrived various alternatives. One of those electric fence thingy's malfunctioning? Too far away. A drip somewhere in the attic? It didn't look as if it had been raining. Some bird pecking at something? Snip, snip snip. There it was again. Followed by the drag of something on gravel. I climbed out of bed and pulling some clothes on, I leaned out of the window. The sound was coming from the far side of the garden. Out of my sightlines. Intrigued, I went down to investigate.

On the West side of the garden there was a walk of sorts between tall box hedges - the one feature of the garden that wasn't totally overgrown. Now forcing my way between the hedges I could see why. Propped precariously on one of those old wooden ladders that splayed out at the base, was a sturdy chap wearing a canvas fishing hat. Intent on his work with the shears, clipping away, he hadn't heard me approach.

I coughed to get his attention. He turned abruptly, wobbled and deftly stepped down, catching the ladder as he did so.

He flushed pink with embarrassment and seemed at a loss for words. I was similarly at a loss. What did you do with a trespasser who appeared to be clipping your hedge for you?

'Bonjour Monsieur,' I tried.

'Madame,' he said, sweeping off his hat in a way that suggested, had he had a forelock he would currently be pulling it.

He had a neat head of grey hair and surprisingly bright blue eyes that were now regarding me in a shy but kindly way. He came forward offering his wrist in a way I've since become accustomed to from working men - not wishing to present a less than clean hand.

'Mademoiselle,' I corrected him.

He cocked his head on one side and repeated. 'Madame. Madame Lefarge?'

'Julia, Mademoiselle Julia Lefarge.' I tried again. And in an attempt to bring things to a head, I added in French: 'May I ask what are you doing, Monsieur?'

He shrugged and indicated the hedge. 'It's the time. The time for trimming. It would be a crime to let it get away.'

It suddenly occured to me that he must be someone Dad had taken on. Odd, he hadn't mentioned a gardener.

'You know that M. Lefarge has passed away?'

He shook his head sadly and stared at the gravel.

'My condolences Madame. It's a very sad affair. And to think he never saw the spring.'

'I know,' despite myself my eyes filled with tears.

His filled too in sympathy. 'Now I've upset you. I am so sorry.' He bent to sweep up the box trimmings. 'I wouldn't have come so soon. But it's the best time. Let box get away and its a tricky customer...'

'But really Monsieur. I don't know what arrangement you had with my father. But I'm afraid I really can't afford...'

He brushed this protest away with a gesture. 'It is not a matter of payment. My father trimmed this hedge all his life. It must be more than two hundred years old. It would be a pity, you see, to let it go back to the wild.'

'I know but...'

'And the garden. The grass will start growing soon and then you'll have a job on your hands. And the orchard hasn't been pruned... You won't be able to manage on your own.'

'But I'm going to sell the place...'

'Sell La Mulatière? But you've only just come...' He said this as if the idea was pure madness on my part.

'I know...'

We both gazed back at the house.

'I ought to prune the wisteria . Then you could get the shutters open. Air the chateau. It must be in need of it'

I turned back to face him. He had a point. The house did need airing. And I certainly wouldn't be able to tackle the wisteria on my own. 'Yes, you're right. But only if I pay you. How much would you charge?'

At that he drew his breath through his teeth and shrugged.

I waited. He didn't look like a rogue but you never could tell.

'Well, we'll have to agree on a price first,' I said firmly.

He started pacing along the front of the house rubbing his chin. 'I'll need a very long ladder,' he said giving me another glimpse of his bright blue eyes.

I suddenly wondered if he'd be all right on a ladder that height. He looked well over sixty.

'Maybe I should get some professionals to do it.'

'I could borrow a long ladder,' he said quickly.

'But I must know how much you'll charge for the job.'

Still he hesitated. It seemed I'd never get a price out of him.

'How would it be if I left you to make your mind up,' I suggested. 'I'll make us a coffee. Come round to the back in a few minutes.'

I left him staring up at the wisteria and went to put the kettle on the stove. I made little cups of black coffee and got out a pack of lump sugar. I had it all laid out on the table when he came and knocked on the back door.

He took his boots off and placed them neatly side by side outside the door, coming in in stockinged feet.

I had to ask him twice before he'd sit down. He reluctantly drew out a chair and sat some way from the table. He looked around the room as if taking in details.

I poured the coffee and passed him the box of sugar. He eased out two cubes neatly with his spoon.

'I was born in the corner of this room,' he said after a moment. 'Over there. Where the fridge is now.'

'Really? So your parents lived here?'

He nodded. 'This was their part of the house. There was no door through to the chateau then. That door over there, into the main house, has been knocked through since. My father was a gardener for Mademoiselle Lamulatière. He was head gardener, there were seven of them in all.'

'Mademoiselle Lamulatière?'

He nodded. 'Mademoiselle Marie. Oh it was a grand place then. You should've seen the gardens.'

'Seven gardeners. It must have been quite something.'

'Oh yes, it was. Mademoiselle had a rose garden, and an aviary. Mulatière was a place to behold. She had swans on the pond. Hunting dogs in the kennels. And horses of course. There was even a winter garden. Fallen down now but you can still see where it joined on to the house. She was good to me, although she always claimed she didn't like children. There was an almighty fuss when she picked up my father and mother from the station and she saw my mother was expecting. But she took to me all the same.'

'She never had children of her own?'

'She never married. Her sister Madamoiselle Louise, she married. She was a very different person, ' he said disapprovingly. 'The house was inherited by her children. Parisiens, Well, they didn't want to know. Let the garden go to wrack and ruin. I used to come by and do a bit here and there. But that box hedge is all I've managed to keep up.'

I wondered if he'd ever been paid for his work. Which reminded me - 'So have you worked out a price for pruning the wisteria?'

He said staring down at his hands. 'I had a friend who did gardening jobs. And he was paid eight euros an hour.'

'But I don't know how long you'll take,' I pointed out. Although it seemed cheap at the price I was worried about taking on an open-ended arrangement with someone I didn't know.

'Oh I'll work fast,' he assured me, getting up from the table as if to prove he was in earnest.

'Very well, it's a deal.' We shook hands on it. It was only one job after all. After that we could see how we got on.

'I'll finish the box hedges this morning,' he said. 'Thank you for the coffee Madame.

'Oh and by the way. I don't know your name?'

'Jerôme,' he said. 'Jerôme Boucheron.'

I watched as he put his boots back on and returned at a hurried pace to the shrubbery. And I realised, that in the gentlest way possible, I'd been inertia-sold - a gardener.

-------- -- -------

I went up to the first floor to have a surreptitious check from the upper windows as to what exactly he was up to. You could see that at some point the box had been laid out in a sort of pattern. Most probably as a '*jardin a la française*' with neat gravel walks between the miniature box hedges. Now all that remained was a long curve of hedge that was thick and bushy and had grown to a height of a good two metres. Two hundred years old, that's what he'd said, maybe he was right. Beyond this hedge, what box remained had grown into stunted trees, their shapes suggesting topiary, something I loathed, poor plants tortured into the shapes of animals or birds. If so, I was glad they'd been allowed to go their own way.

Jerôme was back up his ladder snipping away at the one decent curve. Catching sight of me, he hurriedly upped his pace. I felt a bit guilty at how I'd questionned how fast he could work.

On my way downstairs my attention was caught by more sounds

coming from the back of the house. Perhaps that one-eyed cat had got in. Which was weird because I was sure I'd closed the door behind Jerôme. They were familiar domestic sounds like china being stacked. I tracked them down to the kitchen. Throwing open the door I found a figure leaning over the sink intent on washing up.

The woman turned to pick up a dish and caught sight of me.

'Oh Madame you gave me such a fright,' she said.

I could have said the same to her. She quickly regained her composure and dried her hands on her apron.

'Bonjour Madame. I hope you don't mind. I had the key so I thought I might as well get on. May I present myself, I am Jacqueline...'

She came and shook me briskly by the hand.

I'd only spoken to her on the phone. Her voice had suggested a large lady in a floral overall. But this 'femme de menage' had a smart haircut and satirical glint in her eye.

'I hope you had a pleasant journey. How do you like this little house?'

Remembering my manners, I thanked her for the delicious meal she'd left and for preparing everything so thoughtfully.

She shrugged: 'It's normal. No more trouble to do something well than badly.'

I glanced around the room. She already had all the chairs upturned on the kitchen table. Last night's meal had been washed up and stacked And a fresh baguette protruded from under the cloth on the bread board.

'Oh I used to bring the bread for your father, so I thought...'

'Thank you that's really kind.'

'Now, where shall I start?' she asked.

'Errrm.'

She evidently thought that the deal she'd made with Dad was an on-going arrangement.

'We need to air the place. I'll start on the shutters. Naturally, I closed them when the house was empty. It was a terrible thing... your father... terrible.'

I realised that I couldn't simply dismiss her after all she'd been through.

'Thank you for all your help. It must have been very upsetting for you finding my father like that...'

Jacqueline shrugged and came out with a statement well laced with what I was soon to discover was her habitual dolefulness. 'Eh bien, we never know when our turn will come.'

'But it must have been a shock for you all the same.'

'Life must go on. Now those shutters, do you want me to start upstairs or down?'

'Yes. The shutters. M. Boucheron says he's going to cut back the wisteria so that we can get the whole lot open.'

'Huh. That'll bring the dust to light all right.'

She leaned into the back kitchen and located a broom and set to work brushing the floor with professional briskness. I realised with a sinking feeling that my 'pay-roll' had doubled.

-------- -- -------

When Jacqueline left I ventured down into the now spotless kitchen to fix myself some lunch. The goat's cheese smell was even stronger today. I opened the back door to let some air in. There was camembert left from the night before at the ultimate point of ripeness, maybe that was to blame for the smell. I cut open the crisp baguette Jacqueline had brought and made a big squidgy sandwich. The one-eyed cat walked boldly into the kitchen and mewed, so in spite of the fact I'd told myself severely, that I wasn't going to feed it, I gave it the camembert rind. Then I took my sandwich up through the house and went and sat on my favourite perch in the window of the Art Nouveau room.

I leaned my back on the sun-warmed stone. A frond of wisteria had curled its way up over the windowsill and was opening in the midday heat. A bee droned lazily by.

I looked out over the sunlit garden to where the Sequoia stood sending its dark shadow back towards the house. Two hundred and fifty years old, that was what Dad had said. I wondered who had planted it. There must be a record or legal stuff somewhere which would tell me.

That's when I remembered guiltily I'd totally forgotten to ring the notaire.

Chapter Five

Julia 2009

'Oh come over right away,' he'd said.

I'd been taken aback. I'd been expecting to wait a few days at least for an appointment.

The notaire's office was in the nearest village - Deneville - Number 6, Place Marx Dormoy. I loved the way the French immortalised their heroes in place names. Even tiny Deneville was like a geographical Who's Who – with its Avenue Paul Bert, Place François Péron, rue Emile Guillaumin. Imagine being famous and having a really hideous street named after you. Ave. Julia Lefarge - all mock Swiss chalet-style with 'fifties cement balustrading.

I soon located a polished brass plate inscribed with his name. 'Maitre Thierry Bertrand'. The office was tucked away beyond a double arched doorway, wide enough for a carriage to pass through. When I rang the bell one of the double doors clicked open electronically. It led into a cobbled courtyard.

Maitre Bertrand had come out to greet me. He was dressed in a formal dark suit but had a reassuringly warm handshake and a jovial smile. I'd heard so many horror stories about the stiff formality of the French legal system, I was surprised by his relaxed and kindly manner.

'Mademoiselle Lefarge, welcome. You've come about La Mulatière.'

He led me inside to a study lined with glass fronted bookcases filled to bursting with manila folders. A portrait photo above his desk showed a head balding in exactly the same place, the same smile lines. This was evidently a family business.

Maitre Bertrand expressed his condolences and gave me a minute or two to talk about Dad.

'And now you and your sisters wish to sell the property?'

I hesitated. 'Yes. Yes they do. I mean, yes we do.'

'You're not sure?'

'No... I mean yes. We have to sell it.'

'You realise of course it will take time. Your father's will was made in England but the deeds are registered in France. It's a complicated business.'

'Is it?' How complicated?' My heart started to beat in my chest. A reprieve. The house couldn't be sold immediately. And someone would have to stay here while it was all settled.

He went into details my French could barely follow. It seemed there were duties of various kinds to be paid. Since the house had been owned for less than six years there was some sort of disproportionate tax due, he tutted over that with characteristic French disapproval of money squandered on taxes. Whichever way one looked at it, it was a total waste of money considering it was a house Dad had barely lived in. He went on to point out that the timing would be difficult. Nothing could be done in a hurry. A professional translation of Dad's will was required and someone with the oddly ecclesiastical title of: 'The Apostle of the Hague' had to be consulted.

'How long do you think all this will take?'

He shrugged. 'Three or four months at least. Maybe six.'

'I suppose we could put the house back on the market in the meantime.'

'Tricky,' he said. 'The property itself is not an easy one to sell.' (Was this a polite way of saying Dad was mad to buy the place?)

'No... I suppose not.'

'It was empty for a long time before your father came along.'

I was hardly paying attention. Four months, maybe six.. My mind was racing. Maybe I could take a sabbatical from work. Do the place up a bit, make it more saleable.

'Oh and by the way,' he added. 'The other day I was going through some of my father's papers. I came across something I thought you might like to have. It's the family tree of the Lamulatière family.'

That was the name Jerôme had mentioned. The page he was holding had some kind of coat of arms engraved at the top.

'The family that lived in my house?' 'My house'. It had slipped out inadvertently.

'Yes. As you'll see, they weren't always called Lamulatière. Back in the Eighteenth Century they went by the far grander title of Les Mulatiers de la Grolière.'

'Before the Revolution?'

'Yes, they were nobility up until then. They owned all the land around Deneville. Thousands of hectares, as far as the eye could see.'

He slipped the page into a manila envelope and handed it to me.

'Thank you. Thank you so much. In an odd sort of way I feel as if they're still around.'

The Maitre laughed. 'Ghosts eh? Well I dare say the place is big enough to accomodate the lot of you.'

'So what do we do now?'

'Leave it to me. I'll contact your father's notaire in England and we'll set the wheels in motion. But I warn you, nothing will be done in a hurry. There are all the feast days and the summer holidays...'

'But it's only April.'

'This is the Allier Miss Lefarge. You'll soon get used to it.'

I drove back to La Mulatière with a sense of mounting excitement. Six months, six whole months before the house could be sold! I could take a sabbatical, do some real renovation, take my time to get the place sorted. There'd be a fuss at work, of course. I'd be lucky to get six months. But I deserved a break. I'd been ten or more years in that dead-end job .

Swinging round the intersection into the lane, I took the curve too tightly. There was the blaring of a horn as I narrowly missed a beat-up looking estate car. The guy driving it glared hard at me, then drove on.

I watched his car receding in my rearview mirror. He swung it round the corner into the main road without bothering to signal or stop. He didn't look much older than me, in his 'forties, unshaven. Not bad looking actually. I could still feel his angry glare running through me. But I guess I'd nearly crashed into him, you couldn't blame him. He must have come out of the farm next door. It was a blind corner. I'd have to be more careful in future.

Feeling a little shaken, I turned into La Mulatière's driveway. I drew

to a halt midway where there was the best view of the house. While I had
been away Jacqueline and Jerôme had opened the rest of the shutters. It was
if the house had woken up. The morning sun shone full on the façade,
flattering its creamy stone, masking its disfigurements. I could now see the
proportions of the windows, each finished with its elegant curve of
fashioned stone. La Mulatière wasn't a grand house, there was too much of
the farmhouse about it. But this morning, in the limpid sunlight, it was quite
simply heart-stoppingly beautiful. And for a while, for a few months at
least, it could be mine.

I started the car up again and slowly drove along the drive. Jerôme
and Jacqueline's cars had gone so I was alone. I let myself in through the
front door and was greeted by a delicious smell. Jacqueline must have bees-
waxed the armoire in the hall. It gleamed in the half light bringing back
something of the past grandeur of the house. An incongruous gesture in the
delapidated state of the place. But it was well-meant. It wouldn't take that
much to bring the house back to life. The proportions were there. And the
panelling. Even the floors were intact. Once all the parquet was waxed...

-------- -- -------

Chapter Six

That evening I spread out the Maitre's family tree on the kitchen table. The crest at the top of the page was a kind of shield inscribed with three horses' heads? No not horses, surely they were mules' heads - which fitted of course with the odd name of the house - La Mulatière.

I ran an eye down the network of births deaths and marriages, pausing from time to time, trying to place them in the context of my shaky knowledge of French history.

The first person listed was a fellow called Matthias Mulatier de la Grolière. He was born in 1729, sixty or so years before the Revolution. According to the date over the dormer he would have been twenty-nine by the time the house was built - a rich man in his prime. The dates of his first child Henry, showed that his wife Anne-Marie would have been carrying this child.

-------- -- -------

Later that day, when I was up in the attic, I tried to imagine how Matthias must have felt when his amazing house was newly built.

I leaned out of the dormer and craned upwards. There was the date - 1758 carved into the seamed oak above my head. I realized it must have been Matthias who planted the Sequoia.

I could picture the small group at the far end of the garden gathered around the tiny fragile sapling - most probably on a mild spring day like today, with a West wind promising rain. The women in their bright silks, Anne-Marie's laced high at the waist, to accommodate the bulge of the baby. The men in their sturdy boots... A Priest's white cassock perhaps catching in the breeze as he sprinkles the holy water and intones a prayer.

Famille de la Mulatière

MULATIER de la GROLIERE Matthias
seigneur de la Mulatière b.1729

m. de COURTAIS Ann-Marie 1720-1800

de La Mulatière   de La Mulatière   de La Mulatière
Henri Nicolas   Jean Francois   4 filles
b.1757   b.1756
m. de LONGAUNAY Suzanne
1760 - 1798

de La Mulatière Amisie   Pierre: nommé Lamulatière
b.1790   1806 - 1845
m. Zavier de Godinet

LAMULATIERE   LAMULATIERE
Anselme-Francois   Henriette
1835 – 1893   1834 – 1844
m. LALANDE Elizabeth 1865

LAMULATIERE   LAMULATIERE
Marie-Francoise   Louise-Mathilde   m. P. LECLERC
1885 - 1948   1885 – 1956
Trois filles

Chapter Seven

Matthias Mulatier de la Grolière 1758

The priest gave his benediction and swung the censor. Matthias gave young Auguste a nod and they all stood back as he bedded the tiny sapling into the earth. He rammed the post in beside it and heeled the soil in . Finally he took a strip of veal hide from his pocket and tied the sapling to the post.

Matthias gazed back at his house, now rising proud against the sky as the mason's men dismantled the scaffolding. It smelt of wet limewash and freshly sawn wood. The newly-cut slates gleamed silver in the April sunlight. He could hear the glaziers at work tapping the fragile squares of precious glass into place. Inside the carpenters were adding the final touches to the panelling, sanding and waxing the parquet, ensuring that each key turned freely in each lock.   Soon the furniture would be carried in, the carpets laid, the curtains hung, the first fires lit in the fine stone cheminées.

'A modern house, with every convenience,' he told himself. 'A house built for a new age. An enlightened age when old wrongs would be put to right, ancient feudal traditions swept away and narrow superstitions shown to be the fruit of ignorance and prejudice.

Luc the mason and I planned it together. A house is like a living organism, he'd said, cleverly designed it will profit from the weather. It should be basking in the sun, sheltered from the wind, cooled by water, protected from the cold.

We'd situated it to the south of the forest where a fine row of mature oaks would form a windbreak from the winter winds. Below the house, was a spring whose fresh supply would not only feed our wells but in addition cool our cellar. The man was a scientist for all his rough ways. He explained how water filtering through a the gravel floor, would evaporate providing a natural form of refrigeration to keep my fine wines cool.

I'd wanted a house that was light and well-ventilated. He'd scorned at first the extravagance in terms of glass and heat loss. But at length we'd agreed on long windows facing South West. These would give us the benefit of the morning sun which could be quite strong even in winter. And more windows on to the courtyard at the rear would trap the warmth of the sheltered evening sun.

Above the house, there would be an attic running the full length and width of the house to accomodate the tithe. To access the attic without the inconvenience of the workers passing through the house, it required its own staircase. The design of this was Luc's proudest achievement. I watched as the stairs rose within their cage of wooden scaffolding, each step hewn from a single slab of local stone, forming a strong stable spiral. Its form brought to mind those strange remnants of shell, that the plough would sometimes bring up to the surface. Evidence of the Deluge some say, when Noah's flood covered the Earth. But even that is being questionned these days.

I'd brought Ann one evening and the two of us stood humbled before this work of craftsmanship. Skill that was akin to that of God, the great architect. I could envisage it long in the future. Long after we were gone and the house had fallen, crumbled away into the earth, this staircase would be standing, its spiral still intact, as witness of the house that once was here.

I took Ann's hand in mine and we climbed it, clambering over the mason's scaffolding and entered the attic. The untiled charpente towered over us, tall as a church, dwarfing us with its span. Beneath it was space enough for all the tithe and more besides. I threw back the tarpaulin and drew Ann to me and we leaned out of the dormer gazing out over my land. Five hundred hectares, stretching as far as the blue horizon. My pastures dotted with their slow files of white cows. My fields with their rich furrows ready to receive the seed. The swinging arcs of the sowers pacing up and down, sowing the spring wheat. As I stood there the church clock chimed the angelus and the sowers halted in their tracks and drifted back towards the village as if the bell had set a tide in motion. From now on it will be our bell that rings the hours. The reveil, the midi and the angelus.

Soon, with god's blessing, our children will fill the house. I'd vowed to bring them up according to Rousseau's principles: · They will be breast-fed by their mother. Barefoot until the age of ten. Hungry for knowledge long before they are given lessons. Strong healthy noisy children. My noble savages.

That's when I vowed to plant a tree to commemorate this day. A

Seqouia. A tree from the New World to herald a new age of man.

-------- -- -------

Julia 2009

The Sequoia now stood dark and substantial, dominating the landscape.
What had it witnessed, I wondered, in its two and a half centuries, while
generations in the house were born, lived and died, prospered or suffered,
all within its lifespan?

An idea was starting to form in my mind. What if I researched the
lives of the people who'd lived in the house? It could make a book –
something far more worthwhile than the 'novel' as Dad optimistically called
it – that I'd been trying to write.   If I took that sabbatical I'd have six
months – six whole months to do the research – get something down on
paper...

I was distracted by the sound of a text on my mobile. Hang on I had a
load of texts.   I scrolled through them. Mostly variations on: 'Where are u?'
'Where the fk r u.' Ending with 'R u ded or wt?

Simon! It sounded like trouble.   I made my way down to the end of
the garden and rang him.

.'Hi Simon. It's me Julia.'

The line crackled with interference.

'Thank god.' ....The line was breaking up.... ' in sh...t on Premo.'

'What?'

'Where...ell is the campaign?'

'On Premo? Why?'

'Bast.....d......arry.....!!'

'What?'

'... at   it arry loused up. When will you ...back?'

'Errm?'

'You st..l there. an ... hear me?'

'Only just. Look I'll ring you from a callbox tomorrow. OK?'

'I g..ta ..... b.. back?'

My mobile was out of battery. I flipped it closed. Simon sounded pretty desperate. A Premo repitch. Premo – the *wonder crème* for pre-menstrual cellulite - the biggest money-earner in the agency. We could be losing it. Back in London that bit of news would have had me reaching for the Prozac. But here, looking out on the silent garden in the gathering gloom, it all seemed a million miles away. In another time. On another planet. I realised I didn't care. I didn't give a shit.

I realised guiltily that I'd left the copy for the latest campaign in a drawer in my desk. Well, Simon would have to drag it out, finish it up. It only needed the visuals. Anyway, I'd worry about it tomorrow.

Chapter Eight

The following morning I was up early, standing shivering in the village callbox. Just my luck, it only took France Telecom phone-cards so I was forced to wait in the queue in the Tabac while each small purchase of local paper or cigarettes was accompanied by a run-down of the customer's health, family, veggie patch, bad leg etc. The woman in front of me was trying to get a photo-copy of her ID card and the paper kept jamming. I could feel a slight tightening in my forehead. The return of the tension headache I hadn't had since I'd been here.

Simon was more sympathetic when I eventually got through.

'Yes, well I know you had to sort things out. I understand, about your Dad and everything.'

I had a sudden flashback to that bleak morning. The phone ringing in what seemed like the middle of the night. Still dark, groping for it, answering it groggily. And then trying to make sense of what Jacqueline was trying to tell me. She'd found him at the foot of the stairs when she'd let herself in. She was gabbling on about trying to find names in his address book and the codes and... He must have been drunk I told myself. Yes, that's what it was. Or he'd had a giddy fit. He'd be all right once he came round. Slowly it dawned on me, what she was trying to say. He was lying there at the foot of the stairs. Not drunk, not unconcious - but dead.

There followed that nightmare round of calls. Jane, Sarah, Mummy. Mummy reasserted herself in the position of wife and kept going on about a funeral in England. Well, as she rightly pointed out, no-one knew him *out there*. Sarah didn't seem to react. Jane wanted everything done in rush, as if that would make him less dead somehow. Charles was delegated to go to France and sort things out. Since he was a solicitor he seemed the right person, all the legal stuff and everything. So I'd just got on with work, automatically going through the paces. Until it hit me one morning. Two weeks after the funeral.

I'd hated the way everyone had to give condolences, meeting you in the corridor, not knowing quite what to say. But somehow it was worse when they stopped. Was I meant to forget he'd ever existed? Your Dad's died OK? It's over now, get on with your life. I came in one morning and sat at my desk and nothing seemed to make sense any more. I guess it was a combination of things. The entropic pregnancy, the aftermath and the fact that I'd finally split up with Oliver. I suppose in the circumstances, it wasn't surprising I'd cracked. So that morning, I just walked out of the office, packed the car and took off for France.

'You feeling better then? Getting over it?' asked Simon.

His sympathy made me feel even more guilty.

'Yes... yes I think I am. I'm sorry, you know, about making off like that. But you don't have to worry – I've done all the copy, you've only got to add the visuals.'

I told Simon where to find it and I could hear him riffling round in the drawer making 'hmm' noises.

'Look Julia. I don't feel confident handling this without you,' he said at last.

I gazed out into the watery sunshine. It was Thursday, market day. Outside the callbox the village square had come to life. The stall holders were setting up their wooden tables and laying out rows of home-grown vegetables. The fish man was unpacking fat slabs of fish from his crates of crushed ice. The cheese lady was piling up soft rounds of crumbly goats' cheese. By the look of her, pre-menstrual cellulite was the last thing on her mind.

'When's the presentation?'

'Day after tomorrow.'

'That settles it. It'll take me a day to drive back. There's no point.'

'Fly. Take Eurostar. Rent a private jet if necessary. The company will pay. Barry's got the shits. He says you're the only one who can handle Premo.'

'So I imagine. You're all blokes.'

'Yeah well. I'll keep a bar-stool warm for you at the Five Bells.'

'You'll do nothing of the sort. I've done the copy. All you have to do is get the biggest layout pad you can find and a set of markers and get the whole lot drawn up and on Barry's desk by the end of the day.'

'So you're not coming?'

'No Simon. For once you're going to have to cope on your own.'

I stepped out of the phone booth and took a deep breath. Closing my mind to guilt, I made a round of the market stalls treating myself to free range eggs, a fat succulent artichoke and a bunch of thick white asparagus. As a final impulse purchase I bought a bunch of lettuce seedlings from a chap who had a load of them in a galvanised bucket. The weather was already warm and sunny. With any luck I would have fresh lettuces of my own home-grown within weeks.

------- -- -------

When I got back to the house I found the lettuce seedlings were already wilting in the boot of my car, I'd have to plant them right away if they were going to survive. A brief search found a rusting implement in the barn, something between a pick and a hoe with a long straight handle. Armed with this, I went up to the stretch of land which it seemed had been designated as a vegetable plot. There was a ragged row of brussels sprouts and a couple of cabbages, goodness knows who had planted them, certainly not Dad. I started digging. The soil was rich and black and I had soon carved a little trench in which to bed down the seedlings. I was so engrossed in the job I didn't hear anyone approach. A voice made my jump.

'What are you doing?' It was a deep voice, male and French. The way he asked, brusquely like that, without a formal greeting was pretty rude for a Frenchman.

I straightened up. It was the fellow I'd nearly collided with in the lane, my neighbour from the farm next door. I shaded my eyes against the sun. His body was outlined against the sky, strong and muscular. He stood looking down at me, his face in shadow, unreadable.

'I was planting these lettuces,' I said, similarly not giving him the politeness of a greeting or introduction. If he could be rude, so could I.

'Lettuces? May I?' He made his way down the bank and looked down at my handiwork.

'You're planting them too deep. Anyway there's no use putting them in before Sans Glace.'

'Saint Who?'

'No. Sans Glace. The day of the last frosts.'

'We always plant lettuces in April back home.'

'In England?'

'Yes.'

'Why are you planting lettuces if you're selling the property?'

'Who says I'm selling?'

'It's a small village.'

I had returned to stabbing at the ground with the pick.

'Here, let me do that.'

I let him take it from me. His hand was large, his wrist incredibly strong and hairy. Mummy would have had a fit, I could hear her voice right now: 'For all you know Julia that man might be a rapist or a murderer.' But he didn't seem like either.

I stood and watched as he undid my careful planting. I couldn't help noticing his wide back, narrow hips, his strong jawline...

Stop it Julia Lefarge, you can stop right there. I gave myself a shake. He's nothing but a local yokel – a bit of rough - not your type at all.

'Have you any idea who planted those?' I asked, indicating the sprouts and cabbages.

He grunted with the effort of digging. 'Yes. Me.'

'Oh.' I didn't know how I could politely point out his vegetables were on my land.

He stopped work and leant on the hoe looking at me so intently I had to look away. 'I could put some carrots in for you if you like.'

'Will they be all right before Sans Glace?'

'The frosts should be over by the time they come up.'

'That would be kind.'

'You've been down at the notaire's.'

He must have been watching me. Spying on me.

'Yes. There's a lot to arrange.'

'So you are selling up?' he looked me once again full in the eyes. His eyes, in contrast to his swarthy skin were hazel rimmed with amber.

Idiotically, I could feel myself colouring up. I took the hoe from him and started raking round the seedlings so he wouldn't notice. 'I haven't decided yet.'

Clogged with thick clay, the hoe was doing more harm than good. He stood watching my pathetic efforts with his hands in his pockets.

'I'll put some haricot in for you as well When the time's right. I'm putting some in for myself. It won't take a moment.'

The cheek of it. He was standing there on my land as if he owned it.

'Why don't you grow them on your own land?' I blurted out.

He gave me another very straight look.

'But this is my land.'

'Oh no it's not.'

'Those pickets are the boundary,' he said, indicating them with nod over his shoulder.

I stared at the line of fence posts, they looked pretty new to me.

'I think there's been some misunderstanding. My land goes right up to the hedge,' I insisted.

He stood his ground. 'You can check at the Mairie. Ask to see the plans.'

'I will. I'll do that. Thank you for your help Monsieur err...'

'Ladier, Jacques the name.'

'Julia,' I held out a hand. 'Julia Lefarge.'

He ignored my hand. 'A French name.'

'Yes, my father's family was French. But I'm English.'

'So I noticed. From your accent.'

'I'm doing my best to lose it.'

'That would be a pity. It's very attractive,' he gave me another long look. Humiliatingly, under his gaze, I felt that blush reassert itself. And even more humiliating, I could see he'd noticed.

'I'll put those seeds in then,' he said, turning and walking back towards his house without so much as an *au revoir*. I watched as he whistled to his dog and slammed the door shut after him.

I made my way absent-mindedly back to the kitchen. '*Ladier, Jacques the name*' He had a nice voice, deep and masculine. '*I'm putting some in for myself.*' '*Myself*' implying he was on his own. Was he single, I wondered? The farmhouse looked sad and abandoned. A thin whisp of smoke rose from a single chimney. There wasn't a windowbox or a washing line, nothing to suggest a woman was around.

    I suddenly realised I was standing in the kitchen with the hoe still grasped in my hand. I went and stored it away in the barn.

Chapter Nine

Thursday came and I had no news from Simon. I wondered guiltily how the presentation had gone. But I'd done my bit. More than.

On Friday morning I got a text message not from Simon but the department head - Barry. Ominously it had only two words:'Call me.'

I was put through to Barry immediately: 'How's things. Gets a bit better with time eh? Your Dad and everything.'

'Thanks Barry yes. I'm over it now. What's the news?'

'Not good I'm afraid. Oh they loved the creative work, by the way. But they're streamlining and it looks like Premo's going over to PD&D to join their other brands which means they can make considerable media savings. It was foreseeable, I suppose. But one always hopes...'

'I see...'

'Look Julia. I'm not going to beat around the bush. You know Premo was one of our biggest spenders. There are going to have to be cutbacks.'

I swallowed. 'I see,' I said again. This was going to be a big blow to Simon. It was the first decent job he'd had.

'I'm afraid we've looked at all the options but the long and the short of it is... We're going to have to let you go.'

A sickening giddy feeling ran through my body. Barry was still talking. 'Of course there'll be a nice little bit of compensation. You've been with us how long? Eight years?'

'Nearly ten,' I managed to choke back.

'Yes well. Should be a fair-sized package to tide you over. And you're not going to have any problem finding another... I'll put a word in if you like...'

'But what about Simon? Simon's only been with the company eight months. Is he due anything?'

'Oh Simon's staying. Frankly Julia, the work he did on Premo. Well, it was pretty impressive...'

'The work *he* did on Premo?'

'I know you're a team but..'

'You think he did it all? Is that what he told you?'

'But you were away...'

'Simon pissed around doing sod-all before I left, He came up with crap. I wrote the entire campaign. All he was, was a wrist. And in more ways than one by the sound of it.'

'Of course it's understandable you feel bitter...'

'Bitter. I don't mind being fired Barry. Oh sorry, *made redundant*. I just don't like the creepy way you've gone about it...'

'Believe me, I hate all this as much as you do. My job may well be on the line.'

'My heart bleeds for you, Barry.'

'Look Julia...'

'Goodbye.'

I put the receiver down and made for the car.

I drove at an illegal pace, hurtling down between the two avenues of trees with my mind in a turmoil. Ten years I'd been at M&M. Ten years of writing drivelling copy about piss-awful products. Stuff people didn't really want or need, otherwise they'd've gone and found it for themselves, wouldn't they?

I felt as if I was about to throw up. As I reached the top of the rise I pulled the car into the side of the road and sat there trying to get my composure back.

I could see La Mulatière down in the valley, the sunlight glinting on the slate of the tower, the stone walls glowing with the early morning sun. I wound the window down and took a deep breath. With a rush of fresh air my head seemed miraculously to clear.

Suddenly it was all so simple. Wasn't this what I'd been waiting for? Forget a sabbatical, I could let my flat and stay at La Mulatière for as long as I liked. Redundancy money was just what I needed. I could do the place up properly and maybe I could get Sarah and Jane to chip in too.

I turned the key in the ignition and drove on down the avenue. The flickering sunlight filtered through the trees sent little bursts of excitement fizzing through my veins. I had the exhilerating sense that I'd shrugged something off. A skin? A shedding? A life?

Chapter Ten

I made my way into the house with a hundred projects running through my brain. In my imagination room after room was stripped, painted, papered and had its windows hung with curtains. It would take some furniture to fill this place. But we still didn't know what to do with all father's stuff. He'd been happy to manage with a few basics, plus some pieces that he'd bought with the house. His furniture was still in storage in England which was costing a small fortune. What if we stored it here?

I wandered erratically making a mental note of what would go where. Carrying in my mind a difficult-to-place wardrobe I found myself in one of the back bedrooms filled with the warmth of the afternoon sun.

In places the wallpaper had come unstuck and was hanging in great swathes. I pulled at one and it came off in a single satisfying sheet, powdering me with plaster dust. It would be easy enough to strip this room. Then I could slap on some emulsion and make it look halfway decent. It would be a start.

The rough wooden ladder Jerôme had used had been put away neatly in the barn. Armed with the ladder, a bucket of water and a metal spatula from the kitchen, I was set to attack.

The ancient wallpaper was of a shadowy flower pattern with an interposed stripe, quaintly French. I would have loved to keep it, but even in the better patches it was spotted with mould, too far gone. It tore off in great satisfying sheets round the window. As it fell to the floor I noticed that the wall underneath was lined with some kind of newsprint. I climbed down the ladder and picked up a piece. It was a page from a journal headed: '*Gazette Hebdomadiare de Medecine et de Chirurgie*' It even gave the date *'26 Juillet 1882''*. The hot topic of the day seemed to be : *'Le vertige de la valse'* - the giddiness of the waltz - it conjured up a world of ladies in evening gloves having the vapours. 1882. I considered the faded wallpaper with new respect. It could be forgiven a damp spot or two at its great age.

I tried to imagine the room as it once had been. There was a darker patch where some tall piece of furniture had stood against the wall. The pattern was less faded - showing sinuous flowers and corded ribbons in a surprisingly strong shade of violet. It had most probably been a mirrored armoire. I pictured it reflecting back the image of the room. A dressing table set with its silver backed hair brush and hand mirror, a tortoiseshell comb, a scent spray with its tasselled pump swathed in silk. I now noticed an unfaded rectangle on the parquet and the dents left by four feet. This must be where the bed had once stood. And that square beside it would have been covered by a rug. Look carefully and you could make out the ghost of a room. As if - like those first shadowy photographic images of Fox Talbot - its negative image had been printed by sunlight.

It was with this sense of somehow delving back into the past, peeling back the onion-skin layers of time, that I returned to stripping the wallpaper. Layer after layer of medical journal came to light. They'd been pasted under the wallpaper to serve as a backing, rather in the way professional decorators use lining paper. The paper was harder to shift further from the window. I had to score and soak it and a kitchen spatula wasn't the best tool for the job. By late afternoon I'd reached the hardest part where it would only come off in frustratingly flimsy strips. But I wanted to keep going while the light lasted. The sun was sinking fast, another half hour or so and I could allow myself to break off for some supper and a welcome glass of the bottle of Medoc I'd treated myself to on the way back from the notaire.

I was in the process of scoring, working alongside a chimney breast when my spatula slid deep into the wall. There was a straight vertical crack into which it disappeared up to the handle. I scraped at the paper with my nails. There was fabric underneath. It seemed I'd unearthed some kind of primitive cupboard. Papered over like that and padded out by the pages of medical journal, it had been totally invisible.

Clawing back the fabric with my fingers, I discovered another horizontal crack at the base and sure enough, unearthed some hinges on the far side. It was a door all right. A door papered over how long ago? If the medical journals were contemporary – it must be well over a century.

The light had almost faded from the room. I stood there caught between curiosity and a vague sense of foreboding. What would I find inside? The hidden treasure of the Lamulatières? Or something more sinister? I shivered as my brain conjured up various horror-movie alternatives. Maybe I should leave it till tomorrow. But curiosity was getting the upper hand. I set to work feverishly stripping off the last of the paper inch by inch.

By the time I finished the moon was shining into the room, providing just enough light to see by. With the edge of my spatula, I gingerly eased the door open. At first I thought the cupboard was empty. And then, as my eyes grew accustomed to the gloom, I had a shock which made me almost lose my balance. Something glinted, it was an eye, no two eyes were staring back at me. I steadied myself, leaned inside and drew out a small oil portrait.

I took it downstairs to have a good look at it in the firelight. The canvas was unframed, stained with damp round the edges and the varnish had dulled with age to a treacle colour but the top part had survived in pretty good nick.

The sitter, a young man, stared back at me with an even gaze from his wide grey eyes. He had high cheek bones, and rather an aristocratic nose. There was something sardonic in the way he looked at me. He seemed to be regarding me with mild amusement, as if to say: What do you think you're doing in my house, Julia Lefarge?

Was it his house I wondered? I turned the canvas over. It looked pretty old. On the evidence of the medical journals, it must date from before 1882. I took it downstairs and propped it up on the mantlepiece while I ate some supper. He was a fine looking fellow. Pity he was so much my senior.

Later that evening I took out the family tree and traced back through the names, finding the most recent male - Doctor Anselme Lamulatière, the father of Jerôme's Mademoiselle Marie. A doctor - that made sense of all those medical journals. I stared at the portrait. Was he a bungling country doctor, I wondered, doling out cure-alls like that inept husband of Emma Bovary? Or a man of science? How advanced was the medicine of his day?

I sat up late into the night risking a severe attack of hypochondria piecing scraps of the journals together. Worse than the diseases were the cures - with a predominance of iodine prescribed for the most intimate parts.

Chapter Eleven

Sipping my coffee the following morning, my gaze returned to the portrait. Was this fellow the doctor? In order to know for sure, I needed to get it dated. I was dithering over how to go about this when my eye was caught by a mailing I'd saved propped up on the mantlepiece. It was from some local auctioneers in Moulins. They were offering free valuations, which obviously meant they could date things which hopefully included paintings. I rang them straight away.

They were preparing for a sale. A valuer would be on hand all week. They assured me he would be only too happy to take a look at my portrait. I decided to drive into Moulins that afternoon and take advantage of their offer.

------- -- -------

The auctioneers Saddes et Fils was an old family business with premises on Moulin's main square. Their sales rooms were in a cavernous building, deceptively small from the front, reaching back as wide and as long as a cinema. Friday was viewing day and I found the place packed, milling with dealers and potential buyers. I made my way between crested armoires and gilded consoles, taxing my self restraint to the full, turning a blind eye to pieces that looked *custom made* for La Mulatière.

The expert giving the valuations was seated at a desk at the far end of the room. I waited as he handed back a piece of porcelain to a hopeful vendor. 'No Madame. It's very charming. But I'm afraid, a copy all the same.'

He took my portrait between careful hands and placed it on the desk.

'I'm pretty sure it's pre-1882.' I explained about the medical journals.

Squeezing his eye-glass into place, the fellow nodded. 'Yes Madame, you're right. But it's considerably older than that. Eighteenth Century I should say. Not signed I see, so not of great value. But a nice little portrait. You should have it cleaned. It would be worth it.'

'I'm not really worried about the value. What interests me, is who it's of.'

'You can only establish that through its provenance. By the sound of it, it hasn't moved far in its lifetime. Some chemical tests could give you a more exact idea of the date.'

He handed me the business card of a local restorer, saying. 'Take it to Monsieur Fouquier, he should be able to help.'

------- -- -------

Paul Fouquier's workshop was tucked away in one of Moulins narrow cobbled back streets. By the look of his shop, he was the man for the job. The tiny shopfront with it's hand-painted fascia didn't look as if it had changed in centuries. Inside, the place was stacked with paintings awaiting restoration. My entrance was announced by the ring of an ancient looking bell. A pale white-haired man in a brown dustcoat, bent as if from years of stooping over a workbench, came out from a back room.

'I'm afraid I've got an awful lot on at the moment,' he said apologetically.

'All I really want is to date this painting,' I explained.

He took it from me and held it up to the light.

'Oh yes indeed. Well painted. Where did you find it?'

I explained about the hidden cupboard and he nodded thoughtfully.

'The expert at Sadde's thought it was Eighteenth Century,' I added.

'Well, there's one little thing I could do. If you'll permit me, I'll just remove a little of this varnish. It's all got to come off in the long run.'

'Please. Go ahead.'

He went out to the back and returned with a bottle and a wad of cottonwool.

I watched as he worked at it very gently. He cleaned away a patch above the face.

'Ah ha,' he said. 'As I thought. The hair is powdered, quite grey. And yet this is the face of a young man. So pre-revolutionary. The type of canvas of course confirms this.'

I stared down at the grave grey eyes. 'A dish' that's what Sarah would have called him.

'In that case, I'd definitely like it cleaned.'

'But I'm afraid you'll have to be patient,' said the old fellow. He wouldn't be able to touch it for months. 'Leave it with me and I'll see what I can do.'

Regretfully, I entrusted the portrait to him.

'You'll be surprised how much more will come to light,' he said as he showed me out.

------- -- -------

Eighteenth Century, so not the doctor. I went back to the family tree. There was only one male whose dates coincided with Paul Fourquier's opinion. He had the rather grand name of 'Jean Mulatier de la Grolière – chevalier'. Chevalier!

Chapter Twelve

That evening I sat enjoying my evening glass of wine fantasising about the months to come. I pictured a kind of endless summer where I would spend most of my time outside, planting things and growing things and watching honest and willing workers hard at work doing all the tricky building tasks I couldn't handle myself.

The swallows swooped whistling back and forth across the courtyard. They were flying low, I noticed, catching insects on the wing. Hang on, wasn't that a sign a storm was on the way? Sure enough beyond the gleaming pyramid of the tower, storm clouds were massing overhead.

As I finished my wine I heard the first rumble of thunder. The kitchen light flickered, blinked and then went out. A wind had brewed up out of nowhere and was sweeping around the courtyard. The first heavy drops of rain splattered over the paving. I went back inside, forcing the door closed behind me. I jiggled the lightswitch - no luck. The switch in the dining room didn't work either. It seemed the whole house had gone down. It had got very dark. I located the candelabra that I'd left on the mantlepiece And lit the candles. It had suddenly turned very cold.

For several hours thunder shattered the peace of the countryside and lightning slashed through the garden. Rain lashed against the windows and then finally a torrent of hailstones flew down the chimney to die hissing on the fire. I stoked it up and put on another log but it was too late, the hail had won and extinguished it.

The following morning dawned fresh and clear. I tried a light switch but got no reaction. Downstairs it was the same. The kettle was obstinately dead, so coffee wasn't an option. It seemed the whole house had gone down. I helped myself to a glass of water and took my mobile down to the end of the garden and rang the EDF.

'No Madame, there's no interruption in the supply,' A woman's voice assured me. 'It must be your property that has a problem.'

She said she could send someone out within a week or so.

'But I can't wait a whole week for electricity.'

The woman wanted the number of my electricity account. I explained that I didn't have one. In that case she wanted me to sign on for the supply which meant I needed something called a 'Relève d'Identité' from my bank plus at least three proofs of residence. Bills would do.

'But I don't have a French bank account. Or any bills. I've only just come here.'

'Well, some proof of ownership or a rental agreement...'

'I don't have anything like that. It's a bit complicated.'

The woman gave a disbelieving sigh and enquired the name of the previous owner.

'But that's your name,' she retorted..

'I know, the house was my father's.'

We had a nice little contretemps as she tried to assertain whether he was on direct debit or the date of his last bill. None of which I knew. Eventually with a further sigh the woman took down the full address.

'That explains it,' she said in a deeply disapproving voice. 'He hasn't paid his bill.'

'He couldn't. He's dead.'

'Oh I see.' The woman sounded more sympathetic after that. 'Have you tried pressing the master 'Interrompteur?'

'The what?'

'The red switch on the main panel. Try it Madame, you never know. In the meantime I'll book you in for a safety check. A representative will call.'

I'd spotted an electricity panel in one of the outbuildings during my tour of exploration. A Heath-Robinson affair with lethal looking wires coming out of it. I went and examined it more closely. There was a red button. Let there be light, I prayed as I pressed it. And sure enough when I poked my head out of the door I could see a bulb shining upstairs in the house.

Over the next few days I came to recognise that electricity was a luxury not to be trusted. Stormy weather entailed a violent flickering and if I switched on anything like the vacuum cleaner, the red button would instantly be outraged and turn everything off.

Originally, I'd been lulled into a false kind of confidence, the majority of the rooms had promising looking switches and sockets. But now with a closer look I could see most of the wiring dated back to the dawn of the electrical age. No-one had bothered with the wings, let alone the attics - these lay undisturbed in their Eighteenth Century gloom.

A few mornings later a blue EDF van drew up outside the house and a man with an official looking file under his arm said he'd come to carry out the promised safety check.

He'd barely passed through the door before he slapped a notice on the ancient circuit board saying 'Condamné' The fuse board stood disconnected, sprouting a spaghetti of perished cables. Electricity ceased to be an option for the foreseeable future.

-------- -- -------

I'd settled on the room with the painted panels as my study. I imagined it might have been a sitting room for Jerôme's Mademoiselle Marie. A place where she could sit over her petit point or water colours. Maybe the panels had been painted by her, up a ladder dabbing away with a fine brush, wrapped in a copious apron? As I lugged a table up the stairs I had some pretty self-righteous thoughts about the easy life of pre-liberated woman.

I ranged my papers on it in piles in order of urgency. I was fast accumulating a mini-mountain. Taking a long sheet of lined paper I started listing my priorities. Top of the list came a phone line, there was no way I could continue living here without email. There were promising-looking phone sockets so there must have been a line once. Typically Dad had never got around to reinstating it.

I settled down to make some realistic calculations. I had a stack of bills prised on a nail that I'd been trying to ignore. By the light of the candelbra I set about making sense of them.

A sudden draught made the candles flicker and die. I spun round to find Jacques Ladier leaning into the room, one hand up against the lintel.

'Sorry to disturb you? I hope I didn't make you jump.'

He stood filling the doorway, tall and muscular. I realised sinkingly that had I wanted to, I wouldn't have been able to push past him.

'Yes, you did as a matter of fact,' I said getting up from my chair.

He walked over to the candelbra, took a Bic lighter out of his pocket and lit the three candles.

'You should get a bell. Or a dog. I could find you a good dog.'

'I can't take on a dog. I don't know how long I'm staying.'

'I came to ask if you wanted a pig?'

'A pig?'

'I'm killing the pigs tomorrow.'

'What on earth would I do with a pig?'

'You could fill that freezer you've got in the kitchen,' he said. 'You'd never be at loss for a meal. It's good pork. Free range, fed on nothing but the best.'

I relaxed somewhat, his visit seemed innocent enough.

'Not on. ' I gestured towards the candelbra. ' I've no electricity, you see.'

'I could run a cable over for you if you like. Just to keep you going.'

'Would you? That would really help me out. But I'd have to pay you for the electricity...'

He brushed this away with a wave of his hand.

'Buy the pig. That'll be payment enough.'

'How much?'

'A friend's price.'

'Hmm.'

'Home smoked hams, your own pâté, côte de porc. Filet. Rillettes, épaule salé...'

Epaule salé - the French for bacon. I hadn't had bacon in ages. The thought of the smell of it cooking, almost nicer than the taste really, made my mouth water.

'All right, you've talked me into it.'

'I'll be round with it, day after tomorrow.' He was about to leave so I held out a hand. He took it and made a step or two in my direction as if to kiss me on the cheeks. I took an awkward step back and immediately regretted it. I flushed bright red realising that he must think I was being really stand-offish. Jacques stood there for a moment looking at me assessingly, then he turned on his heel and set off down the stairs.

I hurried down and locked the kitchen door behind him. I leant against it my heart beating violently in my chest. Why did Jacques always have this mortifying effect on me? I peered through the window at him, he was already in his car, revving up the engine. I watched as he drove down the drive and disappeared into the lane.

No, he wasn't my type at all. Scary and hairy that's what Jane and Sarah would say. Oliver's body was smooth, almost hairless, he's always always clean shaven. Jacques had designer stubble you could take a scythe to. He probably had hair down his back! Anyway, what was I thinking of? He was just some clod-hopping farmer – we had absolutely *nothing* in common.

------- -- -------

Next day, when I arrived in the kitchen I found a four point extension flex standing outside the back door. The flex trailed across the courtyard and disappeared under the hedge. Jacques had kept his promise.

Gingerly, I plugged the electric kettle into one of the sockets and was rewarded by a contented kettle noise. '*Brilliant!*' Hot coffee and without having to stoke the wood burning stove.

The pig arrived the following day. I was dressing when I heard the exhaust of the Espace backfire. I hurried down and caught Jacques as he was about to leave.

'Can't stop I'll be late for work.'

'What have you done with the pork?'

'In the barn.'

'How much do I owe you?'

'Don't worry. I'll let you know.' He waved and was off.

He might at least have helped me load the freezer. I wondered how much pork you got off a whole pig.

I picked my way across the overgrown courtyard, unlatched the door and leant my weight against it. The sunlight spread inside the barn, lighting up... No, not a nice pile of cling-filmed joints and sliced rashers. Propped upright in the wheelbarrow was a decapitated pig, it's head resting on its body at a jaunty angle, a cigarette between its lips. I shuddered. Yuck.

What on earth was I meant to do with it now?

------- -- ------

I went and found Jerôme up on the veggie patch. He was mounding up soil in long ridges. When I explained about the pig, Jerôme shrugged. 'He should know what to do with it, he's a butcher by trade.'

'I thought he was a farmer,'

'He's a bit of everything,' he said darkly.

I watched as Jerôme returned to work deftly piling up the soft soil, dropping in a potato and letting the soil slip back, burying it in a single economical movement. 'I had a few seed potatoes left over. I thought I'd put them in for you,' he called over his shoulder

Then he straightened up. 'I see you've sown some carrots.'

'That wasn't me. It was Jacques Ladier.'

'Huh!' Jerôme frowned and went back to work without a word. This wasn't like him. Jerôme was really nice about everybody. I'd never heard him say a harsh word about anyone.

'What have you got against him?'

Jerôme cast a meaningful look at the fence posts. 'How long have those been there?'

'I'm not sure. Anyway he's been really helpful. He's planted loads of stuff. I can't manage this lot on my own.'

Jerôme continued digging obviously thinking that Jacques was doing him out of a job.

'Surely you must know who this land belongs to?' I prompted. 'Can't you remember?'

'In my father's day the farm belonged to the chateau. There wasn't a boundary between the two.'

'So when was the land divided?'

'Must have been when old Ladier died.'

'And was Jacques here then?'

'No he was abroad. Back in his own country.'

'Oh? Where would that be?'

'Somewhere around Marseille, I think.'

'But that's not abroad. That's France.'

'He's a funny fellow. Moody. I'd keep well out of his way Madame.'

I glanced over at the farm. All the shutters were closed. Was there a darker side to Jacques? A man living alone, perhaps I should be on my guard. But maybe this was just Jerôme. Welcoming as the village people had been to me - a total foreigner - they could be hostile to people from other regions of their own country.

I hung around that afternoon fuming, waiting for the sound of the Espace driving into the farmyard. At six thirty I heard the inimitable rattle of its exhaust. Forcing my way through the gap in the hedge I went to confront Jacques.

'Yes?' he said abruptly, no bonjour.

I was similarly brief. 'That pig. What on earth do you expect me to do with it?'

He made no reply but walked round to the back of the Espace. I followed him.

'Well?'

He flung open the boot with a force that made me jump. Inside was a selection of butcher's knives to make your blood run cold. He leaned down and took a great cleaver in his hand. It obviously gave him some satisfaction to see me back away a pace.

'I'll need three kilos of rough salt. Four spices. Pepper. Wine vinegar. Garlic, onions and two good bottles of Bordeaux and I'll do it tomorrow morning. Get the stove stoked good and hot.'

'Right.'

'And bags, you'll have to do the packing. You'll need two sizes, large and small, you can get them at Champion and you'll need something to mark them with.'

'I'll go first thing'

'And sausages. Do you want sausages? Black pudding?'

'Doesn't that involve blood?'

'I've got it here,' he said pointing to a large plastic reservoir, the kind of thing you buy wine in, in bulk. It was filled with something ominously red.'

'Don't worry about the black pudding.'

He shrugged. 'It's your choice.'

Chapter Thirteen

Jerôme was standing in the barn eyeing the pig when I returned next morning from the supermarket.

'Nice beast. What did it cost you?' I could tell by his tone whatever I said he'd think I was being overcharged.

'I'm not sure yet. I'm rather cross actually. I expected it to come in wrapped joints. Just look at it.'

I indicated the head. The rheumy dead eyes had a pale fringe if eyelashes, gross!

'Ah the head. But that's the best bit,' he said.

'In that case, it's yours . Please take it.'

'Thank you. I'll get my wife to make some brawn. Delicious. There's no bit of a pig you can't use you know. Brain, pancreas, heart... Even the bladder.'

I shuddered: 'Please...'

'No this will interest you, Madame. In the old days when people couldn't afford glass they used to blow up the bladder like a child's balloon until it was almost transparent. Then you'd let it dry, slit it down the side and open it out. You could use it like glass for windows. It let the light in, kept the cold out. There's no end of uses for a pig.'

'Well this pig is going to be used for nice chops and joints. Anything else you are more than welcome to.'

We were interrupted by the sound of the Espace coming up the drive. Jacques climbed out of the car and the two men exchanged a curt good morning. There was clearly no love lost between them.

I stood by as Jacques set up his butcher's block on a pair of trestles in the barn. It seemed he'd come fully equipped.

Right!' he said as he wrapped a bloodied apron round his body and sharpened his knife. I was allowed a smile today, although an evil one, as he slashed the blade against the steel. 'Have you got everything I asked for?'

'Yes. I think so.' I showed him my basket.

'Start chopping onions and peel the garlic and I'll bring in the meat for the Rillettes.'

I retired to the kitchen, all too glad to be out of the scene of the cutting. Occasional glances towards the barn revealed his shadow on the wall cleaving and chopping accompanied by horrible sounds of dismemberment. He soon called to me from the barn door. He held out a plastic bucket full of chopped fatty pork.

'Get this cooking in a pan of salted water.'

'Shouldn't I trim the fat off first?'

'No, you've got to render it down. This has to cook for a good two hours.'

By midday the kitchen was a-steam with two great vats of bubbling fat . All my plastic washing up bowls were filled to the top with sliced belly marinating in a snowy mush of onion, garlic, vinegar and coarse salt. A string of sausages fit for a giant's Punch and Judy show was growing in the barn and I had discovered what the two bottles of good Bordeaux were for. Jacques had supplied some five star plonk to soak the belly in. The good Bordeaux was disappearing glass by glass down him.

'Won't you join me?' he asked, indicating the bottles.

I shook my head and said in a prudish fashion. 'No thank you. I never have a drink until the evening.'

'More's the pity,' he said and downed another glass.

At midday Jerôme came to say he was leaving, casting a meaningful glance towards the barn. I found him a large plastic carrier and he left, with a grunt of acknowledgement to Jacques, with the pig's head and a enough pork fat to clog the arteries of Allier.

It was lunch time and I realised I was starving. I'd been up at crack of dawn and on my feet all morning working as butcher's assistant, filling bags and loading the freezer as fast as Jacques cut the pork. It was well past the usual time I grabbed a snack. I felt weak at the knees. I also realised that I couldn't eat while Jacques was here. Or if I did, politeness required I should invite him to join me.

I went into the barn. The place looked like that aftermath of a chain saw massacre. He was busy swabbing down his chopping board.

'I wondered, I mean, I was going to have a sandwich - whether you'd like one too?'

'A sandwich!' he scowled at me.

'And maybe some soup,' I said weakly.

He leaned towards me opening a hand that held two thick loin chops he'd kept to one side.

'What about that salad in the garden?' he asked.

' It's a bit undersize but...'

'Parsley, cheese?'

I nodded.

'Show me the way to the kitchen. You get the salad.'

I picked the most developed lettuce and added a few of my chives and a good bunch of parsley. By the time I got back, he'd found the frying pan and had butter foaming in it. He threw in the chops and a wonderful smell of frying pork filled the room.'

'You cook for yourself or does that woman do it?'

'Oh I do it. When I can be bothered.'

'Have you laid the table? How are you going with the salad?'

'Nearly ready,' I leaped to the sink and started washing it.

I could feel him watching my back. I kept my head bent over the sink concentrating on the salad.

He turned and went back to the cooker. I watched as he slid the chops on to a warm plate and swilled the pan with wine. Then he added more butter and a handful of chopped onion left over from the rillettes. He'd helped himself to the pot of crème frâiche from the fridge. He poured in a good dollop.

I reached for a bowl and was about to dump the lettuce in when he restrained me with a hand. 'Wait!' His hand was large and warm and in spite of its rough texture, surprisingly gentle. He took the bowl from me and poured in olive oil, chopped garlic, salt, pepper and a splash of vinegar. 'Got any mustard?'

Silently, I passed it to him. I watched as he tossed the salad and then using his knife in a rocking motion on the bread board, he delicately chopped the chives and parsley.

'Cut us some bread and we're ready to eat,' he said hitching the bottle of wine under his arm and carrying the two plates to the table.

I followed with the salad. Despite my protests he poured me a glass of wine.

'You can't eat a meal without wine,' he said.

I took a bite of my chop. It was just caramelising on the top and the sauce was delicious. I dipped my bread in it. I was so hungry the chop disappeared in minutes. I picked up the bone and chewed it, making an ignominious kind of slurping noise as I did so. I wiped the juice from my chin. He nodded at me in approval.

'When did you last have a proper meal?'

'Proper meal? Can't remember. That was delicious. My compliments. You're a very good cook.'

The crooked smile returned.

'You're too thin. But you can eat. That's a good sign. Women who don't eat are no use to anyone.'

'Oh?'

Chauvenist sentiments perhaps, but they were a neat turn-around of Oliver's attitude. For Oliver there was no such thing as 'too thin', given the choice he'd like to be seen with a walking skeleton.

I dumped a load of salad in my sauce. What had he done with the dressing? It was brilliant. I usually bought ready-made stuff.

Jacques refilled my glass and I went in search of cheese. The food and more probably the wine seemed to have softened his brusqueness. He was all politeness now. A different person. The monster gone, the man had taken his place. But still I felt there was an iron reserve there. Something I couldn't quite place. A chip on his shoulder perhaps. He always seemed to be talking down to me, trying to prove he had the upper hand.

As soon as he'd downed his coffee he piled his stuff into the Espace, all the while giving me instructions on how to finish the Rillettes – by adding the all-spice and grinding the meat into the right kind of stringy consistency before I potted it.

'You still haven't told me the price of the pig,' I pointed out.

'Seventy euros. That should do it. You can have the butchering for free.'

Seventy euros! A friend's price. Some friend. I realised sinkingly that I could have bought the pork cheaper at the supermarket. However, I suppose, it was free-range.

Chapter Fourteen

Julia 2009

After the pig delivery my sightings of Jacques were rare and brief. He always seemed to be busy, herding cows around or shunting hay or shifting what seemed like mountains of manure. The best I got from him was a hurried wave. But one morning I found an invitation in my post box which promised to bring us face to face. There was to be a reunion in the village hall to celebrate the installation of the '*coq*' on Deneville's newly renovated church spire. Everyone from the village had been invited, so Jacques was bound to be there.

The following Saturday found me in the village hall or 'Salle Polyvalente' as it was called. The coq stood resplendent, if slightly garish in its new coating of gold leaf, set on a table on a dais. Seated at the table was a row of local council 'fonctionnaires'. The mayor was dressed for the occasion with his badge of office on its tricolour ribbon.

I scanned the room for Jacques. No sign of him. After we'd filed by to admire the coq at first hand, the Mayor treated us to a lengthy address. Children clung to knees writhing with boredom but remained obediently silent as he went into an endless series of thank yous. He seemed intent on mentioning everyone involved in the renovation, right down to the chap who'd held the ladder by the sound of it. People were shuffling their feet and casting glances towards a row of trestle tables which had been laid out in readiness with paper tablecloths, glasses and bottles.

I took the opportunity to check out my fellow villagers. The old were seated at the tables dressed in smart clothes, some had even gone as far as hats. The younger generations were in variations of jeans and work wear. I was obviously an object of curiosity – the only stranger at the 'do'. I caught the occasional eye-flick in my direction but no-one was rude enough to stare. As the mayor got into full throttle, I shifted my weight from one foot to the other, wondering if I could politely creep away.

Just as I was about to make a dash for the door, it opened. A latecomer slipped in - it was Jacques. To my surprise, he made straight for the Mayor's dais and slid into an empty seat. There was a slight disturbance as he was greeted along the row of chairs. The Mayor paused long enough to take a breath and shake him by the hand. Jacques had shaved for once and he even had a shirt on – unironed I noticed. I was intrigued. What was he doing up there?

Eventually the Mayor's speech ended to relieved applause. The atmosphere changed up a gear at the sound of bottles being uncorked. Soon tiny glasses of Kir were being passed around. They circulated, I noted, in solemn order of deference, first to the elderly, and then, embarrassingly enough, quite rapidly on to me. Clearly, I was the village's latest celebrity, the new 'chatellaine'.

I took a surreptitious look at Jacques. He'd noted my popularity. I tried a smile and he raised a sardonic eyebrow. He didn't seem inclined to come over and be sociable. With determination I started pushing my way through the crowd towards him. But I was caught midway by the mayor. Still with half an eye on Jacques, I stood there trapped while the Mayor took a deep breath and launched into English. He started on a long tale about how he had been to a place called 'astig when he was a teenager.

Unable to extricate myself, I listened politely to the Mayor's reminiscences. It seemed his most positive and enduring memory of this historic seaside resort was 'Fish and Chips.' Having exhausted his repertoire of English, Monsieur the Mayor slipped back into French and seemed intent on keeping me 'entertained' for the duration of the party. When, at last, I extricated myself, I was just in time to catch a glimpse of Jacques' back as he made his way out through the door. It slammed behind him. So much for sociability.

My attention was distracted by a little old lady who appeared at my elbow offering me a plate of '*pompe au gratin*' - hot and delicious cubes of rich egg dough with chunks of smoky bacon buried in them. The conversation in the Salle had risen to a friendly din. I accepted a wickedly large chunk and caught her eye.

'Please could you tell me, Madame. That Monsieur who just left. What was he doing up there on the dias with the Mayor?'

'You mean Jacques Ladier?'

'Yes, he's my neighbour.'

'He's Deputy Mayor of course. Didn't you know?'

'No. No, I had no idea.'

I stared at the door Jacques had left by. Deputy Mayor. Clearly I was going to have to delete 'clodhopping' from his job description.

Chapter Fifteen

Each evening I went back to my research, trying to tease out every fact I could find about the house. I noticed that the family tree had been torn out of some sort of pamphlet or magazine. At the base of the page it gave its tongue-twisting title: 'La Societé d'Emulation du Bourbonnais.' – the Bourbonnais Appreciation Society and a date: July 1952.

I wondered if the Society still existed, if so maybe they had archives and would have a copy of the pamphlet.

I rang Maitre Bertrand.

'Yes, I'm pretty sure it still exists. It's on the Paris road out of Moulins. The plaque's still there. At least, I think it is. I remember seeing it on a building opposite the graveyard. You could go and check.'

------- -- -------

The next morning found me up early dressed in paint-free clothes for once, ready to drive into Moulins.

After working my way through a tangle of one way streets, I located the Paris road and curb-crawled along it until I found the graveyard. The plaque was still there, along with several others of a civic nature. It was on a bleak building that looked like a hospital or barracks. I left the car half-up on the curb and traced my way via a number of contradictory pointers to a small doorway which had a neat hand-written sign:

La Societé d'Emulation du Bourbonnais.
Bibliotheque
Ouvert Mercredi 14h.- 17h.
sauf fêtes

By a stroke of luck I'd happened on the right day but I'd have to wait until the afternoon for it to open.

I spent the couple of hours or so I had to kill tracing my way through the network of narrow streets in the old town. Moulins is the capital of the

Bourbonnais area and it proudly proclaimed its past on every corner, with brown historic plaques. Joan of Arc had slept here, or slept around by the look of it, as the plaques seemed tellingly numerous.

I allowed myself the rare luxury of a stroll along the wide and shallow Allier which had formed the demarcation line between Vichy France and Free France during the last war, its course marked by a series of monuments to martyrs of the Occupation. Eventually, finding myself back in the main square, I treated myself to a 'plat du jour' and a glass of Saint Pourçain in the Grand Café.

I ate my lunch in its shabby grandeur, enjoying the cafe's painted ceiling and the way its face-to-face acid-etched mirrors reflected the diners in infinite regression. I wondered if Marie and Louise, the two Lamulatière sisters, had sat here as a children, eating an ice-cream or drinking lemonade, entertained by the spectacle of their reflections multiplied endlessly until they dwindled to specks. Or later in life, two women tightly laced in their stays and petticoats, dressed up for a day on the town.

Today my fellow diners were a nicely égalitarian mix of mothers and grandmothers and toddlers, business men, shop girls and blue overalled workmen - all eating their lunch with the seriousness of the French at table.

------- -- -------

Two o'clock found me back at the library door. It was now unlocked and opened on to a bleak corridor which greeted me with the unmistakable smell of old books. I tracked this to an inner room lined with an important looking morocco-bound collection. Beneath the shelves heads were bent over various book-related tasks. There was an atmosphere of rapt concentration.

I made a move towards the first table already aware of the stifling heat and wondering where I could politely dump my raincoat. One of the heads looked up, fixed me with a stare. I started in my very best French.

'Bonjour Monsieur, excusez-moi de vous deranger mais...'

He looked most affronted, got up from his desk and made for a door the led into a further room.and soon re-emerged followed by a slender lady of a certain age. He grumpily informed me that 'Mademoiselle' would help me. Without another word he drew in his chair and returned to his document.

'Mademoiselle' led me to a table at the back of the room. She took my coat, folded it neatly and hung it over a chair, signalling me to sit.

'I'm sorry to disturb you,' I whispered. Four heads raised and stared in my direction. 'But I wondered whether in your archives, you might have a copy of the Bulletin this was torn from.'

She smiled. 'Yes, we should have. Wait here, I'll go and look.' She went into the back room and re-emerged carrying a faded pamphlet. 'La-voilà July 1952' she announced. 'I could photocopy any pages you are interested in.'

I leafed through and found an article by someone called Camille Gagnon. It was headed '*La Domain de la Mulatière.*'

I watched, trying to read over her shoulder as Mademoiselle carefully folded the pages back and placed them on the copier.

As I paid her for the copies she handed me a form and said: 'If you would like to join the library we have quite a collection books on local history, if that is what interests you.'

'Brilliant! That's exactly what I'm looking for.'

Having filled in the form, I hurried back to the car bearing the precious copies, even having a quick leaf through as I walked.

Once back home, I hurried up to my study and settled down at my desk with them..

The first paragraph read:
'*I have seen few tribes that were less inclined to travel. The principle branch of the family never left the parish of Deneville for the past five hundred years. Among the minor branches, most of them were similarly reluctant to leave home. One member of the family only was expatriated, and this it seemed was more from the brutal force of unavoidable events .. than from choice...*'

'*The brutal force of unavoidable events*' that must have been the French

Revolution. Visions of night escapes and bands of marauding villagers leapt to mind. A quick check with the family tree showed that this *'one member of the family'* could only be Jean Mulatier de la Grolière, my famous chevalier, whose portrait was currently in Paul Fouquier's workshop. What had happened to him? Had they guillotined him? Chopped off that noble head?

Forgetting supper, I sat at my desk reading through the article with my big Larousse on hand to look up any terms I wasn't familier with.

According to the Bulletin, Jean and his elder brother Henri had been sent to the militery academy at L'Estissac at the tender ages of thirteen and fourteen respectively. By the age of sixteen they were at Versailles, serving the Light Horse Guards of Louis 16th. But revolution was in the air. In 1793 disorder broke out in the ranks and it became impossible for the officers to control the men under their command. The two brothers resigned their commissions and returned to the Bourbonnais. Jean took up residence at La Mulatière and Henri took over the neighbouring hunting lodge of La Grolière, which was now the home of Maitre Bertrand. As the Revolution swept south from Paris, Jean and Henri left France to join the pro-Royalist armies hoping to launch an invasion to crush the Revolution.

Where had they gone? The article didn't say - Germany, Italy, America? England? And what had happened to La Mulatière? I turned the page over:

'The properties seized from Jean de Mulatière, were put up for auction in the district of Deneville. The sales started on le 12 Vendemiaire an 3 (3rd October 1794). The wife of the emigré, now calling herself plain Suzanne Citoyenne Mulatière, managed to buy back the chateau de La Mulatière in the auctions...

Citoyenne Mulatière - this conjured up visions of Jean's wife Suzanne, now a stalwart supporter of the Revolution, in black peasant apron and shawl, bidding in public for her rightful home. What a story! A nobleman who had fled his country. The wife he left behind, who maybe turned against him, joining the women of the village as they formed bands of rioters fighting for their right to bread at a fair price. Or was it like that? Maybe Suzanne was a staunch royalist, hiding a knife under her apron, biding her time, buying back La Mulatière in the hope of a royalist counter-coup?

I was so absorbed in the article I barely noticed my mobile ringing.

It was Sarah.

'Hi. How are you? What are you doing?' Her familiar voice was fuzzy with interference.

'A bit of research about the house actually.'

'Can't hear you very well.'

I went and leaned perilously out of the window where the phone actually worked.

'Research! About the house.'

'Research! I thought you were meant to be getting the place ready to sell?'

I cast a guilty eye back into the room. My laptop stood on the table under the baleful eye of a battered Anglepoise. The table itself was the only clutter free surface, an island of calm in the wreckage of the house. All around it, the room was strewn with torn wallpaper. The door to the stairwell was hanging on one hinge. And beyond that there was an entire house full of crumbling plasterwork and peeling paint crying out for attention.

'I am. I'm just about to call the mason.'

'Can't you get a proper builder to supervise the whole thing?'

'They don't have proper builders here. They just have different people who do different things.'

'What about an ....then?'

'A what?'

'Architect!'

'I can't see the point in paying someone to tell them what to do.'

'I hope you know what you've taken on Jules.'

'Of course I do. How are you anyway.'

'Huge I feel as if I'm about to burst.'

Sarah then went into details of her planned under-water birth. When she rang off I made a dutiful call to the local mason. As usual, his phone was on answerphone. I left another message.

Half-heartedly I started shoving handfuls of torn wallpaper into a rubbish sack.

Outside, the sunset was putting on a show for me, turning the landscape a hazy golden. The hills had melted into a smudge of cobalt in the distance. The room could wait. I slipped out of the house and indulged in what was now my habitual evening walk to my secret lake. Secret, because it was hidden in a deep copse, lying like a sheet of beaten silver beneath the trees. The moon was already rising. It would be magical tonight. Escapism? Maybe.

------- -- ------

Chapter Sixteen

Sarah was right, Jane was right. I had to get things moving. I began to put the pressure on. After a battle with France Telecom, who demanded an officiously long list of documents, I managed to get the phone line re-instated. Each morning I made the expensive round of calls to roofers, electricians, menuisiers, charpentiers, masons, plumbers and plasterers, trying to get them at least to come and give an estimate.

Over the following weeks I was rewarded with brusque knocks on the door as a succession of workmen turned up to 'take a look.' I was becoming immune to their professional frowns and sighs. One mason actually suggested he could build me a '*nice little pavillon, toute neuf*' for a fraction of the cost of renovating La Mulatière - 'pavillon' being the current French euphemism for hideous new-build semi-bungalow.

------- -- -------

As the days lengthened my days passed in a pleasantly mind-numbing round of DIY tasks. While waiting for the mason I got on with jobs I thought I could tackle myself. Those hideous brown and cream Turkish tiles in the kitchen for example. I went to the local hardware store and invested in a chisel and mallet and set to work, getting a lot of satisfaction from hacking them off and finding some lovely old handmade bricks underneath. I was soon covered in plaster dust and had a growing pyramid of tile shards at my feet. The old bricks were pretty uneven, some needed replacing, and one of them slid out in my hand attached to the tile itself. I paused wondering if I was doing more harm than good. Staring guiltily into the hole, I noticed there was a little roll of paper inside. About the same length as a handrolled cigarette.

I reached inside for it and carefully, enrolled the frail paper. It was cracked with age and falling apart in my hands. But I could make out the words printed on it. It seemed to be some sort of bank note:

ASSIGNAT

de cent francs

Creé le 18 Nivose l'an 3 de La Republique francaise

And it had a signature: *Defau*

Chapter Seventeen

Suzanne Mulatière – 1795

'Take down the casket. Help yourself my dear, there's plenty enough for all, need to stint,' said Belle-mere.

I had not the courage to tell her that the assignats she had invested in were not worth the paper they were printed on.

The servants had left us, one by one, afraid to be seen to serve the wife of a 'traitor to the nation'. At least this made fewer mouths to feed for coinage had virtually disappeared and what goods there were could only be acquired by bartering. Only old Auguste stayed on, still wearing the ragged remnants of his livery, ready to risk his life rather than desert us.
I hid from Belle Mere as best I could the desperate state of our situation.

And then when I thought we could sink no lower, Auguste came back from the village saying the place was awash with rumours of a new edict.
They'd pasted the 'Avertissement' roughly on the church doors. Auguste had seen it and unable to make out more than a few words, he harnessed the horses to the barrouche and took me to read it for myself.

We arrived to find the church doors flung wide open. So this atrocity was in the church! Before the blessed sacrament itself. No, before the altar, the sacrament of course having been removed. I knelt in the doorway to make the sign of the cross and reached automatically for the holy water, forgetting for a moment that the stoup would be dry.

AVERTISSEMENT:

The sale of property of the emigrés, which should procure immense resources to the Republic, being at the same time an action which vividly demonstrates the just revenge of the nation against the traitors who have deserted their country in order to unite with her enemies...

I read the cruel words with disbelief. Below was a list of properties that made my blood run cold. These were the homes and lands of so many or our dear friends. Then nearing the bottom I saw 'La Mulatière'. But this was an outrage. We had not abandoned La Mulatière – Amisie, Belle-Mère and I were still in occupation. They had no right to thrust us out. I read the affiche again. The following properties had been confiscated 'by decree'. By whose decree I did not know. Things changed so rapidly from day to day. But this was theft. It would kill Belle-Mère. I read on: 'the traitors who have deserted their country...'

Deserted! They had condemned all emigrés who returned to death. What did they expect them to do? Come back to put their heads on the block? Hot tears of rage started in my eyes.

Auguste stood rolling his cap in his hands watching as if he could read the words on my lips. His hands trembled as I turned to him.

'Is it so Ma'am. What they're a-saying. It is not so to be sure?' he begged me.

'Yes it is. At least that is what it says. Please now drive me back to La Mulatière.'

-------- -- -------

I took Jean's portrait down from the wall and called to Auguste to bring a step ladder, tacks and a hammer. I made him stay outside the room while I hid away the portrait in the deep niche beside the chimney. I stretched the fabric and tacked it firmly back into place.

We had been given a week to pack up and leave. But what was the point of packing? I would pick up one thing, consider it and discard it. There would be no room for finery in the cottage down the lane. Besides the very possession of anything valuable was risky. In the end I bundled up our simplest clothing, plainest pottery and some basic utensils from the kitchen. I left the precious portrait of Jean in its hiding place. The date has already been set for our 'divorce'. I am to attend the Mairie with a number of other unfortunate wives of the so-called 'traitors' armed with our rings and our papers. I have no choice, unless Jean returns our marriage will be anulled. If Jean returns I will all too soon become a widow.

I tried to make light of the move to Belle Mère, telling her it was a temporary precaution and pretending to Amisie that it was no more than a game. Like they said the Queen had in her pastoral idyll at Versailles, playing at milkmaid with her Sèvres pails. It was summer when we moved and at first the child revelled in the change. I allowed her to go barefoot and she turned brown and rosy in the sun.

But when September came the weather changed. A greasy dampness seemed to settle on the inside of the house. However high we built the fire the damp still seeped back in. The fire seemed to draw the water in through the rough cement walls, up through the fired earth tiles. The tiles were laid on bare earth, irregular where the level sank in places, as if the earth was trying to drag us down into it. When it rained the earth turned to mud. It was the mud that affected our spirits most. Mud always mud. I'd never been aware of it before. The few steps we took from house to carriage, carriage to house in winter time, I'd not encountered mud. But now it clogged everything, making the walk to the well an exhausting task.

Belle Mère sat before the fire wrapped in her shawls as if trying to soak in its warmth. We'd saved her chair. We'd covered its silken brocade with a length of rough home-weave to disguise it.

We lived like the peasants on what we could produce. Yet we were better off than the peasants. While they starved we were allowed to keep all we produced. Auguste, resourceful as ever, arrived with a hen and a rooster. Poor creatures which were hardly fit for the pot. But by dint of scraping and saving peelings and suchlike they were soon transformed into a plump breeding pair. Ducks he trapped from the lake and tamed by daily feeding. The eggs their growing flock produced soon provided the excuse for weekly sorties to the market at Deneville. While Auguste bargained for flour I made my furtive visit to the seamstress. This good woman acted as our poste restante taking in letters secreted in bales of linen. As the eyes of the Committee of Surveillance became ever more vigilant, Jean and other émigrés in a similar sad situation were forced to take further precautions. Letters might be written in lemon juice, only to appear when held up to the fire. Often these would be so faint and damaged we were hard pressed to make out more than a few words. I often used to read out total fictions of my own invention to comfort Belle Mère.

But there was really no solace I could give her. Saddest of all was to see her expression when she walked up the lane to stare at La Mulatière. This was the home of her married life. It was where her children had been born, had grown and prospered. It was where her beloved Matthias had died - her precious home from which she had been so cruelly dispossessed.

Chapter Eighteen

Julia 2009

I drove to Deneville to show Maitre Bertrand my find. He knew exactly what it was.

'Oh an Assignat,' said Maitre Bertrand, taking it to the window to get a better light. 'Originally these were issued as a type of bond. But by 'L'an 3' metal coinage was becoming increasingly rare. Batch after batch of assignats were printed causing massive inflation. They became virtually worthless. Some speculators made a fortune out of them, others lost everything they had.'

'Is it valuable?'

'I doubt it. Not in this condition anyway.'

I was glad actually. I'd found an old glass case in the attic and I was using it to display the collection of what I'd christened my 'objets trouvés'.

That evening I had a call from Oliver. He must have been talking to Jane. He ranted on about 'Burying myself in the country' 'Losing touch.' He finished with: 'Holidays don't last forever you know.'

'It's not a holiday Oliver. I'm working my arse off as a matter of fact.'

'It's the novelty. It'll wear off. One of these days you'll have to get back to real life.'

'Thanks Oliver. I appreciate your concern,'

He must have noted my tone, he made a few more half-hearted comments and then rang off.

Real life? Wasn't this real? Much more real in fact than the life I'd left behind? That oddly surreal world of sales pitches and campaign presentations? I had a sudden flashback to a battle I'd had around the boardroom table with some idiot from middle management who was arguing the case for *talking vegetables*.

I stared out of the window. There was not a building in sight. Just the garden with misty hills beyond, looking glorious in the late afternoon sunlight dappled by the waving branches of the acacias. I suddenly realised that I wanted this house with a fierceness that shocked me. It was totally illogical. What was I thinking of? A single woman in a vast place like this? I've never been particularly coveteous, I'd always scorned the desire for acquisition - cars, jewellery, designer clothes, whatever. But everyone has a weak spot and La Mulatière had found mine.

I gave myself a shake. There must be a name for the mental abberation I was suffering from. The irrational desire to possess a property totally out of scale with one's requirements - a house-aholic perhaps? But it wasn't acquisitiveness. La Mulatière had welcomed me, taken me in, calmed my jangling nerves, soothed the bitter pain of losing Dad, helped fill the gaping void of a future without children. Quite simply I'd fallen in love with the house.

That night I lay in bed unable to sleep, a spiral of contradictory thoughts going round in my brain. Could I buy the others out? I listed my assets – my redundancy money, the value of my flat – I'd have to pay off the mortgage of course. But a third of La Mulatière was mine already.

And hadn't Maitre Bertrand pointed out how much we were going to lose by selling up ? All those ruinous taxes? Charles wasn't going to like those. Maybe we should do as the French do, hang on to it. Jane and Sarah and I could use it as a holiday home, something for us to share. But deep down I knew I could never share La Mulatière. I shuddered at the thought of Jane putting Osborne and Little in the drawing room and Sarah going all Ikea in the attic. And the children would hate it because we couldn't be further from the sea.

No, La Mulatière had to be mine and mine alone. But what on earth would I live on? I could let rooms - 'Chambres d'Hôtes,' the French for 'Bed and Breakfast'. Or a - the West wing would be ideal for a gîte. I'd install a tiny kitchen so it would be self-contained. I'd need more bathrooms of course. Or maybe I could turn La Mulatière into a small hotel?

Mentally, I was sketching in new party walls and fitting in the bathrooms, two by two, economically siting them back to back, when I fell into a fitful sleep.

I dreamed of endless rooms opening one into the other, double doors after double doors. The salon stretched itself out into a ballroom with a grand piano. And beyond that a dining room with all the dishes laid out on the side-table under silver salvers, like the archetypal Victorian house party - smoked haddock, scrambled egg, devilled kidneys...

I woke next morning with the realisation that something that had been tormenting me had been exorcised. For years and years I'd wanted to marry Oliver. I was always thinking he was about to ask. But he never did. There was even that hideous time when I's suggested it myself and he'd gone all morose. Now I wondered why I ever wanted to marry anyone? What was the point of it? Marriage? It mattered, perhaps if you had children. But since I wasn't going to have any...

Tears rolling down my face surprised me. I had a brief and chilling memory of the young surgeon, standing by the bed, trying to explain kindly that something had gone wrong with my uterus, even with IVF, my chances were nil.

With cruel irony, Sarah chose that moment to ring.

'Julia. You Ok?'

'Yes fine why?'

'You don't sound it.'

'Oliver called last night.'

'You didn't let him get to you?'

'No. Quite the contrary.'

'Like we agreed. No retreads?'

'No, I mean, yes.'

'Listen I've made up my mind. I want you to be my birthing partner. To be there you know. At the birth. By the bed holding the limp paw. Telling me when to push.'

'But I thought you were having it under water.'

'No, changed my mind. The only place I could find was miles across London.'

'I thought Mummy would be there...'

'You know what Mummy's like about stuff - you know - below the belt.'

'Or Jane...' I said weakly.

'Tricky with the kids. It could be at night. Charles might be away. Anyway, I thought you'd be pleased.'

'I am. Of course. Really flattered.'

'Oh, it's not going to upset you is it?'

I pulled myself together with an effort. 'No. No of course not. It's just that there's so much to do here.'

'Well that can wait. Babies can't.'

'No I suppose not. Remind me of the definitive date.'

I shuffled through my diary and noted it down..

'So you'll be here?'

'Of course. If you really want me.'

'Thanks Jules.'

Chapter Nineteen

Julia 2009

The following day I made an appointment to see Maitre Bertrand. I needed to know precisely how much the house was worth.

'But of course, it's on the contract which I think...' Maitre Bertrand reached for a file and shuffled through some papers. He gave the answer first in francs and then translated into euros.

'How much?' I repeated.

He wrote it down for me. I couldn't believe how few noughts there were. That was peanuts. It was less than I'd paid for my flat in Fulham ten years back.

'As I told you there'll be estate duty to come off that. And you could be liable for Capital Gains Tax. Of course you can offset this by any improvements your father made.'

'He didn't make any 'improvements', he hardly had time.'

'Improvements could be useful from a tax point of view.'

'What if I bought the others out and didn't sell immediately?'

'You'd still have to pay Inheritance Tax But you could offset the Capital Gains liability if you made the house your primary residence.'

My mind was racing. At that valuation once I'd sold my flat I could easily buy the others out. And I'd have a nice sum over after paying off the mortgage.

'Of course you'd have to sign up with the French Tax system.'

The Maitre smiled a conspiratorial smile. It was him and me against the tax man.

'I can see you like it here in the Bourbonnais, Mademoiselle.'

'Like it? I love it.'

My head was spinning. This was what I'd been praying for. Time to myself. Time to live. And I could live for practically nothing.

Maitre Bertrand continued in a businesslike manner about various legal procedures which needed to be formalised with some people with gloriously vague title of the 'bureau des hypotheques'. But I was barely listening. My mind had gone into overdrive. It was already involved in roofing and flooring, gravel and terraces... and maybe fountains. By the time the Maitre had drawn to a close, I'd planted an entire 'jardin à la française' rimmed with miniature box hedges and I was busy laying out my tasteful selection of herbs in geometric patterns...

------- -- -------

I rang Jane first. My mind was in a such a turmoil I stupidly blurted out.

'You'll never guess what. The house is hardly worth anything.'

'What?'

'Less than two hundred grand and there are taxes and legal costs to come off that.'

'Two hundred grand? You do mean pounds?'

'No. Euros.'

'But it must be worth more. It's huge.'

'No. That's what Dad paid apparently.'

'Divided between the three of us - that'll hardly cover the quote for the loft extension, let alone the extras... like the heating...'

'I know. Sarah's been counting on it too.'

'How long is the whole thing going to take?'

'At least six months. Maybe more.'

'Six months! The builders are demanding a deposit right away.'

'Listen Jane. I've had an idea. I don't know how you and Charles would feel about it. But...' I swallowed. It was now or never. 'I want to buy you and Sarah out...'

'What?'

'Honestly. I think it's the best solution. It means you and Sarah could have the money right away or sooner anyway.'

'But where will you get the money? You couldn't possibly afford to...' she cut in.

'I could if I sold my flat.'

'Julia. Are you mad? You're going to go batty out there living all on your own. We couldn't possibly let you do that.'

I tried to get a word in while Jane ranted on in a wonderful series of mixed metaphors which included property ladders, babies, bathwater and burning boats. She ended by saying that she'd have to speak to Charles about it.

Charles came on the line within minutes. He'd obviously been primed by Jane. But although he made out in the strongest terms that he was against the idea, I could tell from his voice he was tempted. The last thing he needed was to be saddled with a property like La Mulatière - a drain on their resources.

'Be honest Charles. You must agree it's a fair proposition. Buying you out would give me time to get the house in a fit condition to sell. And you could have the money you need much sooner. As soon as my sale goes through, at any rate.'

'We'll think about it. But you won't do anything in a hurry will you Julia? Promise me,' he finished.

'No, I suppose not.'

Then I rang Sarah.

'So what's the verdict?' she demanded as soon as she heard my voice.

I toned down my response for her. 'Well, it's not brilliant news, I'm afraid. The notaire has only valued it at two hundred thousand. Doesn't seem much for a house this size. But I've got a plan. I've already talked to Jane, if I buy you two out I'll have time to do it up. Then if I sell later, I could actually make some money.'

Typically, Sarah said she was hopeless with money and didn't care as long as she had enough to tide her over for a year or so. Until the baby was old enough for her to go back to work at any rate.

I was intentionally vague about about where the money was coming from. I'd had enough of a grilling from Jane and Charles.

Later that evening I got a call on my mobile from my mother.

'Julia. I can't believe what Jane's just told me.'

I held the phone away from my ear while she continued.

'.............. if you must take yourself off to France while there are such lovely places in England. What about the West Country? Or Norfolk?'

'Country places in England cost a fortune, besides I'd be surrounded by empty weekend cottages.'

'I can't think what's got into you... You're just like your father. I blame it all on that time we had to spend in Paris.'

I thought back to our time in Paris, when Dad had the Reuters job and we'd lived in Montparnasse. I went with Jane and Sarah to the Ecole Maternelle. Mummy loathed it, said all the Parisian women treated her like some frump. But I'd loved every minute of it. Big bowls of café au lait and pain chocolat for breakfast. The Cirque d'Hiver. Riding on the carrousel in the park. The heady foreignness of Paris. Even the smell of it, oily 50 franc notes, the exotic mix of Gitane smoke, cacouettes and Parisian drains...

'At least it gave me a good grounding in French. That's coming in really handy right now.'

'But you can't sell your flat, darling. It's your only bit of security.'

'Mummy, trust me. I'm an adult and it's my life. I know what I'm doing. It makes sense financially. We'd be mad to sell Dad's place straight away because of the taxes.'

'But you will sell that house eventually?'

'If it's as ghastly here as you predict, of course– yes.'

At that point luckily my battery ran out.

I walked back into the house and put my mobile on charge.

------- -- -------

My mother's call had confirmed my decision in a way she could hardly have predicted. The alternative - a damp and lonely life in rural England. Or going back to London. Battling with Oliver. Or without Oliver? Having to depend on other friends, mostly paired off now, for company. Working in another dead-end job...

Without giving myself time to back down, I rang the Estate Agents and told them to forget about letting my flat, to put it on the market instead.

They came over all obsequious - it seemed it was a hot property in a very sought-after area. They'd recently renamed the network of streets around the flat 'Briar Village'. As to the price, there'd been a recent recovery in London house prices. They mentioned a figure I'd merely dreamt of. They'd have it sold in no time.

Chapter Twenty

According to the Bulletin, when La Mulatière was confiscated, Suzanne moved into a cottage nearby which was called L'Ombre.

I tried to imagine in the lives of this aristocratic woman forced to live a life without servants - fetching water from the well, dragging her way through the mud on pattens, growing vegetables - muddled and inexperienced - a bit like me I thought wryly.

In my walks around the local country lanes I peered into various derelict cottages. 'L'Ombre' could have been any one of these small 'fermettes' dotted around the surrounding fields. None of them was grand enough to have a name.

A week or so later the mystery of Suzanne's move was solved. I came down to find the postmistress knocking on the kitchen door. She had a registered package for Jacques and since he wasn't in, she asked me to sign for it. It was addressed to L'Ombre.

'Yes, that's Jacques Ladier's farm,' she said.

'It's called L'Ombre?'

'It's the old name, These days people just call it 'The Mulatière Farm.'

The old name - L'Ombre de la Mulatière - in the shadow of La Mulatière – which is exactly what it was.

Later that morning I made my way through the hedge to drop the parcel in on Jacques. The shutters of the farmhouse were still closed. The place looked deserted. The Espace was parked in the garage but his dog was nowhere to be seen and the tractor wasn't there either, so I supposed he was out somewhere in the fields.

I picked my way over the rutted forecourt and knocked on his door. There was no answer. The door wasn't locked. I opened it a slit. It led into a kitchen. I could simply leave the parcel on the kitchen table. I took a step inside giving a loud *'Coo koo'* just in case he should be around after all. No answer.

I put down the parcel. The farmhouse was silent - empty. I looked around taking in the room. By the light of a bare lightbulb, I noted the ancient gas cooker, the original farmhouse sink carved out of a solid piece of stone, a fridge looking incongruously new and white beside it, a table covered by a hideous printed oil-cloth, nothing but a couple of benches by way of seating. How could he live like this?

The floor was of terracotta tiles like the ones at La Mulatière, laid in bare earth by the look of it – it was subsiding in places. Imagine Suzanne and her family decamping here, so cold and damp and miserable after La Mulatière. I could picture Suzanne, standing at the sink, her hands red and chapped in the cold water. Her mother-in-law crouched over the fire wrapped in a shawl. Little Amisie making the rounds of the kitchen reciting the months of the new Revolutionary calendar…

I noted the signs of Jacques' presence. On the table lay a copy of "Le Canard Enchaîné" - the French equivalent of "Private Eye". Beside it was 'Le Réveil du Pays de Tronçais', a free sheet from the local Communist party. And he read 'The Figaro' I noticed – while most farmers round here stuck to La Montagne - the local rag. I tiptoed over to the bookcase. There were the standard paperbacks you'd expect to find in any French house, some classics like Zola, a few detective novels. But there were other books too. Several modern novels, even the latest winner of the Goncourt – a book Oliver had told me I should read. For all his rough manners, Jacques Ladier was not the simple farmer he pretended to be. My curiosity was well and truly aroused now.

Leading off the kitchen, a door was slightly ajar - his bedroom... Was this where Suzanne and Amisie had slept, huddled together for warmth in a sagging feather bed? I crept in. Jacques' bed was unmade, a pile of clothes lay beside it on the floor. I looked around for something more personal - photographs perhaps... I went to the back door and peeped out. If he came back on the tractor, I'd hear him from miles off.

I slipped back through the bedroom door. I knew this was totally out of order, but what I'd gleaned so far had intrigued me. If Jacques was going to behave in such an enigmatic way, he deserved to be spied on.

I crept over to the wardrobe. Fleetingly I could imagine Sarah saying:

'Check if he has any short-sleeved shirts!' which made me want to giggle nervously. But what I found stopped laughter dead in my throat. Hanging up beyond his few jackets and jeans was a cotton dress...

I reached for the dress. It was for someone pretty slender, a size ten I should guess and there were some narrow jeans and a jacket too. A pair of girl's high heeled boots stood beneath them. Going hot and cold, I shoved the cupboard door closed. It had been closed, hadn't it? Had the key been turned in the lock? I stared at it, frantically trying to remember...

'What are you doing?'

Jumping out of my skin would be an understatement. Jacques was standing in the doorway. His approach, bootless and in thick woollen socks had been totally silent.

'Oh my god,' I said. 'I'm so sorry. I was curious... I wanted to know... But I'm really sorry I have absolutely no right...'

I made a move towards the door. But he stood in the doorway barring my way.

'Please. I feel terrible about this. Can I get by?'

He stood there staring at me, saying nothing.

'I was a delivering a parcel. It came this morning, recorded...'

I pushed past to show him where I'd left it on the table. And as I passed him he slid an arm round my body and kissed me firmly on the lips.

Breathlessly I pulled away. But whether I liked it or not, my body had responded. And he'd noticed.

'You must admit. You have expressed interest,' he said.

I backed into the kitchen. 'I was intrigued, that's all.' I was gabbling with embarrassment.

I was down the front steps and heading across the farmyard when he called after me: 'Come and have dinner with me. Tonight.'

He was smiling. No...hang on... He was *laughing* at me. I felt utterly foolish.

'No I can't. I've got something on...' I said

'Rubbish,' He retorted. 'I'll expect you around eight.'

------- -- ------

What was I going to do about Jacques Ladier? I thought of ringing Sarah and asking her advice. But she'd be horrified at me having what she'd call a 'fling with a farmer'. Should I call him and make some excuse? But why should I? I was a grown woman and despite his rough exterior, I was attracted to him. Why was I behaving like some teenaged virgin?

But what did I know about him? As a foreigner I had none of those clues to go on:- taste and humour, background, education - that cruel analysis of consonants and vowels by which we do our callous weighing up process. While my body reacted to him, my mind said – stay well clear.

And what about the clothes in the cupboard? Who was that woman? And was she coming back? Maybe I shouldn't go. But what was all the fuss about? I didn't have to end up in bed with him, did I? No, all I wanted to get to know him better. All I really wanted was friendship. It was going to be a simple meal shared by neighbours.

I treated myself to a long lazy bath, adding a generous dollop of bath essence. Later, when I was rubbing body lotion into my freshly shaven legs, I had to ask myself: 'What are you doing this for *precisely* Julia Lefarge?'

I paused in front of the mirror. I hadn't actually stopped to have a proper look at my reflection for ages. I didn't look that bad actually. I plucked a couple of stray eyebrows and put my hair up with a pony tail band letting a few tendrils escape. Then I raked in a drawer and found some blusher and mascara.

Having exhausted my repertoire of beauty therapy with a splash of Miss Dior, I dressed in my best fitting jeans and a v-kneck. On second thoughts I changed the v-kneck for one of my bulkier jumpers. I wasn't going to throw myself at him.

------- -- -------

Jacques had made an effort. He'd stuck a candle in a bottle and stood it in the centre of the table.

'Can I do anything to help?'

'No. You sit down. It's all under control. Would you like a drink?' he asked.

'That would be nice.'

'It'll have to be wine, it's all I've got.'

He poured a couple of glasses. 'Salut' he said chinking his glass to mine. Our eyes met.

I remembered his arm round my body. That kiss rough and hard on my lips. I looked into my wine glass. 'Nice wine.'

'Côtes du Rhone. Generally reliable.'

He turned away and I watched as he deftly moved around the kitchen, chopping parsley, grating garlic, slicing bread - and noted how efficiently he'd organised everything - bachelor fashion - utensils within reach, knives sharp, chopping board ready, culinder to hand. Was he a bachelor I wondered? Not according to the clothes in the cupboard – watch it Julia Lefarge!

I sat down on the bench at the table - this being the only seat on offer. He leaned over the sink neatly trimming some mushrooms and rubbing them over with kitchen towel. 'Aren't you going to wash those mushrooms?'

He shook his head. 'You don't wash wild ones - they absorb too much moisture.'

'Where did you learn all this? Cooking I mean?'

'One picks it up. Here and there.'

'I haven't.'

He knocked the catch of the oven with a practised gesture, as it slid open a delicious smell wafted out.

'What's cooking?'

'Beef cheeks.'

'I didn't know cows had cheeks.'

'They're delicious, the tenderest bit of the animal, but they take time to cook.'

He threw a slab of butter into a pan and as it foamed, slid in the pile of mushrooms. The garlic and chopped parsley followed. Then two hot plates were produced and without any further ceremony a plate of aromatic mushrooms was placed in front of me. He poured more wine into my glass.

'Bon appetit,' he said and sat down opposite me. He tore off a good length of fresh baguette and handed me the rest.

The mushrooms tasted even better than they smelt. He nodded, seeing my obvious enjoyment: 'They're field mushrooms. You have to get them fresh. Dawn's the best time, before the others get out there.'

'Where did you find them?'

'In the meadows.'

'I know, but whereabouts?'

'I could take you there one day. Maybe... If I got you up in time.' I caught the suggestion in his tone and was careful not to react.

As we ate the beef cheeks, which as he'd promised, were sumptuously tender and in a thick and delicious sauce, I turned the conversation to him.

'Are these from one of your animals?'

He nodded. 'Charolais.'

'How many have you got?'

'Around fifty. Not enough. That's why I do the other job.'

'I know, Jerôme told me...'

'I've done a lot of things. Butchery's not the worst,' he said.

'What was the worst?'

He grinned. 'I made coffins once.'

'God, that must've been depressing.'

'You get used to it.'

'How did you end up here?'

'The farm belonged to my father. When he died I thought I'd better come back and sort things out. I came and looked and I stayed. Maybe I'd just got sick of moving around.'

'Bit like me.'

'But you're planning to sell up?'

'Maybe. I don't know. It depends...'

He poured himself another glass of wine and said: 'You must miss things, things from the city.'

'As a matter of fact. There's very little I miss. Maybe the cinema, but there are DVD's and I can get books and things on Amazon...' I said lightly.

'What do you do with yourself in the evenings. I've seen your light on upstairs?'

'I'm doing some research actually, into the history of the house. The family who owned it is really fascinating.'

'God bless the bourgeoisie,' he said dismissively. I caught an edge in his voice. The word 'bourgeoisie' has a different meaning in French – denoting a far grander class of person than in English.

'Well, I think they're really interesting.'

He made no comment but brought out a platter of cheese with a camembert at the ultimate point of ripeness. He opened another bottle of red.

'Not for me,' I said putting my hand over my glass.

'You can't eat cheese without wine.'

'I've had enough,' I said firmly, my head was starting to swim.

He took a packet of cigarettes out of his pocket.

'You smoke?'

I shook my head. 'Did once, gave up. It was agony. Don't want to go through that again.'

'No sins at all?'

'Oh I do pretty well on gluttony, pride and covetousness.'

He exhaled smoke and sat eyeing me. I looked away. The time had come to leave but I didn't feel I could walk out as soon as I'd eaten.

'How long have you lived here?' I asked.

'Six years on and off. Ever since my father died.'

'Always on your own?' I prompted

'If you mean, is there a women around?' he asked abruptly. 'No, not as such.'

Not as such, what the hell did that mean? I felt annoyed that he couldn't be frank with me? A dark expression had come into his eyes. He stubbed his cigarette out and started to stack the plates. I realised I'd strayed too far into personal territory. Changing the subject, I asked if he'd met Dad when he'd lived at La Mulatière.

Jacques returned to his seat: 'Yes. We had a few drinks together. I liked him.' Our eyes met once again. Unaccountably, I found mine filling with tears.

He stretched out a hand and rested it on mine.

'Look honestly, I should go,' I said.

'Should you?'

'Yes. I've got loads to do in the morning. And...'

'You don't have to give a reason,' he said.

'No... Thank you. Thanks for the meal.'

------- -- -------

I lay in bed that night trying to analyse what had actually happened back there. Jacques had really wanted me to stay, he'd made that pretty clear. Why hadn't I? If he'd been more pressing I probably would have. But what about the clothes in the cupboard?

Chapter Twenty One

Julia 2009

The following morning I caught Jacqueline in one of her chattier moods. She was up a ladder cleaning windows. I grabbed a cloth and started to help her by cleaning the other side. She'd lived in the village all her life. She must know more about Jacques.

'Oh my goodness yes. Jacques Ladier. He was at school with me, right through from Maternelle. What a dare devil he was. Always had his knees covered in Mercurichrome.'

'Has his family always lived next door?'

'No way. They came from the South somewhere. And Jacques - he's been all over the world. What a traveller. His poor father was left with the whole of the farm to deal with on his own. Jacques was a late child, he'd sent him to college and everything. He wanted him to takeover so he could retire.'

'He went to college?'

'He was meant to be studying agriculture at the college in Clermont. But goodness knows what he did with his student days. He was a wild one.'

'So he didn't come back and settle down?' I prompted.

She'd caught my tone, she paused from cleaning and stared through the pane at me.

'If you mean has he ever been married. No, not married as such.'

'But he has had a partner?'

'These days you'd think marriage had gone out of fashion.' I waited for her to go on. 'No, Jacques was a fine young man with a future ahead of him. Until she came along.' She shook her head and squirted more glass cleaner on the window.

'She? Who?'

'She called herself Kattie, though that wasn't her name. Turned up with a suitcase out of nowhere at the bar in the village. She was a beauty, slim like you but with a mass of dark curls. Drove the men wild. The bar had never had so much business.'

She gave her pane a disapproving rub and breathed on it hard.

'They gave her a tiny room at the back, hardly more than a cupboard. Board and lodging and all the tips she could make, that's all they offered. As soon as Jacques set eyes on her he fell head over heels. Made a right fool of himself.'

'So what happened to her?'

'She was never his wife. She moved in to the farm but they never married. They were a fine looking couple they would have had lovely children.'

'But they didn't?'

Jacqueline paused and climbed a couple of steps down the ladder.

'That was the strange part of it. I suppose I shouldn't gossip but I met Kattie early one morning buying bread in the Boulangerie. It was hot in there and all of a sudden she clung to the counter - she'd turned as white as a sheet. She left her money and the bread and had to go out in the street to vomit. I took her purse and the bread out to her while she was having a sit down, recovering. And I couldn't help commenting that maybe we were to have a happy event in a few months. She stared at me like an animal caught in a trap and told me to mind my own business. And I'd known Jacques since school. I hadn't meant any harm. It was very hurtful.'

'What happened to the baby?'

'Who knows. Within a month Kattie had disappeared. No sign of a child. Heaven knows whether it was his or not, the way she went on.'

'What happened to her?'

'All I know is that she disappeared as mysteriously as she'd come. Then Jacques went off travelling. Two years he was away. Left the farm to go to wrack and ruin. That's why the place is in such a state.'

'And there's never been anyone since?'

'Not to my knowledge. Maybe he's taken against women. So much the better. I dare say he's not easy to live with.'

'I see.'

'Not that it's any of my business.'

Jacqueline climbed back up the ladder and started polishing with determination, she obviously felt she'd said enough.

Our talk had left me with a load of conflicting thoughts. Had Jacques made Kattie have an abortion? If so what a bastard! But maybe the baby wasn't his? Even so, people bring up other people's children, don't they? Or maybe she'd kept the baby and she was a single mother struggling to bring it up alone while he swanned off on his travels. Either way it put Jacques in a pretty bad light.

Chapter Twenty Two

Julia 2009

As April drifted into May and the evenings drew longer I slipped into a routine that kept pace with nature. I went to bed when the sun set and rose with it too. I was enjoying a slower pace of life in tune with the seasons. My shrill London alarm clock had been replaced by the most delicious wake-up call imaginable - the sun shining, warm and insistent on my face.

A few telephone calls had miraculously led to the delivery of a Livebox, so I had an internet connection. All I needed now was to sort out the electricity and from a technological point of view I'd be up and running. Several phone calls later proved that electricians were a highly sought-after commodity in the Allier - they were all booked up for months.

I could hear the clink and scrape of metal on soil coming from the direction of the vegetable garden. Jerôme was up there attacking the weeds with a long handled spade that cut deep into the ground. When he stopped long enough to ask about the electrician, he shook his head at the very thought of me squandering money on mere wiring.

'Who've you tried so far?' he asked. He made tutting noises at my list of firms and said his wife had a cousin who could probably sort me out. 'At the weekends,' he said meaningfully.

'I don't care if he comes in the middle of the night as long as he gets the job done.

Jerôme's electrician turned up on my doorstep the following Saturday. I trailed round the house behind him becoming increasingly anxious as his grunts of disapproval over my poor electrical status rose to a crescendo. Most of the wiring had been threaded through old gas conduits. Switches and sockets that had looked promising were joined to cables that led nowhere. At last he announced that all the old wires would have to be stripped out and replaced by an infrastructure of what he called *'gaines'*, plastic tube thingees - I don't even know the name of them in English. Once these were in, I could rewire as often as I liked. Great. From the electrical point of view, things had gone downhill.

The following Saturday the fellow turned up at at seven am and set to work, burrowing with the enthusiasm of a Colditz escapee, drilling through walls four foot thick.

As is the way with renovations, one job led to another. Jerôme's electrician was no surface-mounting bodger. His wiring was a secretive affair, which moved in mysterious ways. Panelling was ruthlessly crow-barred off, floorboards uprooted and skirting set aside to allow his precious 'gaines' to go on their way. One afternoon I came into the salon to find him unashamedly piling up a heap of my beautiful panelling in the centre of the floor.

'You are going to put it back up?' I said.

He shrugged: 'What's the point. It's quite rotten.'

I turned a panel over. Woodwork that I had judged nicely seamed and 'distressed' now revealed its true nature. The hidden side was crumbling to dust. There was nothing for it but to call a carpenter.

A smart green van with Chabrier et Fils emblazoned on the side turned up the following day. A fellow with fine hands and neatly trimmed beard climbed out, he looked more like a musician than a carpenter. I showed him the rotten piece of panelling.

'Hardly surprising,' he said. 'This is the original panelling, You can tell by the rivets, this hasn't been touched for a couple of centuries.'

He shook his head and started to do a tour of the room. I stood by anxiously as he passed judgement on each panel, cruelly burrowing a coin into the precious wood to demonstrate how far gone it was. My heart sank as he measured his way round noting each dimension in neat pencil on a squared pad.

'Of course you'll need to change the doors,' he added. 'They're warped with age. They don't fit anywhere.'

I stared at him in disbelief

'What's wrong with them?'

He held one open and instructed me to take a closer look, narrow side on.

'You can see why it doesn't close properly. It's voilée.'

'Voilée?' It was a word I'd never come across.'

He made a gesture with his hand indicating how it bellied out like a sail. How I loved the French language - so economical and expressive. I could forgive the door its pregnant curve for coming up with such a nice word.

'Well I don't care if it is 'voilée'. There's not a straight line in this house. That's the charm of it.'

'I could probably get it to close if I cheated a bit.'

'Cheat away. I'm keeping these doors. Be careful with them when you take then down. And don't even think about the windows. I can't possibly change them. Look at the glass. See how old it is.'

Some of the panes were quite yellow. They had ripples and bubbles which turned the view outside into a kaleidoscope of dazzling movement. In others the glass was clear as springwater, glossy as a polished wine glass.

He smiled. 'Do you know how they were made? The old panes?'

I shook my head.

'The same way as they made bottles. The glass was blown and then, while it was still hot and flexible, slit and flattened.'

'There you see. That settles it. They're staying.'

'You'll be sorry when winter comes and you're suffering from the draughts.'

'I'll worry about that when the time comes.'

He shook his head and selected the least damaged of the panels – one I was aiming to keep as it happened - and bid me good day, promising he would send me an estimate for replacing the whole lot with perfect copies, no worries, I'd never be able to tell the difference.

I watched his van leave with a sinking feeling, How much were his beautiful authentic-looking panels going to cost? Surely I could keep some of them. I went to double check. I was in the process of shifting one of the larger pieces when I came across something buried underneath. It was a little packet wrapped yellowed oilcloth. Inside there was a pile of folded letters tied around with a faded ribbon. They looked old, very old indeed. I went through them one by one unfolding the fragile paper to find...nothing. Whether it was the damp or the mere passage of time any trace of writing had been erased.

I stared at the panelling, this meant the letters must be two hundred and fifty years old...

Chapter Twenty Three

Jean Mulatier de la Grolière   1794

My dearest, sweetest Suzanne,

I write in haste for the hand and that is to bear this back to you waits below. I send it with little confidence that the blackguards who are paid to deliver it will keep their word.

In short, we have arrived safely which was a miracle in itself. Henri is sojourning with Sir Harry while I have moved in with his daughter and her husband who have kindly contrived to reorder their household to accommodate me.

The journey I hardly like to describe to you. Several times we were so close to being discovered that I doubted that I would ever be writing this letter to you. I can wager that at least double the sum we'd set aside changed hands in bribes. Particularly at Calais, where the safe passage we had been promised did not materialise and the barque which was to carry us became curiously elusive. With the sea at one's face and the devil at one's back, one is in no position to bargain.

London, when we arrived, was awash from a drenching rainstorm and the mud-clogged streets seemed even filthier than those of Paris if that is possible. But we were most courteously and warmly welcomed and set before a roaring fire with every comfort and even the loan of a change of clothes while the servants did what they could to repair the damage to our only vetements.

You should picture us both dressed in Sir Harry's clothes, of fearful cut had they fitted but as he is twice my berth and two thirds my height I made a sorry sight at dinner. The English take their dinner at five pm. A fact we were very glad of that first day. For it had been a good twelve hours since either of us had eaten and what we'd had in Calais had soon been given over to the fishes due to the rolling of the boat.

Tell mother that the lamb was boiled to shreds as she predicted and the sauce was without butter or wine and of a thick white consistency made I surmise with flour and milk all but flavoured with capers. But it was served

with a large complement of potatoes and we set too with almost more
appetite than was polite. We had expected beer or maybe cider but I am
glad to tell you the Sir Harry served a fine Bordeaux and there was plenty of
red Porto supplied after the meal of which he seems inordinately fond. I
noted that he asked our indulgence to place his foot upon a gout stool.

The ladies retired while the Porto was being served and we talked for
an hour or so of matters which I need not disclose here - only to say that
they are close to all our hearts. Sir Harry is of the opinion that the British
are very much caught up in the problems in America and despite the fact
they greatly fear a similar occurence to the French on their own land, their
sympathies may be all that we can hope for.

When we were reunited with the ladies, Lady Sarah announced that
they thought it provident to separate us and that one of us should lodge with
her daughter Charlotte. Henri and I thus tossed a coin for it, which I fear
slightly shocked the company, for the English do seem to be a most
puritanical breed. Those who are genteel are most conscious of the French
as their superior in style and civilisation. They speak our language with
considerable fluidity. Their accent not always of the finest with the
occasional charming but risable mis-pronunciation. But they have made me
shamefully aware of my lack of Engish. The ladies incidentally were most
anxious to hear all they could of the latest fashions. When I replied
somewhat tartly that in Paris the ladies were wearing their necklines low
this season so as not to impede Madame La Guillotine, Lady Sarah blushed
deeply and apologised for her superficiality. Then it was my turn to feel
shamed. For I had been received with such kindness it was cavalier of me to
speak in such a manner. But all was resolved by Sir Harry who brushed the
comment aside with one of his jovial pronouncements.

My room, the one in which I am now seated, my dear Suzanne is up
under the roof. My neighbours are the nursery and a small galley where the
nursery maid has her cot in order to be near the children. You will be glad
to hear that she is well over fifty years old and has a moustache that would
put Auguste's to shame.

Once bedded down I fell into the deepest sleep, having hardly closed
my eyes the night before. And I awoke late the next day to find a small

apparition in my doorway. In my half-waking state I took the child for our sweet Amisie and unthinkingly called out to her in French. Whereupon she marched into my room and told me in no uncertain terms that I talked in a curious way. Once our introduction had been put on a more formal basis, she was identified as Lady Charlotte's five-year old daughter Emma. She has informed me that she will take it upon herself to teach me to speak English in a proper manner. So I dare say I will be coming home with a vocabulary rich in terms for dolls bonnets, ribbons and frills.

After a fine breakfast in which I was expected to eat eggs and salted pork belly washed down with a fair quantity of ale I took myself off on foot to explore the town.

The district I find myself lodged in goes by the quaint name of Holland Park, but I could find nothing remotely Dutch about it, for it is one of the hilliest parts of London and not at all similar to the Pays Bas of its namesake.

That first noon after a hearty dinner, Sir Harry called for me in his carriage on his way to The Parliament in Westminster. As he had a debate of some importance to attend, he left me outside the Parliament Building to wander at my leisure and discover some of the city. A short walk took me into a park called St James's. This rivalled many a park in Paris for its size but not in elegance. It is a wide expanse well cleared for walking and I strolled for a while enjoying the air which was freer of fetid smalls than any part of the town I had yet encountered. A sound of bugles drew my attention to the king's horse guards who were parading in the distance. My eye was also drawn to a vast turkey carpet that had been dragged out and suspended over the balcony railings for a beating. The quality of this made me reassess the standing of the inhabitants for it rivalled any to be seen at Versailles. But the lake of St James's is little more than a duck pond with no statuary or fountains. And my fellow pedestrians were a motley crew. A one legged beggar sat by the pond begging from passers by and there were several ladies of ill-repute loitering around.

From there on I explored a pleasing arrondissement with numerous open squares. The streets of London are for the most part broad but the buildings lack the elegance of ours in France. In daytime the byeways are always busy with cries of vendors offering bread, rabbits, greens, potatoes, all sorts of foodstuffs. When night falls and darkness descends the streets quickly empty and London seems an evil place lit up like hell itself with reddish coal smoke hanging around each lamp post. I was more than glad to find myself safely back at the Parliament Building where Sir Harry had concluded his business for the day.

But enough of my idle discourse. I must make haste to finish for my candle is guttering and my 'facteur' awaits. Surfice to tell all that we are arrived, we are safe and we are most nobly received and cared for.

So my dearest Suzanne. I think of you constantly. I draw you close in my dreams. I pray for your safety and that of Amisie and Mother in these cruel times. And I write in the confidence of God's goodness that it is His will that we will be reunited before very long.

Your loving
Jean

-------- -- -------

When the courrier had left I sat staring into the little coal fire that was kept as a courtesy, burning in my room. I thought back to the days, a mere four years back, but which seemed an age away to me now - when I had brought Suzanne to La Mulatière as my bride.

The marriage took place at Chassignolles, the seat of the Longaunay family some three hour's drive away. The feasting and the dancing had been in full swing for two days but weary of so much revelry and I must admit, more than eager to begin our new conjugal life, I had suggested our early departure. We'd left the revellers still at the height of the wedding festivities and swept away in the carriage with their blessings and hearty well wishings ringing in our ears.

I held Suzanne close, rocking in the rhythm of the carriage and exhausted by the excitement from our days of celebration, she soon slept in my arms. As was the custom in those days, our marriage had been arranged by our parents when we were children. I was a mere boy of nine years when the contract was agreed. But the heavens had been on my side; or perhaps

the foresight of my father (for Suzanne's mother was a fine looking woman)
and the bride that I had returned to claim so reluctantly from the army had
turned out to be a jewel. I could hardly believe my good fortune when this
slender, delicate skinned girl was presented to me. And even more so when
a glance from those brimming blue eyes of hers clearly said that my
affections were returned.

I was too full of joy to sleep and when four or so hours later, we
turned into the avenue of La Mulatière my Suzanne looked so peaceful I
hadn't the heart to wake her.

Here was my home, the scene of my infant games, my boyhood revels,
the home I'd left so eagerly to enter the army and returned to so gratefully
alive to tell the tale of my exploits. Now the house was to be mine. No, ours.
I thought my heart would burst with pride. My life in this place I loved so
fiercely was now to be made complete. I was bringing my bride back with
me.

I signalled to the coachman not to make a sound and lifted Suzanne
still sleeping in my arms. The servants must have heard the carriage.
Auguste had stayed fully dressed in his livery, but the others unable to
contain their curiosity had come with candles and shawls and were huddled
behind him to witness our arrival.

Auguste ran forward to help me. But Suzanne was light as a child in
my arms. Seeing her sleeping, they kept their silence and soon I had swept
up the great arc of stairs and laid her in our bed, still in her wedding dress,
sleeping like a baby.

I sent the maid away. And I confess, such was my fatigue that as soon
as I had thrown off my wedding clothes and lain down beside her, I fell into
the deepest sleep. Such was our wedding night!

The next morning I was woken by the first rays of sunlight shining on
my face. Suzanne was no longer beside me. She had divested herself of her
wedding finery and was sitting in her nightgown by the window gazing out.

'Come back to bed...' I whispered.

She shook her head. 'No.. Not now. Look how the sun is melting
away the mist. Come let's go out in the dawn. Saddle the horses and we'll
ride out. I want to see everything.'

Despite my protests and coaxings she would have her way.

All was quiet in the courtyard. I crept into the stables and saddled our horses myself. By the time I had them at the door, dressed only in her dressing robe and slippers she climbed lightly into the saddle.

We rode out into the fresh sweet dawn. The fields were still clothed in a low mist so that Suzanne, ahead of me seemed to float rather than ride. Her hair not dressed in her habitual coiffure ran down her back in soft tendrils, lifting gently with the motion of the horse, shining golden in the first warm rays of sunlight.

We wove our way through the fields of ripening rye, barley and wheat. I've never seen our harvest more golden, or more green, or more vigorous. As the mist evaporated in the ever growing heat, the smell of the fields rose up to greet us. Everywhere we looked, nature seemed to be bursting into life, reaching for the heavens. Suzanne turned to glance back at me and her face echoed my sentiments. All of this was - ours.

We cantered the horses for a while alongside the brook, my horse familiar with this stage of the ride and straining for his habitual gallop, soon outpaced Suzanne's. But even he held back as if sensing that the two of us were waiting for something. I paced him slowly round the meadow that had been left to grow high for haymaking. The hay was so deep and rich, it was already mounting to the horses withers. Suzanne was not far behind. She arrived, her hair flung back in the breeze, her eyes bright and her compexion rosy with the exertion of the ride.

I dismounted and reached to help her down. As I did so I could feel that she was naked under the fine linen of her gown. Our eyes met and hers said wordlessly: 'Yes. Now.'

And so it was that our marriage was consummated with a tumble in the hay.

'What a fine lady I have married,' I whispered as I disentangled strands of hay from her hair.

She laughed. 'You'll think me nothing better than a peasant girl.'

'I would always have you so.'

'So... let's live like two savages, just with the sun and the wind, with no cares for our attire, or grand entertaining. We'll live off wild things,

mushrooms, nuts and berries and have no need of servants interfering. Let's build ourselves a little hut of leaves and branches just here.'

'I could bring my gun so that we would have the occasional partridge or rabbit to vary our diet.'

She laughed and sighed and lay staring up at the sky. Then suddenly realising the height of the sun she said: 'Come we must make haste. Your mother will rise soon and expect us down.'

'No . Let's stay awhile.' I stroked the inside of her bare arm. 'Let's lie here till dinnertime.'

But Suzanne was already on her feet.

'The workers will be in the fields soon. I'll not have them catch the first glimpse of their new mistress dressed like this!'

The horses had wandered off. Such was the urgency with which we'd thrown ourselves into the soft sweet grass that I hadn't thought to tether them. It took me some time to catch the two beasts. We rode back leaving the imprints of two bodies in a circlet of hay. It wouldn't be the first time that meadow had served as my host.

-------- -- -------

Jean Mulatier de la Grolière – London - April 1794

My dearest sweetest wife

I had long been conscious of outstaying my welcome with Lady Sarah. I have for some time been searching for lodgings appropriate to my purse and my taste. Not an easy task for my purse becomes lighter by the day and my taste is reluctant to change.

However, I am happy to inform you that I have found rooms in Mary-le-Bone above a tavern with a stalwart landlady, name of Susan, which already makes me feel at home. In name only is she like my darling, for her beefy arms are as thick as Old Foisil's and her tongue as free - tho' luckily the English I learned at Lady Sarah's includes few of her favourite phrases. My room, small is it is, is moderately clean and always warm with the heat from the tap room below. I shall not be lonely here because my very sleep has the jovial accompaniment of merry voices well into the early hours and even a song or two if I'm lucky.

From my window I look out over grassy meadows not unlike ours back home in our beloved Mulatière. An industrious market gardener has purchased land adjoining and I am hoping later in the year to profit from his fresh produce as so far my landlady has produced no other vegetable besides potatoes. I heartily miss our fine bread. But I should not talk of this for I know how keenly you are suffering from cruel privations. Please be sure that you and mother and little Amisie eat all you can from nature, apples, berries, nuts should be found in abundance. Sell anything you have left for milk and cheese for Amisie. How I wish I could send you some substantial British fare.

But enough of idle wishing. I know you will want to hear all of my doings and news of London to pass on to others with unfortunate relations in exile.

On the first morning at the Tavern I set out to explore my new surroundings. My progress was arrested not far down the street by the sound of a jovial discourse in our own native language. Peering over a parapet I found a group of priests at work, their shovel hats bobbing up and down as they industriously dug in a ditch.

On enquiring of the Father who seemed to be in charge of this curious equipe, I found that they are building a Roman Catholic chapel where we the French community can worship in our own fashion. The Protestants have generously being vacating their churches and turning a blind eye to our pope-ish rituals for essential services but the French community here feels the need of our own place of worship.

Since then I have found Mary-le-Bone to be a veritable little France - in fact the locals refer to it in gest as 'Normandy' after a tavern of the same name in the High Street. The Huguenots had established their presence so effectively both here and in neighbouring Soho that I find our native language is spoken almost as commonly as it is in Paris.

A great camaraderie has grown up among those forced into circumstances similar to my own. Indeed now the flow of exchange has been cut off from France there is little opportunity for flaunting fine garments or wealth as all of us are now suffering to a greater or lesser extent from lack of funds.

In order to relieve this 'financial embarrassment' a series of divertissements have been set up. There are morning ateliers where the ladies gather to embroider muslin and the Comtesse de F. has actually turned her hand to millinery! She told me with some pride that she could make a fine straw hat in three mornings. I replied that I wished that I could make myself as useful. 'But you can,' she retorted. 'We need strong fellows like you to go up to the market at Cornhill and fetch materials.'

Picture me, my dear Suzanne, on a wet morning, barely dawn, bartering for straw and having such success I secure a vast bundle at a good price. This I discover to my chagrin, I can barely lift - but cannot leave in the street for fear of it being stolen. The way back being a good two kilometers, I am forced to carry it any way I can contrive. There I am with the bundle, not knowing which arm to take it under, or whether to strap it to my back - then in the long run engineering to balance it on my head so keeping off the driving rain. I have done a small drawing of this to amuse Amisie.

Now my love remember as we promised at the Angelus we share a single prayer. That we shall be reunited. That this madness that has overtaken our country shall subside. That peace, tranquillity and the rule of God shall return to our beloved homeland.

Kiss my mother's hands and hold close my little Amisie for me.

Remember as ever I love and worship you.

Your loving Jean.

-------- -- -------

Jean Mulatier de la Grolière - 1795

My dearest sweetest Suzanne.

I fear this may be the last missive you receive from me for quite some time. According to the 'Courrier de Londres' the Comité de Surveillance from now on will open all packets and read all letters. I therefore feel it prudent, deeply as it saddens me, for us to desist from all correspondence. I do not need to remind you that your letters are the one joy and sustenance of my life. Yet to continue, my darling, could put my precious family in jeopardy.

So here in this one letter, I must attempt to compact all my love and all my hopes for the future and all my faith in the belief that we will ride this time of torment and be together once again in this life. If not my beloved Suzanne, sadly and certainly, in the next. May this faith sustain you through the terrible privations and terrors that I know you suffer although you complain so little. How many times have I bowed on my knee and prayed I had not fled the country but stayed at your side or taken you and mother and little Amisie with me. But it is idle to regret what cannot be changed.

I will try and give you a picture of my life here to supply the want of the letters which were to follow.

Most of us try to continue our lives with as little alteration as possible to our accustomed habitudes and tastes. Thus we gather each evening at one house or another to enjoy civilised conversation. I for one have spent many a pleasant evening in the salon of Mme de B. who is related distantly to my great aunts in Bourges. Mostly we chat and naturally our conversation turns to politics. Every man has his project for the future when, God willing, times of peace and tranquillity will be restored in our beloved homeland. Our Country is always central to our thoughts, to all discussions and to our hearts. As to lighter pleasures - should the household be furnished with an instrument, we enjoy music from the ladies. Cards are not favoured pastime. I hazard that we all have a new respect for the few coins we have in our pockets and I myself feel it would be ignoble to take winnings off a chap who is as destitute as myself.

My fellow emigrés have come up with numerous solutions to relieve their financial difficulties. The ladies, as I have mentioned before, tend to be eternally resourceful making hats or dresses or embroidering muslin. The young girls are reluctantly forced into the position of saleswomen, taking their wares from haberdasher to haberdasher. The men are less adapted to pecuniary skills. There are some who read at the play, in London currently, French drama has become all the rage. Others who teach French or music. There are some who have come up with devilishly cunning employments such as a M. d'Albagnac who is much in demand for his skill at tossing salads at elegant parties. Such is his success that he has even hired an assistant to hand him his assortment of vinegars, truffles and condiments. There is another cynical fellow who has ordered the construction of a miniature guillotine of walnut wood and entertains rapt audiences daily with a demonstration of its efficacity with a reluctant cast of unfortunate ducks and geese. Both theatrical and economical, the fellow contrives to supply the pot each evening with the former day's repertoire.

As to my own pecunary situation, I long cast about for some way to gain a living suitable to a gentleman. But country fellow as I am, having no talents for painting miniatures, playing an instrument, or reading at the theatre, I despondently thought that I would forever be condemned as a beast of burden beneath my load of straw. But then I encountered a M. de Polignaux who has opened a school of fencing in a room above a tavern in Soho. Little did I think that my training with the epée and sabre at d'Estissac would prove so valuable. How we young bloods fooled around with the poor M d'Alemberd our fencing master, all being of the firm opinion that in modern warefare a man is likely to have a bullet though his head before he has a chance draw his sabre.

So now I spend my mornings coaching young gentlemen from the best of British families on the French manner of fencing. Through this I have struck up a friendship with one of my pupils - a jovial fellow with whom I manage well to communicate despite our lack of each other's language. Last week he invited me to a fine soirée at a magnificent country residence in Chiswick. We were treated to a sumptuous dinner such as I have not seen since departing the shores of my beloved France. To which you can be sure my dearest Suzanne I did more than justice.

So my darling you can see that my lot is not one of physical privation. The privation is in my heart, from the pain of missing you, my darling Amisie and dear mother. My fears for you, I must confess often bring me very low.

Kiss my mother's hands, hold Amisie to you and hold me in your heart my dearest little wife. Remember that my love, my constancy, my hopes and prayers are with you always.

Until we are together
Your loving husband
Jean

PS: Please bless old Auguste for me, and remember me to the Curé.

-------- -- -------

How different my life was from this happy fiction I felt compelled to send to Suzanne. In truth I had squandered my money in the very first week. Within a month, confident in my imminent return, I had sold the snuff boxes which I had brought with me as security, for a set of fine clothes.

In truth our soirées were often sad affairs as news filtered through of loved ones who had met their end on the guillotine. Death and poverty was all around us and we in Mary le Bone were the fortunate ones. The poorer emigrés have installed themselves South of the River Thames in Cheapside where lodgings of a kind can be found for pennies. Here there is little hope of commerce or employment as their British neighbours are as poor as they are. Pitiful stories have come to light in a pamphlet published by two benevolent British noblewomen. It tells of Mme de L who has lost her reason following an awful birth just admitted to the hospital of St Luke leaving five children, the oldest seven, without provision. Mme de D dead of hunger leaving a paralysed husband and three sick sons. Mme la Comtesse de B herself sick with an old husband suffering from gout who could not leave his bed.

These benevolent English women have set up a women's committee organising a relief in kind which provides beds, linen and clothes for children. Food and medical aid when they can. A fund has been created designed to provide the poorest widows with an income of ten pounds per annum.

I feel shamed by all this, remembering that such a sum is one that I might frequently lose at the gambling tables without turning a hair. Now French gentlewomen are contriving to keep a family for a year on such a sum. And yet they too are the fortunate ones, as in the homeland we have fled from many of their relatives have lost everything including their heads.

In the descending spiral of misery it seems there is an infinite regression of suffering. No end to it but merciful death.

Julia 2009

I went and had a good moan to Maitre Bertrand about the letters.

'They were totally illegible, every one of them.'

'It's understandable. Those emigrés didn't want to implicate their families. In order to escape detection they used all sorts of ruses. Like writing in lemon juice, for instance. You held the paper up to the fire and the juice changed colour. Once read the writing disappeared, for ever.'

Chapter Twenty Four

Julia 2009

Rain had set in over the last few days and I could almost sense the grass growing at a speed fast enough to see, like one of those-time lapse nature films. At night my sleep was troubled by dreams in which the garden had turned into a dense jungle with phallic fronds swelling and bursting open in a frenzied rite of Spring. I'd never seen plants shoot up like this in England. Soon the meadows would be waist deep. Woods impenetrable. Paths impassable. How was I going to cope?

In a break between showers I dragged on a pair of wellingtons and went out to check the paths. Anything that was green or sharp or spikey was thrusting itself out of the ground. The wood was already clogged with dense thickets of cow parsley. Beds of nettles had shot up from nowhere. Young brambles were snaking their way through the undergrowth, everything was fighting its way towards the light.

A sound caught my attention. A swish, swish, swish over from the far side of the pond. *Jerôme.* I tracked it down. Sure enough, there he was in the wood, swinging a scythe in a great arc. How long had he been there? And how much had he done so far? With a sinking feeling I tried to estimate how many euros-worth he'd already cut.

'Bonjour Madame,' he said catching sight of me and putting down his scythe. He wiped his hands on his trousers and came to greet me.

'Bonjour. Wow you've got a job on your hands,' I said meaningfully.

He shrugged and smiled. 'This is the Allier. Nature doesn't to things by halves eh?'

'It certainly doesn't.'

'Let it get out of hand,' he said, bringing out his now familiar threat. 'And you'll have no end of trouble. The brambles, the nettles... ' he drew breath disapprovingly through his teeth.

I felt like pointing out that nature had happily been left to its own devices in the wood so far. I was more interested in the veggie patch and the lawn.

'I was wondering about a mower...' I started.

'Oh you'll need a proper tractor mower for this lot. And then of course there are the meadows.'

'I see.' Jerôme picked up his scythe and started slashing at the blade with some sort of medieval-looking sharpening stone.

'I was thinking of getting a hover mower, an electric one.'

He thought this was a fine joke. 'Take weeks to mow this with a hover,' he said. 'And imagine what it would cost in electricity.'

He shook his head with typical French disapproval of wasting money on such a commodity. He swished his scythe through a clump of grass testing the blade, clearly indicating that he had his meter running.

'I'll have to think about it,' I said.

I walked back into the house feeling shaken. The expense of it, just to keep the garden under control. I could see why that Lamulatière woman had seven gardeners. But there must be a better solution. I needed animals, I decided - four-legged lawn-mowers.

I suggested this to Jerôme when he came in to be paid. He grudgingly agreed this might be a solution.

'Can you tell me where I can buy them?'

'Saincoins. That's the place. The biggest live animal market in France, every Wednesday morning.' He was amazed I didn't know this important piece of local information.

I immediately started fantasising about long-haired donkeys with soft ears and the cross of St Michel on their backs. Or calves, maybe, which I could fatten and sell - they might even be a money-making proposition. Or sheep, a small flock which I could use to clear the land and sell the wool. I'd check out the animal situation the following Wednesday.

------- -- -------

Jerôme, it seemed, had different ideas. The following afternoon I found him in the garden with a man I'd never seen before. The stranger came forward cockily and shook me by the hand.

'Antoine Berrichon. Bonjour, Jerôme tells me you need equipment for the garden.'

I eyed them both. This was a conspiracy. I wondered if Jerôme was getting a rake off.

'You've got a nice property here Madame...But large...' continued Antoine.

'I took the liberty to show him round the park,' interrupted Jerôme. 'I hope you don't mind. But he needed to know the size, the area to be mown.'

In unison they turned to the park and eyed it assessingly. The recent rain was on their side, the grass looked ominously lush and healthy.

'What about the orchard?' asked Antoine. 'That needs to be done as well. You'll need a pretty big machine.'

'I don't know,' I said weakly 'I thought maybe I'd get some animals.'

Antoine looked dubious. He muttered something about fencing. And water of course. Maybe a shed. I was starting to feel rather helpless. He sounded as if he wanted to sell me a tractor.

'Well let's say the lawn has to be mown, and the orchard,' I conceded. 'Leave the meadows. I'll think of something.'

The two of them started pacing out the lawn. There was a lot of sucking of breath through teeth. Eventually they walked back to me with the verdict.

'It'll need to be deisel,' said Antoine. 'And nothing less than 6 cylinder.'

'How much will that cost? Round about?'

'Round about?' he squeezed up his eyes. 'I could do you a good price.'

'Umm?'

'Round about ten thousand.'

'Euros?'

'For a good machine made to last.'

'But I can't afford that.'

'I do happen to have something d'occasion (the French for second-hand). Done up of course by me. Six months guarantee. It's a nice machine. Just what you need.'

'It is,' agreed Jerôme nodding. 'I just happened to notice it when passing the shop.'

'I see.'

'Well you can't leave it to grow like this. It'll be unmowable soon. Then I'll have to do the whole lot with the scythe.'

It would take hours, expensive hours, for Jerôme to scythe the lawn.

'How much is it? This wonderful second hand machine of yours.'

'I could let you have it for five thousand. That's a good price.'

'I suppose I'd better come and have a look at it,' I said.

The two of them seemed content with this. They climbed into Jerôme's car and drove off.

I looked back at the garden despondently. Five thousand euros! That was over four thousand pounds. I certainly wasn't going to fork out that much until I'd looked into all the options. No. What I needed was a cheaper solution, and one that recycled the cuttings – four-legged lawn mowers.

------ -- -------

The following Wednesday I emerged groggily into the dawn. I'd set the alarm for a horribly early start as according to Jerôme the market would be in full swing by six am. With the combination of alarm and nightingales, I was awake in good time.

Searching the streets of a grey Saincoins, thick with morning mist, frustratingly enough, the animal market was nowhere to be found. I made a couple of rounds of the village and started wondering whether maybe Jêrome had got it wrong and the market was a once a month affair. At length, I located an old man with a dog and shopping basket which indicated he was a resident. He directed me back to a market square jam-packed with fruit and veg. stalls and booths full of wine-drinking and sausage-eating farmers. But still no sign of animals for sale.

A set of conflicting directions delivered with wine and garlicky breath sent me out of town again and into an area of grey steel hangars where I came across a car park filled with vast double-decker animal conveyors. My nose told me I'd found the right place.

As I made my way between vast pens of Charolais calves, and bleary eyed sheep, cold reason started to take hold. My grasp of animal husbandry was nil. What of innoculations and dipping? The size and location of sheds, heated or unheated? Feed in winter? Running water? What sort of fencing? Electric? How did you choose a good animal? Hooves, teeth, the whites of their eyes?

And I couldn't see any donkeys. I realised I hadn't the faintest idea what a donkey cost:- Fifty euros? Five hundred? A thousand?

Determined to at least find out the price of a donkey, I set out on a systematic search of the pens. I was getting in everyone's way, red-faced farmers armed with electric prods constantly redirected me into new alleys divided off by scaffolding poles. I hadn't come dressed for the event, this was gumboot terrain, slippery underfoot and exceedingly smelly. I groped my way back towards the entrance, threatened by wild eyed calves and blindly pushing and shoving sheep. I was just about to give up and go home when I found one lone specimen.

I stood eyeing this donkey. He hung his head sadly. This was the animal nobody wanted. And following his gaze I saw why. He was a reject donkey, one that had come off nature's conveyor belt and been set to one side. The poor beast's front hooves turned up like wooden clogs, horribly deformed. I shuddered, it might have been kinder to put the animal out of its misery. For a moment I was tempted to take him on, give the poor creature a home, after all I already had a one-eyed cat.

But the sight of this donkey brought me down to earth. The responsibility of animals was too much. Particularly a disabled donkey whose resale value was probably nil. Should I go back to England I'd never find another home for him.

Chastened, I made my way back to the car. Retracing my way back through Saincoins streets, I came across the food and vegetable market again and stopped to console myself with humbler purchases:- a loaf of pain de campagne and some fresh spinach. Soon my eye had been caught by a handmade local basket and as is the way with markets such a basket must been filled. In went a bunch of white and purple turnips, their skin as soft as a baby's. This was soon followed by a pot of golden miel 'toute fleurs', a saucisson sec crusted with dried chilli, and a deep golden soft cheese, half cows' milk half goats'.

As my basket grew heavier I was tempted into the covered market by the sound of crowing and clucking. This was where the small animals were sold. Vendors patiently sat with their wire baskets of tiny baby rabbits. One was held out for me and it's potential described as 'good tender meat for the pot.' It wiffled its velvety nose at me. I was tempted, if only to save it from an early gravy. But my tender townee sensitivities were in the minority here. Chickens passed hands bound upside down, three at a time, in squawking bunches. Frantically cheeping chicks were going by the dozen. I paused again tempted. Fresh eggs in the morning? But I'd have to build a henhouse first. I dithered over a pair of delicate white fan-tailed pigeons but even I knew that without a lock-up dovecote, pigeons are a short term purchase.

I was about to turn and head back to the car when a pair of malard ducks caught my eye. The two of them were crouched together in a cardboard box their gleaming heads of iridescent feathers curved one around the other. Poor things, they looked petrified. Now wild ducks were a possibility. If I left I could simply repatriate them to a neighbouring lake. And they wouldn't need any care at all.

'Are they really wild?' I asked the vendor.

He took a breath quite obviously trying to guage what I wanted to hear.

'No no, quite tame really,' he said.

'Oh? But they are malards?'

'Oh yes, pure malards,' he held one out to me for examination.

'Won't they fly away if I take them home?' I asked guardedly.

'Not if I clip their wings for you,' he said producing a lethal looking knife.

'No! Please.' I backed away.

'No Madame look. Only the feathers. It doesn't hurt the bird. And they'll soon grow back.'

'But won't they fly away then?'

'Not if you feed them and keep them happy. Look at this beautiful duck. They'll fatten up in no time,' he reached for the other.

'I wasn't going to eat them,' I said. 'I just want them for my pond.'

He thought this was a tremendous joke, he raised an eyebrow at his neighbour. 'Oh well then. You couldn't have a prettier pair than these.'

He announced the price as eight euros each. I didn't even bother to haggle. Malards it was going to be. Hawk-eyed as an RSPB inspector I watched as he neatly clipped a few centimetres of flight feathers from one wing of each duck. It didn't seem to bother the bird.

Now the proud owner of a neatly tied cardboard box of malards, I made for home. Not quite the purchase of stock I'd envisaged but it was a start. I drove back worried about how hot it was in the car and wondering how long the birds had been out of water. There was not a movement from the box. They were absolutely silent. I had horrible visions of opening it to find two dead ducks inside.

I drove the car as near as I could to the pond and did a mercy dash to the water with the box. No sooner had I undone the string than the malards leapt into life, squeezing their way out before I'd had a chance to lift the lid. With a great deal of quacking and flapping they shot into the water. I watched as they did a kind of victory roll round the pond then started dipping their heads and sending showers of water over their backs. Dead ducks indeed.

------- -- -------

I'd given in of course. Who wouldn't faced by the combined pressure of Jerôme, Antoine and burgeoning nature? Nature being the most persuasive. In fact 'burgeoning' had taken on a whole new meaning for me.

The lawnmower was delivered the following Friday. I found it standing outside the house in all its garish orange splendour with Jerôme and Antoine hovering over it in admiration, as if it were some thoroughbred. They were fussing about where to store it.

Jerôme stared towards Jacques' farm with a frown on his face.

'If you still had the chapel Madame. That would've been the place.'

'Chapel? What chapel?'

'Didn't you know? That barn Ladier keeps his car in. It was the chapel that belonged to the house.'

'I had no idea. Are you sure?'

'You go and take a look at it. It's in a dreadful state. A shocking shame. But what do you expect from people like him.'

'What do you mean? People like him?'

'He's part of that lot, down at the Mairie.'

'What lot?'

'Communists,' he said darkly.

'Really?' I knew the commune was socialist, like most of the the rural communities round about. But by the way Jerôme said it, he made them sound like radical extremists.

'What's wrong with them?'

'In the old days, things were done properly. Take this place. In my father's day you could be proud of it. Now look at it. It takes a foreigner like you Madame to try and put the place back in order.'

I stared at him. I hadn't expected to hear such reactionary views in this day and age. He was talking like some faithful old retainer.

'So you think things were better in the old days?'

Jerôme nodded as if there were no contest. 'Progress? All the changes they say they've made – we're no better off.'

.

I tentatively suggested the ancient kennels as home for the mower. Currently they were stacked from floor to ceiling with rubbish. This brought on another bate of sucking through teeth and measuring. But at last Jerôme admitted it was a solution. Twenty or so barrow-loads later, he'd cleared an area large enough to house the expensive beast and he came to the kitchen door to inform me that it was properly bedded down.

When he'd left I went to check out the 'chapel'. I took a quick look into the farmyard double-checking Jacques wasn't around. I didn't want to be caught spying on him a second time. I tiptoed over to the barn. The doors stood open. The clapped-out Espace was nowhere to be seen. I ventured inside. The interior walls were of crumbling lime cement and the oil-stained floor was paved in octagonal terracotta tiles just like the ones in the bathroom of La Mulatière. At the far end there was a niche for a statue and on the right of the door an unmistakable stoup for holy water.

I stood back from it and ran my eye over the rough stonework of the façade, High up there was a little rounded romanesque window half hidden by ivy. And under that there was a date carved into the stone. 1866. Not as old as the house so a bit of a mystery.

------- -- -------

My trespassing was interrupted by my phone ringing. I looked around nervously to see if it had been overheard then forced my way back through the hedge and answered it.

'Jules. You all right?'

It was Jane.

'Yes fine why?'

'You haven't called in ages.'

'I've been so busy. Up to my eyes.'

'We worry about you. All alone there. Anything could happen.'

'Like what?'

'I don't know – burglars, axe-murderers. And you must be so lonely.'

'Rubbish. I haven't got time to be lonely. There's too much to do.'

'What about that neighbour of yours?' Jane's voice suggested that she and Sarah had been jumping to conclusions.

'I think there's another woman around.'

'So what do with yourself all evening? You haven't even got a tele.'

'I've got a radio which gets Radio Four in a muffled sort of way. And I've got books... And I'm writing again.'

'What on earth is there to write about, stuck out there?'

'Stuff about the house mainly. Or rather the people who've lived here. I keep imagining their voices. It's as if the house wants to tell me something.'

There was a pause the other end of the phone: 'That's it. You've totally lost it. I said you'd go potty living there on your own.'

'I've never felt so sane in my life.'

'But you must be lonely. It's so quiet in the country.'

'Not at all. It's positively deafening. Listen.' I held up my mobile to the open window. A nightingale was belting out its repertoire in the wisteria above the window-frame and the frogs had set up their nightly chant.

'What's that bird.'

'A nightingale.'

'Cool and what else? Are those grass-hoppers?'

'Frogs.'

'Brilliant. Miranda's doing frogs at school, you could bring her back some frogspawn. What's happening with the notaire?'

''Spose he's doing whatever notaires do. He said it'd take ages.'

'Shouldn't you check?'

'He'll probably take even longer if I interfere.'

'Well he better get things moving soon. I want you back here. I've got someone you've got to meet.'

'Uh-uh.'

'Well. You must miss having Oliver. Even if its only for sex.'

'I'm sure he'd love to hear you say that.'

'You know what I mean.'

'Thanks Jane but I can look after myself. I don't want any of your boring bachelors.'

'What I had in mind was a dishy divorcee.'

'Same thing. Listen, I've got things to do. I'm coming back for Sarah's baby - we can talk about it then.'

'Don't forget the frog-spawn.'

'Probably be frogs by then.'

I rang off and went down to the pond to check. Last week there had been plenty of frogspawn. Some had already hatched out. A few days ago the pond had been rimmed with little black commas nibbling and wriggling their tails in delight. Now there wasn't a single one to be seen.

The ducks, as usual, belly flopped into the pond on my approach. I watched as they swam round dipping their beaks in the water and tossing their heads back obviously enjoying something slippery and delicious, a bit like a diner eating oysters. Miranda had definitely missed her chance of frog spawn.

Chapter Twenty Five

Julia 2009

The work Jerôme was putting in on the vegetable garden was starting to pay off. One afternoon he proudly presented me with a lettuce, stripping back the outer leaves showing me how dense and crisp the centre was.

'Keep the outer leaves for the ducks,' he said

'I can't think why they're not laying. I was looking forward to eggs.'

'Eggs! But you've got two males Madame,' he said, showing a rare burst of amusement. 'The females look quite different.'

'Do they?' I felt really foolish.

'I could find you some females if you like. You'll need two mères for every père.'

'Oh would you?' My dreams of self-sufficiency came a step nearer, if the ducks started laying I might even consider chickens. 'I was thinking of putting more seeds in. Radishes and spinach. Maybe while you're up here you could...'

'Oh dear no. Not this week.'

This was the first time he'd refused me anything.

'But you'll soon be through with the digging.'

'You'll have to wait till at least the end of next week. It's the moon you see.'

'The moon?'

'It has to be in the first quarter. Plant them any other time and radishes? You'll have nothing but leaves.'

'Surely not. That's simply superstition, sounds like black magic to me.'

Jerôme reached in his pocket and pulled out a packet of seeds. He showed me the back. Sure enough the phase of the moon was indicated by a slim crescent. Printed proof. He shook his head at my sad ignorance of horticultural matters

A few days later he turned up with a sackful of female ducks in the boot of his car. God knows where he'd got them. They looked suspiciously like ones I'd seen on Deneville's municipal pond. But he announced that they were good breeding females and only five euros each.

They were brown and speckled, dull-looking creatures compared with the dashing males but my two ducks soon had them sorted into two wives each, paddling at a respectful distance in their wake.

Sarah had been updating me on the progress of the pregnancy with a nightly phone call. I was fast mastering the jargon. The baby had 'engaged' so it seemed intent on delivery on the due date. I could delay no longer.

I made the rounds of the house, locking all the doors and closing the shutters. Some of them were warped and hard to shift and I needed Jerôme to help me.

'So you're off to England,' he commented. 'I'll keep an eye on the house if you like.'

I didn't like to accept this offer not knowing how much I should pay him.

'That would be kind. But there's really no need. The builders will be here and Jacques Ladier's next door.'

'Huh!' said Jerôme. 'I wouldn't trust him if I were you.'

I paused from tugging at a shutter. 'Why not?'

Jerôme shook his head evidently not wanting to answer.

'Come on. Tell me.'

'He should keep himself to himself, that's all.'

'He's Deputy Mayor, he should be trustworthy enough.'

'He likes to poke his nose in.'

'Poke his nose in - where?'

'All right. If you must know. Before your father bought the chateau, that agent gave me the key. He asked me to look round from time to time. Check for leaks and things. One day I came across that fellow Ladier - in the house.'

I remembered the time Jacques had made his way upstairs uninvited to my study.

'How did he get in?'

'It's easy enough to find a way into this house if you've a mind to.'

'But what was he doing here?'

'He said he was looking for something.'

'Looking for something? What?'

Jerôme shrugged. 'Oh it was just some excuse. Take my advice, Madame. Lock up well.' And he disappeared down the stairs.

I gave the shutters a final push and slammed the big hook down to fasten them. As I did so I caught sight of a childish scrawl on the inside of one of them. I made out two names: *Marie* and *Louise*, first scratched in chalk and then above, the same names extravagantly looped, in pencil. Marie, Louise. – the two Lamulatière sisters. Was this writing of their names an annual ritual like Sarah, Jane and and I, measuring ourselves on the doorjamb, stretching every sinew for that competitive noting of the passing of the years? Or were they left there in the primitive way of children, making their mark in order to be remembered, intending them to be found by someone long after they'd grown up and gone. Someone like me?

But I hardly had time to linger. I wanted to have everything loaded in the car ready to leave first thing next morning.

The extension flex Jacques had leant me was still in the kitchen, trailing out across the yard. I unplugged it and winding the flex on the roller made my way down to the hedge.

I could see Jacques across the yard, shovelling manure-clogged straw out of the barn. I could smell it too.

'Hi,' I called, holding up the roller.

Jacques stretched up to his full height and called back. 'Those electricians of yours finished then?'

'No, but I'm going away for a while.'

'Oh? Where?'

'London.'

'How long for?'

'Not sure yet. My sister's having a baby. And...' I added as an afterthought, 'I've friends to see.'

He came over wiping his filthy hands on his trousers.

He frowned as he took the extension flex. 'So you won't be needing this then.'

'No... thank you. The electricians should've finished by the time I get back. Thanks though, it's really helped me out. I really do feel I should pay you for the electricity.'

Jacques brushed this aside with a gesture. 'You paid for the pig.'

'Well that's kind of you...'

I paused not quite knowing how to end the conversation. He could obviously see that with his hands in their current state, a handshake was out of the question. And I certainly wasn't going to kiss him on the cheeks. He grinned his lop-sided grin at me and turning on his heel, went back to work.

------- -- -------

The plan was for me to stay at Sarah's so as to be 'on tap'. I arrived in London in the early evening feeling stiff and bug-eyed from the drive, unprepared for the nightmare of finding a parking place in Baron's Court. After a steaming hour or so, I left the car three streets away and toiled up to Sarah's flat with my suitcase.

She'd left the front door on the latch, so I let myself in. Sarah was laid out on the sofa with her feet up on cushions.

'Methusellah has come to the mountain,' I bent down to give her a kiss.'

'You were ages parking. I thought you'd crashed.'

'My god Sarah! You're enormous!'

'Tell me about it. I'm having to pee every half hour. The brat seems to be leaning on my bladder. Do you want tea or something?'

'I'll make it.'

When I came back with the mugs of tea, Sarah started on a stream of instructions: 'I'm all packed and ready to go. We'll have to do a trial run to the hospital to see how long it takes. And you've got to be sure your mobile's charged and you've got the hospital number. And I'll have to show you where all the baby's stuff is...' she was hoisting herself off the sofa.

    'Sarah, calm down. I'm here now. It's not about to drop out is it?'

    'No I guess not.'

    'Come on. Here's a cuppa. Haven't you got anything stronger?'

    'No. Not good for baby.'

    'Well I'm popping out to the 'offie' for a bottle of something later. God what a drive that was.'

------- -- -------

The next day I left Sarah propped up in front of morning television and drove over to Fulham. The removal people were coming to give a quote. As I parked in my street I noted that during my absence"Briar Village" had moved a knotch or two up the residential scale. My cluttered little corner shop had turned into a deli. In place of their usual boxes of ageing fruit and veg., it was now flanked by stylish zinc buckets full of Dutch flowers. My local pub. had transformed itself into a Wine Bar, its hearty roasts and shepherds' pies replaced by a slate offering sun-dried veggies, seared tuna, everything 'drizzled' in balsamic vinegar.

    Letting myself into my flat, I found it had unaccountably shrunk. How had I ever lived in a place so tiny? I drew up a blind. Hadn't I ever noticed that view? The soot-stained wall and that hideous central heating vent? I sank down on to the sofa with a feeling of relief. Selling-up? I'd definitely made the right decision.

------- -- -------

I went to see Jane the following day.

    'I've got something in the car for you. From Dad.'

    'From Dad?'

    'I found it stashed away in a cupboard, with his clothes...' In my mind's eye I was standing in the half light at La Mulatière, in the Art Nouveau room with its softly gleaming panels, holding his jacket in my arms breathing in the smell of the wool.

Jane was already heaving the crate out of the boot: 'Oh the Beaujolais. Charles'll be pleased. Fancy him remembering. Dear Dad.'

'There was something for Sarah as well. Baby clothes.'

'She's like a mountain isn't she? Can't talk about anything but the baby...'

'Poor thing,' I cut in.

'Oh Jules I'm sorry,' Jane rubbed my arm. 'It'll get better with time.'

'I'm not sure I'd want Oliver's sprog anyway.'

'Come on let's have a drink. I've made us spag. arrabiata with tons of chilli. The twins are being picked up from Nursery. Give us a chance to have some peace. Fancy a glass of wine?'

'Shall I open one of these?' I indicated the crate.

'No way. Charles would have a fit. They're for laying down. I've got a bottle of Aussie Chardonnay in the fridge.'

She poured us each a glass and we took them over to the bay window. Jane swept an armful of toys on to the floor clearing a place for us to sit.

I stared out at their back garden. A tiny square of grass and a grubby sandpit littered with an upturned tricycle and bright plastic beakers. I had a fleeting glimpse of the life Jane envisaged for me - with a similar toy strewn pocket handkerchief of lawn.

I noted that the blackened lilac tree in the far corner was just coming into bloom. There were lilacs at La Mulatière, great banks of them, the air would be heady with their scent by now. In my mind's eye I was walking down the avenue of trees and coming face to face with the house. I could hear the frogs discordant chorus from the fish pond. Would the wisteria still be in bloom when I got back, I wondered?

'As for that job,' Jane was saying. 'You know you loathed it, you'll soon find something else.'

'Well as a matter of fact, I...'

'Charles says don't accept their pay-off until you've consulted him. Talking of money, he says it's a good time to invest. And there'll be the money from Dad's place too when you sell it. You'll be fine - for the future, you know.'

'For my lonely old age, you mean?'

'No! I bet you anything you'll get back with Oliver.' She caught my warning glance. 'Anyway your redundancy money should tide you over, till you find something.'

We were half way through lunch by the time I plucked up the courage to ask Jane if she and Charles could help with some cash for the renovations.

'Not on I'm afraid. Can't those agents of yours get a move on? Charles has got what money there is tied up and with the market in its current state he can't sell anything. We'll go bonkers if we don't get that extra space for the kids soon.'

------- -- -------

Sarah was even less help. She said with the baby coming she couldn't even think about it.

'I'll only get maternity pay for three months and after that god knows how I'll manage. I was counting on the money from the house.'

I tried to explain about the problems with the will and the taxes, but she was only listened with half an ear. She was already cooeing over the contents of the box of Baby Dior.

'Oh look at this Julia. It's all interlined with tiny check, isn't that adorable?'

------- -- -------

It was alarming how quickly I slipped back into the routine of London. La Mulatière seemed to fade from existence like some impossible fantasy. Like something that had never been. Some kind of vivid dream that I had woken from and believed was real.

No sooner was I back in London than Jane and Sarah resumed match-making with renewed determination. Their conversations were punctuated with terribly obvious references to any available single man. In the first week of my visit, Jane even contrived a party for me.

'Just a few friends round for drinks and kind of mezze thingummees,' was how she described it.

'You will go, won't you?' insisted Sarah.

'Only if you come.'

'No frankly, I don't think I can face it. Everyone'll be standing, I can't keep upright for that long.'

'I won't go then.'

'No you must. I'll be fine. Keep your mobile on. I'll ring if there's the slightest twinge.'

'I don't know why you're so keen to get me out of here?'

Sarah rolled her eyes. 'I'm not. Go and have a good time. How long is it precisely since you've been to a party?'

'Ages. I've forgotten how to talk to people.'

'That settles it. You're going.'

------- -- ------

Jane had asked me to arrive early, so I could give her a hand with the food while she put the children to bed. But the minute I was through the door she hustled me into the living room where I found Oliver installed on the sofa. So that was why Sarah had been so keen for me to go, they were in it together.

'Julia,' he said getting up to greet me. 'What a surprise. You're looking great. Lovely tan,.'

'Builder's tan, ends at the vest marks,' I said.

Jane popped her head round the door. 'Just going to tuck in the twins,' she said in an oh-so-obvious leaving us alone tone of voice.

Oliver put an arm round my waist and kissed me, but only on the cheek.

He settled back on the sofa and patted the seat beside him: 'So how's that little place of yours?'

'Are you really interested?'

'I know you're dying to tell me, so yes...'

'Too large, too run-down, too expensive... But I still love it.'

'Making any friends?'

'Yes actually,'

'The parson, the doctor, the old folks in the 'grace and favour' home?'

'And more besides. But tell me about you. How's everything at Cornell's?'

'Cornell's is thriving. Taken on more staff. Just had another equity hand-out as a matter of fact. I believe I'm quite a catch.'

'Weren't you always?'

We were interrupted by the door opening. Charles led in a girl I hadn't seen before.

Oliver leapt to his feet: 'And voilà - a new colleague, Julia meet Veronica.'

'Hi. Wow! I've heard so much about you. About that wonderful house of yours...' Veronica slid over to Oliver and gave him a very un-colleague-like kiss and he gave her a squeeze.

I caught Oliver's eye and raised an eyebrow. He gave me a negative response behind Veronica's back.

'Is it really miles away from anywhere?' asked Veronica. 'Must be so scary living there on your own.'

'No, as a matter of fact, it's not scary at all. I've a farm within shouting distance.'

'Inhabited by a hairy hunchbacked ogre, according to Jane,' said Oliver.

'Really?'

'He's not hunchbacked, only a bit unshaven.'

More people were arriving. Derek an old pal of Oliver's pressed his way across the room, saying: 'Oliver and how's the lovely Veronica? (The two of them in one sentence, I noted). 'Oh and my goodness *Julia* - you're back.'

'Only temporarily. Look, I better go and find Jane, she must need a hand with the food.'

I forced my way through to the kitchen.

'How long's this been going on with *Veronica.*'

Jane straightened up hot from the oven.

'Veronica? She's meant to be in Hay-on-Wye this weekend.'

'Hay-on-Wye?'

'Book Festival. Not long. And it's not serious. Oliver told me she's just keeping your side of the bed warm.'

'Sure she'd be thrilled to hear that.'

'Do you think these look burnt?' Jane pointed at the baking tray of canapés she'd just removed from the oven.

'Caramelised. They're fine. Want me to put them on a plate?'

'You're a star. Anyway,' she said looking at me archly: 'You don't want Oliver, so you've told me.'

'No, I know I don't, but...'

'...you don't want anyone else to have him?'

'It'll take time to get used to, that's all.'

'Well. Veronica will be history by the time you've got used to her.'

'What makes you say that?'

'She's not as tolerant as you are,' said Jane pushing the door open and disappearing into the living room with the plate of canapés.

I stood staring at the door. Tolerant? Wasn't that how you described a *doormat*?

------- -- -------

We had a couple of false alarms before the actual birth. The second time, I'd actually driven Sarah to the hospital, but the contractions stopped and I had to bring her home.

By the time she went into labour for real, we were experts at counting the seconds between contractions.

'This is it this time,' I said.

Sarah's face was flushed from the pain. 'God, I bloody well hope so. I was starting to think I was gestating an elephant.'

Sarah had insisted on a 'natural birth'. I hadn't realised how *primitive* the whole thing was. It seemed to take forever. We'd gone into hospital very gung ho at seven in the morning. By mid-day the pains were obviously excruciating. By night time, I was begging Sarah to have an epidural, I couldn't stand watching her suffer. But they said it was too late by then. At last, at around two in the morning, I was trailing anxiously behind as they wheeled her into the delivery room.

Suddenly all was tense, efficient, under control. I was given a mask and sent to the non-baby end where Sarah clung to my hand so hard I thought she was going to crush it.

And then quite suddenly, it was all over. A tiny screaming, bloodied form was being held up wrapped in a towel.

'It's a lovely boy,' announced the midwife.

I wanted to melt into background as Sarah, calm now, her face bathed in sweat, received the squalling bundle.

'Hush now... shush...' she whispered. Then she looked up, her face ecstatic... 'Jules... Look... Isn't he...? Jules, you're not crying..?'

It was all too much. We all know about birth, the official version - the pink and blue sanitised affair that's marketed to us. The actual thing is raw, primeval, intensely humbling.

------- -- -------

The following morning I slept until midday. I woke feeling muggy and somewhat shaken by the night before. But I had a hot bath and pulled myself together. A call to the hospital found Sarah far more in control than I was. It seemed she would be fully occupied all day with visits from the rest of the family, so I took charge of preparing for her return.

I opened a bottle of wine at lunchtime to celebrate and put on a CD, then started pushing the Hoover round the flat. The baby's room didn't need touching. Everything stood, pristine, ready - cot, changing mat, disposable nappies - a chest of drawers stuffed with baby clothes.

I slid open the top drawer - there was the gift from Dad - the Baby Dior outfit with its check interlining. The sight of it made my eyes sting with tears. Another grandchild. One he wouldn't see. A boy.

I shoved the drawer closed and went back to hoovering. Not for me the joys of motherhood. I thought of Oliver and the baby we might have had. Then I went and slopped more wine into the glass and told myself firmly not to engage in maudlin and useless self-pity.

------- -- -------

I stayed on for a week after the birth and settled Sarah and little Ernest back in the flat.

Jane called in several times with the twins and Miranda. The girls bossily took charge, treating little Ernest like a large and rather damp doll.

While Sarah was busy feeding, Jane caught me in the kitchen and had a big moan about the cost of their building work. I tried to reassure her that I was doing everything I could to get Briarmount sold.

'So when do you think you'll have Dad's place ready to market?' she asked. I hadn't actually broached my idea of keeping the house.

'The legal side's got to be sorted first,' I said.

Jane leaned on the worktop and eyed me assessingly: 'That French notaire chappie. I suppose he knows what he's doing?'

'Of course he does. It's complicated, that's all.'

'How complicated? You can't stay stranded out there forever.'

'Look...' I said, turning to face her. 'I've been meaning to tell you. Jane, you've got to back me up on this one. I've decided not to sell the house.'

'*Not* sell La Mulatière?'

'No.'

'You mean you're going to live there? In that vast house? Alone?'

'I might not be alone forever.'

'Who are you going to meet out there for godsake? Some local yokel?'

'Maybe.'

'You've got someone out there already!'

'No, I haven't. I don't need anyone. Why can't people understand. I *want* to be on my own. I love it there. I want to write. And for once in my life I've found something to write about.'

'*What* precisely are you going to live on?'

'I'm going to do summer lets. And I've other ideas too.'

'Such as?'

'Not fully formulated yet.'

So I'd committed myself. The news circulated through the family bringing with it all the expected warnings and recriminations. Mummy was the worst. I had to spend a conciliatory weekend with her in Edenhurst as penance. Two days which confirmed in my mind, beyond a shadow doubt, I was doing the right thing.

------- -- -------

The following days in London I was flat out making arrangements for the removal firm. Packing stuff in boxes and labelling them. Sorting through books and making a pile for Oxfam, having a blitz on my wardrobe. I was hardly going to need my 'Presentation Suits' at La Mulatière. All my heels went into a rubbish sack that sat in the hall sagging spikily, threatening to split at any moment.

Like a lover separated from their loved one, I bought the house ridiculously extravagant presents. On the way to pick up the duvet from the dry cleaners, I found myself in Christopher Wray making out a cheque for an extortionately-priced pair of Arts and Crafts wall lights for the Art Nouveau room.

I tracked down an architectural salvage merchant in the Goldhawk Road and did a deal for a pair of Victorian wash basins complete with brass taps. I dithered over a marble vanity top and regretted it later. The final totally irrelevant purchase was a sea-green trug and apron kit with its own matching trowel and fork from Conran's garden department.

The truth was, wherever I might be, my heart was still at La Mulatière. I could picture the house, all locked and shuttered - the narrow bands of sunlight slanting through the dusky air - the rooms still... silent... empty ....unobserved. Or were they empty? I remembered that sensation of the people from the past still being there. Maybe the past was forever replaying itself... light footsteps on the parquet, the distant sound of laughter, a few notes on a spinette...

When the agents rang to say they had a couple of clients they wanted to show round, I decided to leave them to it. I simply couldn't hold out any longer.

------- -- -------

I left Fulham in the grey dawn of the following Sunday. I had the car packed to the roof with everything from toilet roll holders to fire irons. As I climbed into the driving seat a lone blackbird was singing its heart out on the telegraph wire outside my flat. I drew my coat closer round me. Wryly, I pictured an alternative Sunday morning. Lying in the warmth of Oliver's bed while he popped out with his overcoat over his pyjamas to buy the Sundays and fresh croissants from the corner deli.. A long, lazy, sexy morning followed by brunch out maybe, the two of us alone, or lunch in the pub with a load of his friends. We'd have a walk in the park or take in an exhibition at some gallery followed by a film at the Curzon and then supper somewhere. And then it would be Monday again - and again and again. That's what I was giving up.

I drove on with determination through the outer suburbs, streets lined by endless trails of 'thirties semis and hypermarkets with their car parks already filling up for Sunday service. Then somewhere on the M25 the sun broke though and as it melted the last trailing fingers of mist over the fields, I saw a herd of white Charolais cows. I thought of Allier and my heart rose. I stepped harder on the accelerator.

Chapter Twenty Six

Once over the Channel I could hardly contain my rising excitement. I didn't even want to stop for petrol as every kilometer drew me closer to La Mulatière.

I ground my way round Paris on the outer Peripherique counting myself lucky that it was Sunday so no lorries to contend with. I was round the city in record time and soon speeding through the open plains of Orléans. There I opened the window and was rewarded by the scent of manure, disgustingly pungent yet somehow welcoming.

A couple of hours later I left the motorway and plunged into the forest of Tronçais. While I'd been away, the trees had progressed from their first lacy covering of shy green into full blown leaf. Between the foliage I caught glimpses of bright lakes and russet tiles, and then as I approached Deneville I was greeted by the delicious scent of woodsmoke from the saw mills.

A few minutes later, tingling with anticipation, I swung the car down the two long avenues of trees to catch my first glimpse of La Mulatière's sharp pyramid of slate.

The house was still there. It hadn't burnt down, or disappeared into thin air like those castles in folk tales. There was the tower followed by the full sweep of the slate roof. As I crunched up the drive, there it was, standing in the dappled green, the sun bathing the weathered stone with warmth, welcoming me.

------- -- -------

Not bothering to unload the car, I made a tour of the garden. There had been rain while was away and heat as well by the look of it. The 'lawn' had grown a good ten centimetres, it stretched away in a lush green oval. Around the lawn, the trees wereweighed down with new leaves. The box hedges Jerôme had clipped so neatly, were already due for another haircut. Even the cedar of Lebanon, that I'd thought well beyond its sell-by, had a flush of blue green growth at the tips of its boughs

I made my way round to the orchard. The ancient fruit trees were scattering a snow of blossom. I could see tiny immature pears were starting to form and more trees sprouted what looked like bunches of minute green cherries. Brilliant, I'd have my own fruit in the summer.

------- -- -------

I peered over the hedge, wondering if Jacques was around. No smoke rose from the chimney. All the shutters were closed. There was nothing to suggest the farmhouse was even inhabited. That's when I noticed a sign had been roughly tacked on the gate.

A VENDRE

My heart missed a beat. So Jacques was selling up. I tried analyse how I felt about this. Surprised. Sorry. Yes, I had to admit I was going to miss him.

The following morning when I returned from my trip for the bread, I saw Jacques come out of the farmhouse carrying a bucket of something. He disappeared into the barn.

On impulse, I forced my way through and pushed open the gate. I picked my way over the rutted yard to the barn door. It was dark inside and it took a moment or so for my eyes to adjust to the gloom. Jacques was hunched over a stall, feeding a young calf with a bottle. I could hear the calf sucking hungrily. He was talking softly to the creature and stroking its back.

As I approached, Jacques looked up and caught sight of me.

'Bonjour,' he said. 'What can I do for you?'

I bent down beside him. 'Is it an orphan?'

He nodded. 'The cow died last night. Difficult birth. Often are - these Charolais have such wide shoulders.'

'Poor little thing. May I?'

He looked at me doubtfully and then passed the bottle. The calf rolled its eyes but continued sucking for all it was worth.

'Don't they drink fast!'

'Thank goodness, they can down a good few litres.'

'Can't you get another cow to adopt it?'

'In time. I may get a cow with a stillbirth.'

When the calf had had its fill, we walked back towards the farmhouse. Jacques paused awkwardly at his door. 'So you're selling up?' I said.

He shrugged. 'I don't have much option.'

'Why?'

'Feeding these beasts on hay, I'm running at a loss.'

'But if you had more land?'

Jacques frowned and stared at the ground.

'Listen Jacques. I've got more land than I can cope with. Why don't you put your cows to graze on my meadows. The grass is going crazy. You'd be doing me a favour. I'm going to have to pay someone soon to mow them.'

He avoided my eyes and said. 'I wouldn't want to get into a legal dispute.'

'What do you mean, a legal dispute?'

'That rogue your father bought from. He had the law on me for having cattle on his land.'

'Well you won't have a problem with me. I need them there to keep the grass down.'

He still looked doubtful.

'Please Jacques,' I continued. 'If it would make you feel better I'll rent the land to you if you like. Some small sum, a peppercorn rent - a few euros a week.'

'If it's really what you want...'

'For godsake, can't you see, it suits us both!'

His face softened. He held out a hand 'Let's shake on it then.'

His hand was large and warm in mine

------- -- -------

A few hours later I heard the frantic lowing of cattle. I went to the window and saw Jacques herding his cows through the gap in the hedge. The young calves rushed forward cantering on wobbly legs, revelling in their new found freedom. The cows followed, their heads already bent as they ate their way into the field.

------- -- -------

During my absence a huge pile of letters had built up in my postbox. Among them I found a card from Paul Fouquier. For a moment I couldn't place who he was and then I remembered the portrait. He'd finished cleaning it and I arranged to go and pick it up that afternoon.

He unwrapped the canvas from a folded piece of linen. The face was handsomer than ever. The grey eyes faced me levelly and now the lower half of the portrait was cleaned I could see the sardonic curl of his mouth.

'The colour of the jacket has come up really nicely, you can tell by the braiding it's an expensive item and you see that the stock is of a very fine lace. I must say I'm very pleased indeed.'

I nodded. 'And what about the date?'

'Oh late Eighteenth Century, shortly before the Revolution I should say. And judging by the powdered wig - a nobleman.'

A young man, shortly before the Revolution Jean Mulatier de la Grolière, chevalier – my charismatic emigré.

-------- -- --------

Back home I stood the portrait up on the mantlepiece. His cool grey eyes seemed to watch me as I moved around preparing my evening meal. And when I sat at the table he gazed down from his superior height as I ate.

That night I lay in my bed in the Art Nouveau room, staring up into its tattered draperies. I left the window open to allow the freshness of the garden in. Somewhere in the distance, I could hear the gentle drone of a tractor working its way across the meadows. Jacques, I thought.

I turned over on my back and listened to its pulsing rhythm as it made its way back and forth across the field. I pictured him in the warm night working under the stars. There was a delicious sense of the living and breathing countryside outside, of things growing and people at work in a landscape that was ordered and safe and productive.

At well past midnight I heard Jacques' tractor turn into the farmyard. His dog barked and his door slammed and then there was silence.

That night I dreamed I was in the past. The house was in its heyday. Fine tapestries hung on the walls, the parquet was polished with sweet beeswax, fires burned in all the grates, I lay staring up and the silk of my hung bed, marvelling at how it had been restored to its full glory. I was dreaming I was Suzanne and Jean had returned in the night and no-one had woken me. He had slipped into the bed. I could feel the heat of his body against mine.

Suddenly I woke bathed in sweat. I lay staring up into the tattered silk in disbelief. What had woken me was an orgasm. Impossible. I was alone.

I couldn't sleep after that. I got up and perched at the window. The sun was rising in a dazzling ball of orange through the branches of the Sequoia. Infinitely slowly, it detaching itself and rose, bloated and misshapen, in the morning mist. It was going to be a beautiful day.

------- -- -------

All the following week I was haunted by the curious sense of Jean Mulatier's presence. It was as if during my absense he'd repossessed the house. In the dawn I could hear his horse's hooves on the gravel, moving restlessly held in check by the sleepy stable boy, as he waited for his master to set off for the hunt.

I kept coming across reminders of him. Here was the ring where he tethered his horse, there was the worn stone he'd used as a step up as he flung himself into the saddle. At odd moments he would creep into my mind - sometimes as a young man, charging down the stairs in riding boots. I could almost hear him shouting from the windows to his brothers with some wager, some taunt, some male prank.

Or at the pump, at dusk, flinging his bridle to a servant, stripping his

clothes off, plunging his head under the spout. In my mind's eye, I could
see the water running down his back.

------- -- -------

I'd returned with renewed enthusiasm to my research.

According to the Bulletin, Jean had arrived back in France aboard one
of the ships that made the ill-fated invasion at Quiberon. The ships had set
sail from England carrying the cream of French nobility planning to fight
their way back into France and reinstate the monarchy. But there had been
tip-off. They were met on the beach by a savage Revolutionary force and
there was a bloody massacre. Jean was one of the few lucky ones to survive.
Somehow he made his way across France, travelling incognito from safe
house to safe house until at last, when the amnesty was announced, he
returned to La Mulatière.

I pictured his homecoming, finding his precious home had been saved
for him by the astute bargaining of Suzanne. His mother still alive and the
daughter he left as a tiny child having grown into a fine young woman.

------- -- -------

These thoughts were interrupted by a ring on the doorbell. Who could it be
at this hour? I leaned out of the window.

'It's me, Jacques.'

I went downstairs and found him standing outside.

'Are you working?' he asked.

'I was just doing some research but...'

'But you could break off?'

He was in a good mood, smiling. It was one of his sunny spells.

'I suppose I could. Do you want to come in? Can I offer you a coffee
or a glass of something?'

He shook his head. 'No. Why don't you come out? It's a wonderful
evening.'

'Why aren't you looking after your cows? Tucking them in or

whatever you do at night?'

'With your meadows there's plenty of new grass. They'll feed themselves from now on.'

'OK, why not? Wait here, I'll go and get a sweater.'

It was companionable walking in the gloom. Soothing. Earlier that evening I'd received a load of photos by e-mail of little Ernest. Each one tugged at the heartstrings.

As we reached the lake, Jacques slowed his pace. He pulled some branches apart. There was a pathway leading along the bank which was thick with foliage.

'Come,' he said holding out a hand.

'I didn't know this path was here.'

'A secret path.'

'I've always called this my secret lake.'

The path narrowed and we walked in single file. I was conscious of his gaze on the back of my neck, I could feel the closeness of him. The path ended in a grassy clearing where there was a weir. The sound of water rushing through it was somehow hypnotic. The moon was reflected in the inky depths of the lake. I leant on the weir staring at its pale disk waxing and waning in the ripples.

'Julia?' I could barely hear Jacques' voice above the rushing of the water. I turned and leaned closer to catch what he was saying.

All of a sudden he was kissing me deeply and meaningfully. I responded. My body starved of affection for so long pressed into his. Before I knew it we had sunk down in the grass. Everything that was sane and responsible told me this shouldn't be happening. But there was no resisting. It felt totally right. It was spontaneous brilliant, blissful - in fact I'd never had sex like it.

'It's getting late. Where shall we finish the night? Your bed or mine?' asked Jacques.

So we slept that night under the great baldican. The windows were open to the warm air. The passing owls had competition to their soft night sounds

As is the way of relationships, there was no way but forward. The next day, as soon as he arrived back from work, Jacques made his way through the hedge. I found him cooking in my kitchen.

From then on he was in my bed practically every night. Without anything being said we fell into a routine. As summer ripened and the fields turned from green into a parched and hazy gold, I let things drift. I didn't allow myself to question whether or not I should be enjoying those deliciously langourous nights. I closed my mind to the future. Unlike Oliver, Jacques never questionned or demanded anything. He just let me be. While he worked at Champion or on the farm I'd write. We'd cook and eat together. Then late in the evening we'd often take a walk or on hot nights even a swim in our secret lake.

Chapter Twenty Seven

Julia 2009

My love affair with the house was still in its 'honeymoon period' - in my eyes La Mulatière could do no wrong. Currently it stood bathed in glorious early summer weather. All day long the windows were left wide open, allowing the warmth to flood inside. I could feel it healing the house, drying out the damp, easing warped parquet back into place, lighting musty corners where spiders had been engaged in a campaign of intensive colinization for generations.

Day by day, more workers turned up at La Mulatière. From eight in the morning till midday and two in the afternoon till six the house gave off a happy discord of whistling, jangling radios, hammering and drilling. The two hours in between were dedicated to the serious business of lunch. The workers had set up a kind of field kitchen in the barn. At twelve o'clock sharp they would knock off and within a very short time wonderful smells of cooking would start wafting across the courtyard. They'd ranged deckchairs around a garden table and fitted up a microwave and a two ring burner. I felt quite envious at the sound of bottles being uncorked and low murmured conversation. No one would reappear until two o'clock after coffee had been consumed and their newspapers read.

It was all part of the French 'quality of life' obsession that I was starting to respect. It was even reflected in their work. Locks fitted, doors opened and closed with a smooth satisfying clunk, pipework was neatly channelled into the wall, woodwork fitted tongue into groove. Nothing dripped or dragged or snagged. There was none of that slovenly workmanship I'd come to expect of 'Bob the builder' back home.

With Jacqueline I had a tireless ally. Up ladders or down on her knees, she was on a ceiling to floor crusade to rid the house of dirt . With missionary zeal she was intent on chucking out anything she didn't regard as useful. I caught her one day coming down the main staircase with a look of satisfaction on her face. She was carrying a crate of something which clinked.

'I had a go at the top attic. What a state the place was in…'

'You didn't throw anything out, did you?' I asked warningly.

'No I didn't, but the sooner you take a look through this lot the better.'
She was getting fed up with my obsessive hoarding.

'Come on, let me see, open it up.'

Inside was the most wonderful collection of bottles.

'There's no way you're throwing these out!'

That evening I spend a delicious hour sorting through them. They were old
bottles, a hundred or so years old by the look of them, the kind of thing
people go fossaking for in rubbish dumps. Many of them still had their
labels intact: Sulphate of Ammoniaque. Ashes of Roses. Valerianate de
Pierlot. And there were some a beautiful hazy blue-mauve ones labelled as
ether. I was selecting the better ones for my little cabinet when I came
across a tiny phail meshed in gold complete with a minute stopper. I took it
to the kitchen and rinsed it under the tap. Drying it carefully I held it up to
the light. It sent out sparks of colour, a whole prism of blue red and gold. It
was real cut crystal.

The following Friday I took my find to the expert at Sadde's. He took it in
his hand and squinted at it through his eye-glass.

'It's a perfume bottle, quite old, I'd say late Eighteenth Century. But
not French, this is English crystalware. I can't really tell you much about it.
Did you bring it from England?'

'No, it was found in my house here, in with a load of old bottles.'

'A bit of a mystery then?' He handed it back with a smile. 'I could
put it into auction for you. I'm not sure how much it would fetch.
You noticed the initials?'

'No, where?'

He lent me his eye-glass. Sure enough, etched minutely into the
crystal, were the letters A.M.G.

'Thank you. I'll think about it.'

I slipped the phail back in my bag. I had no intention of selling it. Late Eighteenth Century and English! Valuable, light and portable, just the sort of thing an émigré might bring back for a loved one.

That evening I searched through the family tree and was rewarded with A.M.G. – Amisie Mulatier de la Grolière – Jean Mulatier's daughter.

Chapter Twenty Eight

Amisie de la Mulatière 1800

The little perfume bottle was a gift from Papa. Thus it was more precious to me than you can imagine.

All my young life had been spent in waiting. Waiting for the troubles to be over. Waiting for our move back into the big house. Above all else - waiting for the return of Father.

As a child I could barely remember my father. Only the feeling of a presence, the shadow of a memory. A tall figure riding up to the house. The glimpse of a face seen through a carriage window - tiny fragments which I tried in vain to piece together. In his absence, my father had taken on the aspect of some mythical figure, some godlike being I had created from what could be gleaned from Grand-Mere and Maman.

We were poor but I did not mind the privations of my early life. I slept in the same bed as Maman, it felt safe and warm. I can still remember summer days when I was allowed to play outside and no-one fussed about my skin getting brown in the sun. I didn't understand why Grandmere cried and cried. The only thing I didn't like was having to wear clothes of rough linen which chafed my skin and horrible wooden clogs like the common farm people. But Maman said that everything had changed and this was a new life which we had to enjoy like a game until the old life came back again. And that this would be very soon.

Maman took charge of my education, she taught me to read and to write and to calculate. Grandmere taught me how to pray and to sew.

I realise now that there were many points of conflict between Maman and Grandmere. I remember one occasion in particular when I was trying to memorise the months of the year, walking round and round the room reciting haltingly: ....Thermidor.... Pluvieux.... Nivôse.. when Grandmere flew into a fury. I clung to Maman tearfully not understanding how I had displeased her. Maman spoke in my defence, saying things I did not understand. I know now that what I witnessed went deep into their relationship.

Maman and Papa had tried to embrace the reforms that led to our unhappy situation. Indeed it was with some pride that Maman called herself Citoyenne Mulatière. I remember dragging behind her skirts as she marched with the other women demanding our right to bread at a fair price. Grandmere said she would rather go without than see her family subjected to such shame.

But it was that last winter - that final winter before Papa returned that I remember most. Maman had contrived to buy back the big house in the auctions. We returned in winter, old faithful Auguste driving us with our few sticks of furniture in farm cart. You can imagine the impression this made on me - at that time still a child aged around seven years. The building stood, shuttered as I had always known it. In fact in my fancy the park , now overgrown with nettles and brambles and all manner of scrubby trees gave the house the allure of some sleeping castle or a palace from the beloved tales of Perrault that Maman read to me in the evenings - leaning the book to catch the firelight.

Grandmere and I watched from the cart as Maman took the great key and turned it in the lock. The door swung open and she let out a cry of distress.

I ran to her and stared inside. Here was not the fairy palace of my childish imagination. The great entrée had been used as a store for hay. Beasts also must have been lodged there for the stench was like that of an uncleaned barn. The stairway was impassable as all manner of furniture had been tossed down and lay in pieces on the filthy steps. The walls were besmirched where quite clearly there had been some savage riot. Draperies and silks were similarly defaced with excrement of what origin I dare not think. A portrait on the wall was slashed through, books lay in piles torn and partially blackened where an attempt had been made to burn them.

How different this sad return was from the one we had envisaged. But Auguste turned to and forced his way to the back kitchens where the devastation was a little less extreme. He soon had a fire burning in the grate and sweeping the worst of the debris aside we found a place for Grandmere's fauteuil.

Day by day our old servants or members of their families turned up at

*the door and were willing to help for a bowl of soup or a half loaf of bread
such was the misery in which these people found themselves.*

*Grandmère insisted on installing herself once more in what had been
her apartments in the house. Maman and I slept in the kitchens which were
the only rooms we managed to keep served by a fire. But we never could get
the house warm. The cold seemed to have seeped into those great thick
walls and no amount of fires burning could bring us comfort.*

*I watched as Maman now weakened from the constant toil and no
doubt the toll taken by our poor diet fell into a feverish decline. The doctor
came and bled her but the new blood seemed to do her little good. We wrote
to father of course, although letters had been opened and censored for quite
some time. I had little hope of a reply as such posts the there were would
take the minimum of ten days each way. Maman rallied a little when one
morning, the long awaited and longed-for news arrived saying that father
was coming home.*

Julia 2009

I'd borrowed a load of books on French history from the Society
d'Emulation's library. Each evening I muddled my way through them
trying to match events to the framework of the family tree.

According to the Bulletin, Jean Mulatier had returned under the
'Consulat'. I wasn't sure what the 'Consulat' was. But a check through an
index showed it was the first period of Napoleon's reign. The dates were
given as 1801-1804 (check!) I went back to the family tree and discovered
the sad fact that Suzanne had not survived to see her precious Jean. She died
in 1798. Jean must have come home to find his mother and his daughter
Amisie grieving for her loss.

Chapter Twenty Nine

Julia 2009

It had became a kind of obsessive pastime, imagining the voices of the people from the past. Even the drudgery of painting La Mulatière's endless metres of skirting boards was made bearable by tales of the bitter-sweet lives of my imaginary companions.

One afternoon, I was down on my knees working my way backwards along the upper landing when I heard a movement in the house below. Footsteps. Too late for Jacqueline or Jerôme. It must be Jacques. I got to my feet and leaning over the bannisters, shouted down in French. 'Hi there, I'll be down in a minute.''

'Julia?'

Oliver! What was he doing here?

Instinctively I glanced in the mirror. What a sight I looked.

'Oliver?'

'Where are you?'

'Hang on a minute, '

It was too late he was already on his way up the stairs.

'Julia! My god. Look at you. What a house. Honestly Julia, what do you look like?'

'Thank you Oliver. Hello.'

'I mean. Hello.'

I offered a cheek. He ignored it and kissed me awkwardly on the lips.

'Sorry that was about the only really clean bit I could locate.'

'What on earth are you doing here?'

'Since you wouldn't answer my calls I decided this was the only way... You're angry that I came?'

'You might have asked if you could first. People do as a rule.'

'If I could have got through to you. And anyway you would have refused.'

'Yes. I suppose I would.'

'So...?'

'Look, you can't stay. I'm expecting someone as a matter of fact.'

'Who?'

'A neighbour… for dinner.'

'What sort of neighbour?'

'The farmer from next door. He's been um.. helping me out.'

'Can't you put him off? I've come all the way from England.'

I suddenly had a vision of how excruciating a dinner would be with Oliver and Jacques - Oliver being typically condescending and Jacques putting on a real macho act bristling with hostility.

'I suppose I'll have to.'

'Good, I'll go and get my stuff in and you go and rub yourself down with white spirit or something.'

'Oh? You think you're going to stay, do you?'

He looked at me sideways. 'You wouldn't send me to a hotel?'

'There's one in the village.'

'Oh for god's sake.'

'What's happened to Veronica?'

'Ah…Veronica.'

'She hasn't dumped you, surely?'

'I think you'd call the dumping mutual.'

'Jane said it wouldn't last.'

While Oliver went out to his car, I rang Jacques. 'Look Jacques, this is really embarrassing. Do you mind if we don't see each other tonight? An old friend's turned up unexpectedly from England and we've got a lot to catch up on.'

I could hear by his tone this was pissing him off.

'I'm really sorry. But we'll be talking English and… Look I'll catch up with you tomorrow, OK?'

------- -- -------

I made Oliver take me to the restaurant in the village, as far away from Jacques as possible.

As luck would have it turning out of the driveway we practically collided with the Espace in the lane. Jacques came to an abrupt halt giving Oliver an aggressive stare.

'Who the hell was that?'

'My neighbour.'

'Not the one you were having to dinner?'

'Yes, as a matter of fact.'

'Christ Julia. I don't like the idea of him living next door. Does he live alone?'

'Yes. At least I've never seen anyone else there.'

Oliver shook his head and frowned at the road ahead.

We were in row mode. It raged in the car and then rumbled on in an uneasy truce through the meal.

Over a brandy Oliver softened his approach.

'The truth is I really miss you Julia,' he leaned towards me. 'Listen. I've taken a week off. We can spend some quality time together.'

I stared at him. *A whole week.* What was I going to do about Jacques?

------- -- -------

That night we slept together my bed - it being the only bed on offer. Inevitably we made love - for old time's sake as Oliver put it. It was a pretty one-sided affair and afterwards I couldn't get to sleep. I lay there listening to Oliver's familiar breathing, thinking what a rotter I was with Jacques sleeping alone next door. At length I climbed out of bed and wrapping my towelling robe round me sat at the window.

Oliver's voice came from the bed.

'Come back to bed.'

'For *old time's* sake?'

Oliver yawned, 'Well, you're a very nice old-timer to be with.'

'Thank you, but I think there's been enough of that for one night.'

'I reckon it's stress. Look we'll spend a few days in Paris. I'll book us somewhere plush. You need a break.'

'This is a break.'

'No it's not, you're working flat out.'

'I haven't got the time to rush off to Paris. I've got plumbers, roofers, the mason coming...'

'I don't know why you're doing all this. You'll never sell this place at a profit you know.'

'Who says I'm going to sell it?'

------- -- -------

The next morning while Oliver was in the bath I rang Jacques. His phone was on answerphone, so I left an apologetic message saying my friend was staying on.

Oliver stayed three days in all. I was starting to get panicky. Every time I rang Jacques I got his message service. He was barring my calls. The longer I left it the worse it got. Why oh why, hadn't I told Oliver about Jacques in the first place, and sent him packing. I was saved by a call Oliver received from London.

He clipped his mobile shut. 'Bad news I'm afraid. I'll have to go back. Something's come up. And it seems they can't solve it without me.'

'Oh dear.'

I helped him pack, finding various things he'd left dotted around the house.

Within an hour I was standing in the doorway waving him off. As the sound of his car crunched away down the driveway I felt as if a weight had been lifted from over my head. Something that had been hanging over me, threateningly.

His car turned at the end of the lane. He'd gone. I was alone. Alone with the house.

I left the door wide open and walked back inside. The morning sun was streaming in through the windows, I could see it repeated in bright trapezoids on the parquet, room after room after room. It was going to be a glorious day.

I took a deep breath. Now to face Jacques. I found him forking hay up into the barn.

'Hi,'

He didn't turn to face me he just continued doggedly working.

'Your 'little friend' gone then?'

'Little friend' was slang in French for lover. I pretended not to understand.

'He had to go back to London.'

'What does he do there?'

'He runs a publishing company.'

'He won't have much time to come down here then.'

'No, I doubt if he'll ever come back.'

'Oh?'

'It's over Jacques. He used to be my boyfriend. But it's been over for some time. That's why I came here.'

Jacques turned to face me. 'It's not been over for the last three nights.' His eyes were bloodshot, he looked as if he'd been drinking heavily. My eyes met his. I couldn't lie to him.

'Look, I'm sorry. We'd been together for ages. But we'd broken up before I came. It didn't mean anything.'

'No,' he said bitterly. 'It doesn't mean anything, does it? What do you call it? Shagging? Bonking? Like with me?'

'No of course not.'

'Oh no, hang on. He's a publisher. With me you were just having a bit of rough.'

I stared at him. 'God you've got a chip on your shoulder.'

He paused for a moment while my meaning sank in then he turned his back on me and started work again. His voice was thrown back at me loaded with anger.

'Goodbye Julia.'

Chapter Thirty

I felt entirely wretched. Bother and blast Oliver. Why did he have to turn up and ruin everything? I thought of going over to the farm, begging, pleading, even writing a letter of apology. Nothing I could think of seemed appropriate. A sneaky little voice reasoned the other way. Jacques didn't own me. We'd never even talked about the future. It was just an affair. This was the Twentieth Centurey for godsake. Jacques was being totally unreasonable. But deep in my heart I knew I'd hurt him. And that made me hate myself.

Even the sight of Jacques' cows in my meadows made me feel sick with misery. The poor beats were hardly better off than they had been with him. Summer was taking its toll. The meadows had turned bottle blond overnight. The grass had stopped growing and they had taken to wandering miserably from one shady patch to another.

Summer in Allier had ferocious Continental intensity, that had taken me by surprise. The thermometer kept rising to frightening levels. Each morning I'd get up to find the same cloudless sky. As the sun inched its way round from East to West I'd go from room to room closing the shutters against its relentless glare.

I'd been watching the level of the fish pond sink lower as the temperature rose. The ducks wives, stood on the side making a lot of noisy quacking, clearly indicated that their new home wasn't up to scratch. They waddled back and forth on the island and had even taken a few tentative flights around the garden.

I took a basket of stale bread for them, leaning precariously over the edge to soak it in pond water as directed by Jerôme. The ducks watched from the far side.

'We'll be in trouble soon,' Jerôme said coming up behind me, 'When that water goes stagnant.'

'I know, but what can I do about it?'

'It used to fed with fresh water from the chateau d'eau.'

'How did it get here?'

'By pipes underground, installed by The Doctor or so I was told.'

'What doctor?'

'Mademoiselle Marie's father. He did no end of modernisation.'

'Do you think they're still there?'

'Most probably but they'll take some finding.'

'You mean you'll have to dig for them.'

'Difficult,' he said screwing up his eyes: 'As far as I can remember, they go right across Ladier's farmyard.'

'Well that's a lot of use.' With our current relationship digging up his farmyard was totally out of the question.

Luckily Jerôme came up with an alternative plan to supply water to the pond. He remembered, way back in his father's time, there had been talk of a well at the front of ther house. It had been covered over when mains water arrived, but if we could locate it, we should be able to sink a pump and have as much water as we wanted.

'Where was it exactly?'

He shrugged and said he'd take a look. Several days passed and the garden became pockmarked with the holes he'd made with a long metal pole. At last he admitted that he couldn't locate it. 'But!' he announced – he had a friend who could divine water, he'd ask him to drop by. More witchcraft, I commented. But Jerôme insisted this fellow truly had the gift.

Next morning I awoke to the sound of footsteps on the gravel and looked out of the window to see Jerôme in front of the house with an old fellow wearing an ancient black suit shiny from wear, complete with waistcoat. The two of them had their heads together going from hole to hole swinging something on the end of a chain.

I dressed and hurried downstairs, intrigued.

'Ça y est!' I heard Jerôme announce in delight. 'Madame, we've found it!'

I joined them. The 'thing on the chain' was an old pocket watch. It was swinging in a gentle circle over the hole that, by coincidence, Jerôme had said was the most likely location. He scuttled off to find a spade.

The 'diviner' and I stood by as Jerôme shovelled for all he was worth. About a metre down he hit rock. Undismayed he made the pit wider and uncovered what looked like a long flat boulder.

Delighted noises from the couple implied this was good news. I left them to it and went to have breakfast. I was on my second cup of coffee when Jerôme arrived at the back door his face wreathed in smiles.

Back at the pit the old boy stood at the edge holding on to a piece of string.

'Six metres of good sweet water,' announced Jerôme, passing the string to me. 'Get a pump down there, link it to the pond with a bit of piping and you'll have plenty of water to keep that pond of yours filled.'

I thanked the old fellow and asked what I owed him. As ever I got the polite but unhelpful answer that I could give what I liked. I led them both back to the kitchen for a coffee. As I poured it, I tried to work out what one paid for water divining? Was there a going rate? Were they in this together. Had their find been sheer luck? I opened my purse to see how much I had in it. There was a fifty euro note. I held it out 'Would that be all right?'

In seconds it was slipped into the old fellow's pocket and my hand was being vigourously pumped. I reckoned I'd been conned, but I couldn't complain. Later that morning I went down to tell the ducks the good news and was rewarded to find a single beautiful greeny white duck egg in the grass. Still warm.

Chapter Thirty One

That night I had a call from Maitre Bertrand. He'd been driving past the farm and noticed Jacques' cattle on my land. He nearly hit the roof when I told him what I'd agreed.

'Oh no, Julia, I must stop you there. That's not at all wise.'

'Why not? It's doing me a service. I can't keep those meadows mown. And I certainly can't manage animals myself.'

He insisted that I drove in to see him right away.

'You really can't have Ladier grazing beasts on your land,' he said as soon as I got through his door.

'Why ever not?'

'I hadn't wanted to worry you with old grievances. It was all settled before your father bought the house.'

'What grievances?'

'Here in France, when someone dies, property is divided equally between their children. When Marie Lamulatière's died, since she had no heir, the property was inherited by her sister Louise's children. They lived mainly in Paris. They spent a month or so at most here in the summer. They took no interest in the land, left the Ladiers to look after it. Well, you can't let animals roam free. Over time, the Ladiers installed fencing, gates. But that meant in effect they'd moved the boundaries. The Ladiers claimed the land was theirs.'

'Did they have any right to it?'

'There's an old law, dating back to the Enlightenment. "As much land as a man tills, plants, improves, cultivates, and can use the product of, so much is his property".'

'But all that sort of thing finished ages ago, surely?'

'It's been tightened up. But there's still a grey area. It can cause problems.

'I see.'

I drove home feeling chastened. It was horribly awkward. On top of everything else I couldn't face telling Jacques I'd changed my mind about the meadows. Bother Maitre Bertrand. It was my land, I could do what I liked with it. I'd let Jacques leave his cattle where they were but I'd better make sure he agreed the land was mine legally.

------- -- -------

I left a message on Jacques answerphone saying I had to see him urgently. It wasn't until late that evening that I heard the Espace return. A few minutes later I found him standing in the dark on my kitchen doorstep.

'Bonsoir,' his voice sounded slurred as it came out of the gloom. He sounded as if he'd had a lot to drink.

'Bonsoir. Thank you for coming.' I came out on to the doorstep to meet him. 'I went to see the notaire this morning...' I started.

He interrupted: 'Aren't you going to invite me in?'

'It's late, but yes, of course.'

He lurched as he passed through the door. I could smell the alcohol on his breath.

'Would you like a coffee or something?'

'Haven't you got anything stronger?'

'A glass of wine?'

'That would be fine.'

I poured two glasses and brought them to the table.

'Look Jacques please. I'm sorry. Can't we put this whole thing behind us?'

He ignored this and said gruffly: 'What was so urgent you had to see me about it?'

I took a breath. Clearly this was not the moment to try to make up.

'It's Maitre Bertrand the notaire. I'm afraid he's making a terrible fuss about having your cattle on my land.'

'There you are you see,' said Jacques. 'They're all in it. The bourgeois always stick together. It's given with one hand and taken back with the other.'

I could see that temper of his flaring up again.

'Look, it's fine by me. You're more than welcome to leave them there. I just that Maitre Bertrand wants to be sure you know the land is mine legally, that's all.'

'I'll get them moving right away,' he said gruffly. His face had flushed an angry red. 'I'll take them off, the whole damn lot of them.'

'No honestly, please don't move them on my account.'

'It's your land as you've pointed out. I don't need charity.' The last word was flung at me. He was already reaching in his pocket for his keys.

'Jacques, I wasn't being charitable.'

But Jacques was already stumbling out into the darkness. He was far more drunk than I'd realised.

During the night I woke to hear the disturbed mooing of cows. I leaned out of the window. Jacques was at work with the tractor headlights full on - he was rounding up the cattle with the help of his dog. I watched as he herded them off my land and closed the gap in the hedge with a strap of electric fence. He cast a last glance over the meadows now still and empty in the moonlight. Then he turned and whistled to the dog.

------- -- ------

Jacques kept to himself after that. I'd see him in the distance from time to time, coming out of the Tabac with a newspaper or buying bread in the Boulangerie. When our paths crossed, he just nodded or gave me a sardonic *'Bonjour Madame'* as if nothing had ever happened between us. The sight of him always made me feel utterly wretched..

I could hardly bear to look into the farmyard. His bullocks were trapped in a compound so small they'd trampled the ground to bare earth. They stood pulling disconsolately at a miserable bale of hay. It was a hateful situation. I longed to grab him by the arm and tell him to snap out of it. But I'd seen the proud side of him. And the angry side. Frankly, when he was in one of his moods, he scared me.

Chapter Thirty Two

I was getting through money at the rate of knots and had no idea how long my savings would last. I didn't have anything put away for the unexpected.

One afternoon Jacqueline came down to be paid and announced proudly that she'd finished clearing the attic over the East wing and that I should go and take a look.

It was eerily quiet in the house. A glance through the fanlight showed the parking area was empty. With clockwork precision the workers had knocked off at the stroke of six.

Jacqueline had made a miraculous clearance. She'd even swept the floor. Now I could see where there must once have been windows in the roof. Tiled over I presumed for economy. There were the remains of a pathetic cupboard in one corner - a rough wooden frame with a few strips of rag clinging to it. And there was a bit of zinc piping slotted in between the floor boards. Used for the slops of the wash bowl no doubt. Or worse. These must have been the servant's quarters once. The attic had probably been some kind of dormitory. With the roof unlined like this the poor things must have been freezing in winter, broiling in summer. I could picture them lying on rough paillasses stuffed with straw. Work-weary bodies, fragrant with sweat, huddled together no doubt in winter. Whispered voices in the gloom. All very Hardyesque.

With proper insulation and a few veluxes I could make more rooms up here - more money-earning 'chambres d'hotes'. I examined the floor, it was made of wide planks of solid oak, shiny with wear, I wouldn't even need to carpet these rooms. Then I noticed something. I knelt down, fresh dust had appeared out of nowhere. I felt myself go hot and cold. '*Woodworm*'. I stared up at the beams. Some of them did look a bit nibbled. What if the whole house was infested? I could could imagine them. Tens of thousands of miniscule beasts, their mandibles crunching away, inching their way through the centuries' old timbers, hollowing them out, so that at any moment now the roof might *cave in*.

I hurried downstairs for the telephone directory and searched through the Yellow Pages. There was no lack of companies that dealt with infestation. A few phone calls later, I'd managed to fix an appointment for the very next day.

The representative of a wood treatment firm turned up on the dot of eight. I'd spent an anxious night tossing and turning, imagining that I could hear the sound of infinitesimal chomping accompanied by the somber creak and groan of diseased timbers. I was up and dressed and breakfasted well before he arrived. He'd come in a smart white van with a picture of evil-looking insects on the side. I led him up to the smallest attic. He took a pinch of the dust and rubbed it in a professional way between two fingers. Then he gave it sniff and stared up at the beams.

'*Well?*'

He shook his head and said he'd have to get a ladder from his van. I watched, my palms going wet with the tension, as he ran his torch beam along the timbers making noises of disapproval through his teeth.

'What do you think?'

Still reluctant to give a verdict he started measuring the width of the wood. At last he snapped his measure shut and said he could deal with it - no problem.

'What are you going to do? Spray it?'

He shook his head. 'No spraying won't do anything. We'll have to impregnate.'

'What's the difference?'

He climbed down from the ladder and took a glossy leaflet from his briefcase. It had pictures of their van and men in uniform and details about guarantees. It all looked horribly expensive.

'There's more,' I said.

I lead him up to the attic over the West wing. He sounded less confident this time. 'Yes we could do this too. It'll take time of course.'

Reluctantly, I took him up the spiral stone staircase to the top attic - the showpiece with its the massive charpente built like ships' timbers. He looked up and literally blanched. 'No,' he admitted. 'It's really too much work.'

But this was the one that mattered. 'Surely if you can do the others...'

'It would take months, Madame.'

'So what do you do exactly. When you impregnate?'

He came out with his standard patter. They inserted coloured plastic plugs, not very large, about the size of golf tees, at ten centimetre intervals throughout the charpente and the chemical was injected into them.

It was my turn to blanch now. My beautiful hand-hewn timbers! 'And then you take them out? Doesn't that leave holes?'

'No, no, we leave them in. After four or five years we'll need to inject again.'

Seeing the look of horror on my face, the fellow started to pack up his leaflets. I followed him down the stone staircase. All the way down, he was still valiantly making a sales pitch for the treatment of the first attic.

But as I pointed out, what was the point in treating one attic and leaving the others? I watched as he climbed into his van with a look of professional defeat. Then he drove off with a wave and an expression I could only interpret as relief.

I stood in my gateway feeling defeated. Jerôme arrived at that point. He must have passed the fellow's van in the lane.

'What did he want?' he asked.

I explained about the infestation, he could see how upset I was.

'I know a thing or two about timber,' he said marching up the stairs.

I followed him and pointed out the dust.

Jerôme knelt down took a handful and stared at it, then licked a finger and tasted it

'Woodworm,' he pronounced getting to his feet. 'Nothing to worry about'

'Woodworm? But it puts the fear of god in us in England.'

'Madame no, what you need to worry about is capricornes. They march in straight lines eating everything in their path. And then there are termites. They say they eat whole houses.'

'How can we be sure it's not capricornes - or termites? That fellow said he could inject the beams.' I explained about the chemical treatment.

Jerôme gave a contemptuous guffaw. 'First of all, if you did that, you'd be weakening the beams by drilling holes. Secondly, wood this old won't absorb chemicals.' He slapped a beam. 'This is chestnut. Insects won't touch the stuff - that's why it's used for charpentes.'

Jerôme made his way downstairs chuckling to himself, delighted that he's shown up these upstarts with their new fangled ways for the rogues they were.

Chapter Thirty Three

I was making a determined effort *not* to look at the farm. Jacques had his own life, it was no concern of mine. I concentrated on the research I was doing for my book. My section on Amisie was taking shape. According to the family tree she had married a man called Zavier de Godinet. A fellow a good twenty years older than her, a contemporary of her father's. I was wondering about this strange alliance when by sheer chance I came across some first hand source material.

I'd had a mailing from a The Societé d'Emulation du Bourbonnais. They were arranging an outing to local places of interest. I knew I needed to get out and meet more people and this seemed like the ideal opportunity. So I rang and asked if I could join them and managed to get the last place on the coach.

We spent the morning in an earnest group, trailing in and out of the coach, visiting various churches and other sights, mainly ecclesiastical. It was a scorching day and standing in the heat staring up at various chuch façades rather eclipsed their finer architectural points, which our guide was eager to point out to us at great length.

I was relieved when at last we arrived at a cool restaurant in Montluçon and the rest of the party visibly perked up as key business of the day began. A special menu had been ordered and while the others studied the choices on offer, I took the opportunity to read the pin-on name tags that had been handed out to us at the start of the day.

A large and animated person opposite me had a badge with 'de Godinet' written on it. The name rang a bell – it was the family Jean's daughter, Amisie Mulatière had married into.

I immediately homed in on her and when there was a pause in her conversation long enough for interruption, I leaned over and asked if she was by any chance related to the de Godinet family who'd lived at La Mulatière. She replied that not hers but her late husband's family were indeed from the manoir. We chatted on during the meal and exchanged cards. 'I will be in touch,' Madame de Godinet said firmly, as we parted company at the end of the day.

She kept her word. A few weeks later I received a card from her inviting me to a lunch to meet her brother-in-law who she promised could tell me more about her husband's ancestors.

The following Saturday I drove into Moulins dressed in what I hoped would be appropriate style for a formal French luncheon. This was most definitely a skirt occasion which meant foraging in drawers for unsnagged tights.

Madame de Godinet lived in one of the elegant Eighteenth Century houses in old Moulins. These *'Hotels Particuliers'* as they were called, were the town-house versions of country manoirs like La Mulatière – lovely old buildings that gave Moulins its air of faded grandeur.

The de Godinet house was a tall flat-fronted building set back from a long tree-lined square. It was protected by a high wall and had a set of iron gates fit to keep a mob out. I was glad I'd made the effort from the clothing point of view, for once inside a uniformed maid led me upstairs to where aperitifs were being served in a drawing room overlooking the square. Here I found I was one of a party of ten. All the men were in formal dark suits complete with ties. When introduced they were decidedly of the click-of-heels and brush-of-lips-on-hand class. After the round of introductions, the attention fell on me and I made a big effort with my French, summoning all the relevant tenses and even having the subjunctive on standby.

The room was furnished with French antiques polished to what Jane and I always called a'marron-glacé' finish. Once the initial interest had switched from me, I hovered quietly trying to work out who was who and to take an intelligent interest in the conversation, which was mainly of French politics, without displaying my shameful lack of knowledge. Over the past months La Mulatière had absorbed all my energy leaving little room for current affairs.

Luncheon was served downstairs in a dining room filled with family heirlooms. Thoughtfully, Madame de Godinet had seated me next to her brother -in-law, in the place of honour. As the maid circulated with the dishes they came first to me and I served myself with the tiny morsels French politeness required.

Unfortunately, the attention of M. de Godinet, who must have been well into his eighties, was totally occupied by a garrulous lady on his other side. She boomed at him at decibels that implied he was extremely deaf. Left to my own devices, I examined the room, taking in details and noting how an authentic French 18th Century room should be decorated. My eye was drawn to the panelling. I sat trying to memorize how it was picked out in three subtly different shades of grey - light, dark and intermediate – each carefully applied to accentuate the depth of the mouldings.

'What do you think Mademoiselle...?' M. de Godinet suddenly demanded.

'I'm so sorry I was miles away.'

The lady beyond him, boomed even louder, kindly trying to draw me into their discussion on the indiscretions of some minister. Luckily, before I was forced into a display of ignorance, the main course was served.

Monsieur de Godinet now turned to me and I managed to redirect the conversation to his ancestors. But my delving was less productive than I'd hoped. When I brought up the subject of Zavier de Godinet, the old fellow launched into a long discourse detailing the countless marriages and descendencies that linked him to this ancestor.

I drove back to La Mulatière rather disappointed. I'd learned practically nothing about Amisie's husband but on the plus side it had been a delicious lunch and I'd gained some first hand insights into traditional French paint effects.

----- -- -----

I got back from Moulins to find the parking area jammed with a promising selection of vans and lorries. Brilliant - the mason was there, and the carpenter. I could hear the plasterers' whistling coming from the attic over the east wing. And there was a strange throbbing sound coming from round the back.

I tracked down the source of the throbbing – a vast cylindrical monster sprouting a flexible tube like something out of a painting by de Chirico. The plumber, was leaning over staring down into a manhole that was stuffed to the top with something that looked like christmas pudding.

'I've found out what the problem is,' he said. 'That smell...'

'The goat's cheese smell? It comes and goes...'

'Full to the top it is.'

'What?'

'La fosse septique.'

It took me a moment to translate this into septic tank.

He continued. 'Hasn't been cleaned in years. But we'll soon have this lot out.'

'Yukk,' I said backing off.

-------- -- -------

Promising noises were coming from the kitchen wing, the thud of a sledge hammer and intermittent bursts from a pneumatic drill.

I stuck my head round the door and quickly retracted it. The floor had gone and one of the party walls was crumbling into clouds of dust before my eyes.

'Sorry about that. No use you know. It was quite rotten,' explained the mason emerging through the dust and wiping his hands on his trousers for the customary wrist shake.

'But that was a wall...' I protested.

'Merely a cloison,' he replied. 'Don't worry we'll have a new one back up in no time.'

Jacqueline came up behind me and stood with her hands on her hips and an expression of deep disapproval.

'How do you expect me to clean with all the dust they're making?' she grumbled.

'You're right, you can't. There's no point.'

She shrugged and waited. I realised she wasn't simply going to pack up and go home. She had a right to her couple of hours' work. No doubt she needed the money.

I racked my brains to find her something to do.

'There's still the attic over the West wing,' I said. 'I'm afraid it's heavy work and horribly dirty.'

'Huh,' she said. 'That doesn't bother me. Hard work never killed anyone.'

'Well, I'd better get changed first.' Still dressed in my smart skirt I felt somewhat of an anomaly on site.

'I'll make a start ,' said Jacqueline, tying her overall more tightly round her.

When I got up to the attic dressed in what had become my standard uniform - paint-stained jeans, hideous promotional T-shirt, sweater with the elbows out - I considered Jacqueline with new respect. Pooh-poohing the rubbish bags I offered she had a makeshift chute set up though one of the tiny roof lights. Resolutely ignoring the clouds of age old dust she worked untiringly. Within half an hour my eyes were sore and my throat was dry. I felt as if my back was breaking.

'Would you like a coffee?' I suggested weakly.

'Coffee?' said Jacqueline, as if I'd suggested strychnine. 'Certainly not. I can't stop now.'

I didn't like to simply leave her so I made a big play of re-rigging the lights so we could see better. In so doing I kicked over one of her buckets of debris.

Jacqueline straightened up. 'You look really tired Madame.'

'Do I?'

'Yes. You should go and sit down.'

'Oh well yes maybe. I need to make some phone calls.'

I had been dismissed. I made myself a coffee and went and hid with it in my study feeling really guilty. I was never going to get used to sitting around while other people were working.

After an hour or so Jacqueline came and knocked on the door. I made a great play of being on the phone.

'I've finished for the day. That was a job and a half.' I could see from her expression that she was pretty pleased with herself at showing me up for the wimp I was.

She dumped a black bag on the table.

'You better have a look through this lot,' she said. 'They're only fit to be burned. I've put them in a rubbish sack.' she said meaningfully.

Inside were a load of mouldy paperbacks falling apart with age. They were mostly deadly dull devout works, like sermons and prayer books and lives of the saints. There were three books of the same title. These were in a better condition. In fact, they'd never been read. Their pages were still uncut like the books I remembered Dad buying in the Boulevard St Michel, when I was a child. I stored them away in the bookcase meaning to get back to them when I had more time.

At the bottom of the bag there were some exercise books, their manila covers fluffy with age. One in particular caught my eye. The child's name on the front was M-F Lamulatière. It was Marie Lamulatière's school book. I was certainly going to keep that.

Chapter Thirty Four

I'd underestimated George de Godinet. A few days later a large manila envelope arrived. Inside there was a wadge of papers with an accompanying note:

Mademoiselle

I have pleasure in enclosing a transcript of my great-great-great grandfather's journal...

There was a photocopy of an elegant but illegible handwritten text which George had thoughtfully accompanied by a typewritten transcript. It described what had happened after the Revolution, when the Royalist counter-revolutionary armies were being disbanded. Zavier was an officer in the army of the Prince de Condé. He and his fellow officers had been drawn from the cream of the aristocracy. Now the Royalist cause was lost and they were deprived of their rôle as defenders of the realm, these men found themselves in a sorry state.

------- -- -------

'Emigré a vingt ans'
Journal de Zavier de Godinet 1795.

"It is difficult to express the impression that this disastrous and unexpected news gave us. Almost all of us were totally without money; our own country had closed its borders to us and death awaited those who attempted to return. Many fell victim to their own hands; some totally lost their reason, others put a bullet through their brains or flung themselves to a watery death. Imagine our predicament for a moment - ten or twelve thousand persons, all accustomed since childhood to a life of idle luxury, who with youthful enthusiasm had taken up a cause which forced them to abandon their homeland - now reduced at a stroke to utter destitution and forced to wander back and forth in a foreign land, without friends or relations, chased from town to town, village to village like criminals. In summary, it seemed almost impossible to find a safe haven in the entire continent of Europe in

which we could take refuge. Holland at that time, was the only country willing to turn a blind eye to the ingress of a fair number of us on its territory. For my part, I found kindness and humanity in a pretty little village called Boxmeer. This was situated on the banks of the river Meuse and was under the sovereignty of a prince of Hohenzollern, who himself was under the protection of Holland. On arriving at an inn, the inhabitants came out of curiosity to take a look and me and my fellows - and seeing the state of our apparel, took us for deserters. Finding that I was the youngest of the group, our host offered me the job of apprentice miller - there was a windmill near to his house. Not feeling myself strong enough to carry the sacks, I thanked him profusely but declined. Then a master tailor offered me work, but, not knowing how to use a needle, I felt it imprudent to accept his offer. Fodder for our horses was at an extortionate price which made me decide the next morning to put my horse up for sale. I let the beast go for a mere twenty ecus complete with its saddle and bridle. The market was flooded with horses at that time which meant I could only get a moderate price. With money in my pocket my imagination suggested a thousand different projects at once - which made it difficult to come to a decision; I chose at length to abandon all my former ambitions and to go to London, capital of England and demand from some English Milords a passage to the Indies. So I left on foot bound for Helvetsluik, a seaport on the coast of Holland meaning to take the first package available across the Channel. Arriving there, I met many of my fellow countrymen, a few of whom I recognised, and confided in them my intentions. They held forth at such length that they managed in the end to dissuade me and under their tutelage I felt the rebirth in my bosom of those elusive sentiments that had originally sent me abroad in the quest of laurels...

------- -- -------

Julia 2009

I read on, finding a long account of Zavier's trials. Having sold his horse, he had no alternative but to take his pack on his back and walk. His long trek must have had ended at La Mulatière where according to the family tree he married Amisie. She was only sixteen – whilst Zavier de Godinet was nearer her father's age –*nineteen* years older than her.   It made me wonder what their marriage could have been like.

Chapter Thirty Five

Amisie de Godinet née Mulatière – 1809

Unhappily, M. de Godinet had lost his entire fortune in our troubled times. When father offered him a place under our roof, he accepted without hesitation. The fact was, he had little choice in the matter - the alternative being a state of destitution quite unsuited to a gentleman.

Thanks to the persistence of Maman's residence in the region, we had not only managed to buy back La Mulatière in the auctions but had retained the greater part of our lands and property. Under the Consulat, Father was even offered restitution, which he in his republican spirit decided not to accept.

M. de Godinet was not so fortunate, he had little more then the clothes he wore on his back. Our first meeting was hardly propitious. M. de Godinet had arrived from Moulins to dine with my father. The journey had taken him all of two days as he was forced by his precarious financial state to make the journey on foot. As you can imagine, on arrival his garments were of a fearful state. Auguste had at first denied him access to the property assuming him to be some vagrant. Yet M. de Godinet seemed quite unconcerned by his appearance or his unconventional behaviour. When my father was called and he greeted him as a long-lost comrade, the servants were quite put to shame. Their friendship went back a long way. M. de Godinet had met my father when they were military cadets at the Academy of Estissac and subsequently they had served alongside one another in the King's Light Horse Guards.

That first evening I sat by father's knee while the two of them reminisced on the days of their youth and their many daring exploits. Often these tales were of a nature quite unsuited to my ears and I was forced to rise and find some excuse to leave the room to address a servant, for since the death of beloved Maman, I had taken on the responsibilities of mistress of my father's household. Grandmère being deeply affected by all that she had endured, was now of feeble mind and seldom left her room.

And so our little household took on a new inhabitant and fell into a new rhythm of life. Here we were, a grand dame confined to her room, a nobleman, a veteran soldier and a girl of thirteen years.

I was young and alas unconscious of the allure of a young girl to a gentleman who I viewed with very much the same respect as I did my father. But by the time I had attained the age of fifteen, I was dismayed to find that M. de Godinet had already asked father for my hand and that father in his wisdom had accepted his offer.

Woe to a girl who imagines she can resist her father. And in particular a father like mine who was so dear to me. M. Godinet's rights and his passions might perhaps have been eluded, had he been far away, but I was daily subjected to his entreaties.

At every turn I would be faced by a comparison with my father's noble bearing and dignity - his intelligent and even-handed opinions and fairness to all, while the discourse of M. de Godinet was full of ramblings and contradictory conclusions. And yet it was Father who promoted this alliance. And a father who speaks as a friend, who appeals at once to nature and to the heart, cannot be denied. I knew this marriage was in my best interest. For what other well-born suitor was likely to appear? You have to understand that so many of our young noblemen had been lost through emigration, fallen prey to the guillotine or been slain in the counter-revolutionary battles. But how I wished things could have stayed as they were. That I could have kept my place quietly at father's table, watching over him and caring for him and helping to heal the gaping wound left by the loss of dearest Maman.

I had no-one to turn to. No woman to advise me. Grandmère had taken to barely audible muttering to herself. I knew nothing of men or marriage. All I knew was that it was my duty to obey my father's wishes.

We were married on the morning of my sixteenth birthday. In the end it was one fact alone that persuaded me: had I married elsewhere I might have been forced to bear a separation from my beloved father. In marrying M. de Godinet, I could stay with the person I most loved in the world, in the home of my birth, once cruelly lost but now regained, where all was familiar to me.

Julia 2009

I wondered how happy Amisie's marriage could have been with a husband so much older. I checked the family tree to see if there had been any children. None was listed. But on closer scrutiny, the family tree held a further surprise. It showed that Amisie had a younger brother - *eighteen* years younger. A bit of a mystery since Suzanne had died in 1792 and no further marriage was recorded for Jean Mulatier.

A quick calculation told me he would only have been about forty-five when he returned to La Mulatière to find himself a widower. You could hardly expect him to remain celibate for the rest of his life.

-------- -- -------

Amisie Lamulatière – 1813

I was the one who first perceived Colinette was with child. She was a pretty girl with gentle ways and despite her simple country birth, I had taken her and trained her up as a my own maid rather than send to Moulins for one. Indeed, dressed as she often was in my own passed-down apparel, she could easily be mistaken for a gentlewoman. One day, searching for her to do some errand, I found her sobbing in the back kitchen.

My many kind entreaties as to the cause of this sorrow were at length answered by a confession of her condition. I immediately insisted that the young man responsible should be spoken to by father and a marriage swiftly arranged.

'Come now, dry your eyes. It is not as bad as all that. We will have music and dancing at your wedding and make merry.'

But the poor girl continued to sob and insist as I might I could not wring a confession as to who was the father of this child. I left her disconcerted with the growing conviction that all was not as it should be. I confess that my suspicions fell on my husband who had been known to stray from our conjugal bedchamber before. There ensued an argument with accusations and counter accusations on his part - the usual thing about my coldness to him, we do not need to go into that. But he said on his honour that he was not responsible.

Then he made a suggestion that offended me deeply. My father in his kindness had endeavoured to teach Colinette to read and write. She was a bright girl and quick at her lessons. As my husband pointed out, this had necessitated some considerable time spent alone together.

'I believe the cause is more closely related to yourself.' he said with an ironic laugh.

'No!' I exclaimed.

Of course, I went to father immediately and told him of Colinette's plight, avoiding the calumny that my husband had insinuated. 'Colinette must leave us. I cannot keep a maid in her condition,' I protested.

'She is to stay,' was all father said.

I was silent for a minute and moved to where I could see his face in a better light. His gentle face told me that my husband's suspicions were indeed well-founded.

'What is to happen to the child?' I asked.

He put out a hand and stroked my hair. 'Do you not think we have room enough in this house to accomodate another soul. And food enough to nourish one?'

And so it was that my tiny brother was born. Oh how we loved that child. What joy little Pierre brought into the house. It was a strange menage indeed. My father, my husband, Colinette and I. Grandmère, who passed away before the child was born, happily never suspected. As to other people, most assumed that the child was mine and Zavier's and that Colinette was no more than his wet-nurse. We left them under this delusion, Pierre himself was not told of his true parentage until his fifteenth birthday.

As the years went by I was in all but natural birth a mother to him. Of course we spoiled him, indulging him in all his moods and fancies. As a young man he went to study in Bourges. I regret, as spoilt children often are, that he was profligate, a lover of gambling and the pleasures of life. He married a milliner's daughter and they had two children: Anselme and Henriette. The cities at the time were ravaged by cholera, so the children often came to stay at La Mulatière to avoid infection. Colinette and I revelled in these children. The sewing we did, the visits to the cobbler and to the haberdasher for yards of material. They would always be sent home with a fine new set of clothes and underwear and well-fitting shoes for I fear they had often arrived in a very sorry state. My brother's financial dealings were always a source of worry to us.

While father was alive he was constantly troubled by requests from Pierre for money. The excuses were many, he'd been robbed, the doctor's bills had mounted up, he'd been unlucky in some business enterprise. Father always complied with these request. Money was sent, no questions were asked. But when father passed away and this task was delegated to my husband Zavier, the matter changed. Each begging letter was followed by days of argument and recrimination. I would support Pierre, pointing out how easy our life was, childess and in the country and with all the conforts of servants while he had so many charges on his pocket.

Eventually when Zavier flatly refused to send further money I determined to go to see for myself the true state of my brother's needs. I secreted the small sum I had of my own in my reticule. A return journey to Bourges in those days could be achieved in barely a day thanks to the opening of the new 'chemin de fer'.

I confess I was more than a little fearful of this new mode of transport and when the chaise had deposited me at the railway station at St Amand I stood positively quaking in my boots as this great smoke-belching monster shunted to a stop at the platform. All the way to Bourges I sat clutching my reticule with the precious bank notes inside believing that at any minute the fire that was fuelling the dizzying speed at which we were being swept through the countryside would blast us to kingdom-come. In less time than I would have believed possible, we arrived at Bourges and I made my shaky descent to terra firma.

There were handsome cabs waiting outside the station. When I gave the driver the address of my dear brother he looked at me uncertainly and asked me to repeat it.

Our journey took us through a fine part of the city were tall buidings of a certain elegance led up to the cathedral. But soon he turned down a side street, long narrow and winding, which lead out into a district of a *mean and impoverished character. We passed tall factory buildings from which I could hear the clatter and drone of machinery. The streets were dirty, with filthy water running down the gutters. Ragged children who looked sadly undernourished were playing on the steps of the tenements.*

I had a picture in my mind of Pierre's establishment. A modest milliner's shop with a fine selection of hats displayed in the window. The family probably living in a neat back salon with bedrooms above. I knew their situation was difficult but nothing had prepared me for the state of dissolution in which I was to find them. There was no milliner's shop. I had to climb to the fifth floor to reach Pierre's apartment. When the door eventually was opened in answer to my anxious knocking, I found myself face to face with Annette, Pierre's wife, her hair was awry, her dress was stained, the room behind her was a chaotic mess of materials for her hat-making business. She asked me in and brushed a chair free. Henriette came running to me and clutched my knees, crying silently.

'And where is Pierre,' I asked.

'He's in the back room, sleeping. He's not been well.'

'Take me to him,' I said in alarm.

Annette was silent. But Henriette took me by the hand and led me into a back room that was if anything more dissolute than the first. Pierre indeed was asleep. He lay on his back breathing heavily and the reason for his sleep was only too apparent. A half full bottle of some spirit stood on the table by the bed and others empty rolled on the floor beneath it.

'How long has he been like this?' I asked Annette when I recovered myself.

She dissolved in tears. It wasn't the drinking as much as the gambling. The worse his debts became the more wildly he bet, thinking to gain more if he risked more. I sank back on the chair again holding the reticule tightly to me. Was this to be the future of my carefully hoarded money?

'And where is Anselme?'

Anselme was at school. He was a good boy keen on his studies. Henriette it seemed was of more use to her mother at home. Even as we sat there she took up some straw and her tiny fingers set to work weaving a band for a hat.

'And the shop?'

Annette started on a long diatribe. The competiton of cheap mass-produced hats had ruined her trade. They could no longer afford to rent the shop. Now she was doing piece-work, trimmings and finishings for a hat factory for a pittance. Oh how wonderfully this new world of mechanisation has transformed the lives of the poor!

Of course I gave Annette the money. Telling her to keep it well away from Pierre. She thanked me a thousand times. I had to leave before Pieere regained consciousness. The hansome conveyed me back to the station. That was the last time I saw Annette or Pierre or little Henriette. The next time the fever took its toll of the city, the three of them succombed.

Anselme was the only member of the family to survive. He was sixteen by that time. The death of his family determined the young lad to make medicine his career. So I provided for him. Zavier by this time had followed Father to his grave, so I had charge of my finances. I was able to finance the fees for the Faculty of Medicine in Paris and lodge him handsomely while he studied to become a doctor.

Chapter Thirty Six

Julia 2009

As summer waned and the first showers of Autumn cleared the air, I was starting to see results from all our hard work. The garden was coming under control. Jerôme had made it his preserve. He was always coming up with little initiatives. I'd catch staking out a new flowerbed or planting a tree he'd 'just happened to come across'. He seemed intent in getting the place back to the state it had been in its heyday when his father was head gardener. Jane and Sarah had nick-named him 'Widmerpool'.

The hours, expensive hours, he spent riding his beloved orange monster were paying off. The lawn – as it could now be described - was comparatively weed free and lay in a perfect oval spreading away from the front of the house. The mature trees stood free from their shaggy fetlocks of undergrowth, spaced around it at intervals. Framing the house on each side was a mini maze of clipped box hedges. To the right, deep under years of tangled ivy and compounded leaf mould Jerôme had unearthed a path that wound its way between box plants so overgrown they'd turned into trees. The path led tellingly towards Jacques farm, where it was cut off abruptly by his hedge.

When Jerôme came at the end of a day, looking very pleased with himself, to announce that the path was clear, I added a bonus to his pay 'for petrol'. Pride prevented him from ever taking more than the carefully noted hours he'd earned.

Once he'd driven off, I treated myself to a 'victory walk' down the path. He'd levelled it and neatly edged it with stones – all it needed now was a bit of gravel and - *lacking the chapel* - maybe a feature like a statue or something at the far end.

I was stopped short by the hedge. I parted the branches and stared at Jacques 'garage'. As ever I felt a flush of annoyance. To make it worse my shin had caught on something sharp. A nasty bruise was forming and it had actually broken the skin. A piece of ironwork was lodged in the hedge and covered in creeper. No doubt some rusting piece of farm machinery, I'd probably get tetanus.

I pushed crossly at whatever it was and noticed some decorative scrollwork in the iron. Dragging the ivy off I uncovered an ornamental cast iron cross - about a metre tall. I stared up at the chapel. There was a tell-tale bracket under the gable, no doubt where the cross belonged.

How and when did the chapel become Jacques'? I'd like to have it back. Not that I'm religious or anything. But it belonged to the house.

Chapter Thirty Seven

Dr Anselme Lamulatière – 1855

I stared up at the iron cross conscious of all its connotations of narrow superstition and idolatory and thought what a pretty pass I'd come to.

Three years earlier, I had arrived at La Mulatière, to find my inheritance in a sorry condition. Imagine me that first evening, travel-weary after the long journey from Paris, arriving at the gates of the manoir.

I'd come dressed for the part. I'd had my tailor furnish me with a jacket and waistcoat in imported English tweed and a pair of stout new breeches and I'd completed the ensemble with a pair of sturdy boots in fine morocco leather. I felt in every way the country gentleman as I proudly arrived to take possession of my new estate.

The house stood silent and shuttered. No servant came out to greet me. Not a dog barked. Nothing stirred. The driver of the carriage I'd hired to convey me from Moulins refused to enter the driveway for fear of sinking up to the wheel hubs in the mud. So I approached the house on foot, besmirching my boots and fine new breeches on the way. My calls were in vain. There was not so much as a sound to signal life inside.

Unlatching the door of the kitchen, I became all too aware of the sorry state of the place. It seemed my Aunt had taken little interest in the house in the latter years of her life. She had apparently taken to her room and seldom emerged except for funerals.

Downstairs the servants had long ceased to serve in anything but name. Most of them being as old or older than Aunt Amisie. I found only the last surviving one, Colinette, who I remembered as a fine slender straight-backed woman from my childhood had transformed into a frail bent old crone. The poor creature was sitting over a miserable fire of sticks in the icy kitchen. She looked as if she was unlikely to survive the year.

For the past decade the two old women must have been living in conditions that were positively medieval. The water for the house had to be pumped by hand and the only form of heating was wood which Colinette had to drag from the park and chop herself. Clearly she and Aunt Amisie had been reduced to the lowest of circumstances. Chickens had been roosting in the kitchen - the table was quite white with their droppings. The cooking area was black with grease.

Realising that I would need more able servants for my care, I braced myself to tell Colinette that I would have to send her to be cared for at the convent of the good sisters. To my amazement she grasped my hands and bathed them in tears of thanks. The poor old dear was pitifully grateful. On reflection, I realised that this was probably the only rest she would have had in her entire life.

I made it my first priority to visit all my farms and small holdings and assess the living conditions of the workers. Those first rounds of La Mulatière's farms, taken by necessity on horseback, for many of the farm tracks were in such a state a carriage was out of the question, revealed people living in conditions barely fit for beasts. I had to remind myself that Aunt Amisie had been born during the Ancien Règime. She had survived famine, Revolution, the Terror, the Empire and lived to see the Restoration. A certain eccentricity in her notions as a proprietress could be understood, if perhaps not forgiven.

When Aunt Amisie died she left no children. As her nearest surviving relative all her property and lands were left to me. I knew she had been fond of me as a child. My sister and I had been sent to La Mulatière several times when there had been an epidemic in our home town of Bourges. Henriette and I had spent many happy summer days playing in the park of La Mulatière while cholera took its sad toll in the city.

It was thus that at a tender age of twenty five I found myself responsible for her entire estate, which comprised around two thousand hectares with no less than thirty farms. I had barely completed my studies at the Faculty of Medicine in Paris. Barely completed, for I confess I had made a poor show of it. It was only at a second botched attempt that I was awarded my M.D. The truth of the matter was that the calling of physician had never been to my liking. To this day the smell of embalming fluid turns my stomach and the sights of the dissecting rooms haunt my dreams. But *worse than these were the operations, which in my student days were brutal, bloody and accompanied by the fearsome screams of the poor sufferers. I'm afraid that I fled from one poor fellow's ill-fated amputation with such horror, I swore never again to enter the operating rooms.*

I found solace in attending the lectures on "Comparative Anatomy" at the Academie des Sciences. Here I was lucky enough to encounter the theories of such great minds as Lamarck and Cuvier. Their breadth of vision and free thinking were a total revelation to me. I soon became a regular at the lecture halls at the Jardin des Plantes and found myself immersed in a world of fascinating scientific speculation. Here was intellectual freedom. Bravely flouting the constraints of Church dogma, great men theorized on a universe in which life began spontaneously, without divine intervention. I listened with rapt attention to their descriptions of a primeval world where filaments of simple cells snaked their way across a watery globe; dividing - combining - multiplying into more complex organisms; advancing by self-generated variation to populate the world with its plethora of species; diversifying into plants and molluscs, fish and the fowls of the air; to arrive at creatures as diverse and as specialised as the camel and the great carnivores of the savanna and in time to Man himself. All living creatures, in short, being generated through a natural process of 'transmutation'. In the immortal words of Lamarck: "Species are mutable. Allied species are co-descendants of common stock."

It did not take a great bound of the understanding to recognise that this was a theory that had been used in selective farming since the dawn of cultivation. I wanted to see nature at work, test this thesis for myself. So when I received my aunt's bequest, in my mind's eye the lands of La Mulatière became a model farm in which I could radically advance the current practices of agriculture. It would become a veritable laboratory of new horticultural methods, where by applying the scientific principles I had gleaned in my studies I would improve yields, better the lives of the working man and create a shining example of modern husbandry.

The farming economy around La Mulatière was based on the metayer, or tied-labourer system. It was an ignominious arrangement which extended across the entire Bourbonnais region, and one that I could sense was sowing the seeds of discontent in a workforce beginning to emerge from a state of feudal servitude.

A typical metayer's contract stipulated that half the fruit from their trees, one hundred eggs a year, eight capons, half of their turkeys, their geese and their ducks were due to the landlord. Generally the provision of such goods would be task of the farmer's wife. At la Mulatière the good women had had an easy time of it recently as Aunt Amisie's frugal diet would not have absorbed one tenth of this.

Drinking water for these peasants was hand pumped from a well. These wells were often poorly sited near the slurry from the cowhouse. Any notion of human sanitation was quite beyond question, the normal arrangement being a bucket which would be carried out into some secluded spot on the land.

My first forays soon confirmed the decision I had taken. My duty as proprietor should take priority over any notion of a career as a medical practitioner. What medical knowledge I had gleaned from my studies in Paris would be put to good use helping to improve the health and well-being of the labourers working on my land.

The most urgent matter was the lack of trustworthy drinking water. Countless diseases could be tracked back to this one source, and I admit it had become somewhat of an obsession with me. In fact, to this day I never let anything but boiled water pass my lips.

From the very start I'd suspected the siting of the wells at the manoir to be the cause of numerous ills. The water looked clear enough but it was plain to see that the water table drained downhill from fields where cattle grazed.

I was pondering on this problem when the pigeonnière caught my eye. Within hours I had drawn up a plan for the plumber. By a simple system of zinc gutterings the conical roof could be used as a catchment area. Clean and safe drinking water thus collected would be conveyed into a large reservoir inside the upper chamber of the pigeonnière, this was at a height elevated enough for water to feed the taps in the house at a fairly decent pressure merely by the power of gravity.

I must confess I felt rather proud of my design. The application of *science in a domestic context. The workers I employed to carry out this project were doubtful and came up with several counter proposals for filtering the well water. But I stood firm. As is contrary way of nature; we experienced the driest Spring in decades, so it took time to verify the wisdom of my invention.*

With the onset of the winter rains I had enough water to supply two paved chambres de toilette. The mason thought it a fine joke - a gentleman concerning himself with such humble domestic matters. But I had vowed to drag La Mulatière out of its medieval gloom and make it a house fit for a family living in the modern age. All it lacked was the pretty woman who was going to make my dream complete.

I need hardly say that a young man, single and with a fair amount of property does not stay unnoticed in a small village like Deneville. Soon cards accompanied by discreet handwritten notes began to arrive by the day from attentive members of the bourgeoisie anxious to 'integrate me into the community'.

Little did I have need of a cook for I could have dined out on a nightly basis on the sumptuous dinners they laid before me. And it was not only comestibles on offer. There were their daughters too, tight-laced and decolletée, their hair sprung fresh from curling papers, their cheeks pinched to pinkness; I was clearly being invited to take my pick of these as well. One by one they were paraded before me and put through their paces displaying their many and varied accomplishments. Oh the singing and the piano playing - the painted miniatures, the petit-point. I fear I was fast earning myself a poor reputation with my yawning and early departures, for often I had been up and about my farms since sunrise.

I suspect that not a few hot tears were shed into pillows over my indifference. But what could I do? Never in Paris had I attracted such interest. The women I had 'known' there, were of another type entirely and by no means so tightly corsetted.

After a few months I could see heads nodding and tongues wagging as I passed by on market day. It was made all too apparent that I was expected to do my duty and choose from among the ripe young daughters on offer. Such gentle pressure has its effect over time. I was a young healthy male and I missed what female contact I had been accustomed to hitherto.

Almost despite myself, I started to assess the choice on offer. I have never been one for flirtation and frivolous conversations and bit by bit I found myself withdrawing to the outer circle of the salons where a quiet girl sat neatly dressed, her hair parted and demurely smoothed away from her forehead.

It clearly amazed everyone that I should have singled out Elizabeth. Quiet, dull Elizabeth with her bookish ways. But indeed talking with her was a relief after all the empty chitter-chatter of their soirées. She shared my enthusiasm for reform. Admittedly her benevolence was linked more with the Church than was perhaps to my liking. But she was an intelligent girl and in time and with maturity I felt sure that she would come around to my way of thinking.

The turning point came one day when I was out visiting a farm where one of my workers lay on his sickbed. I arrived to find Elizabeth leaning over the bed, in no way disgusted by the condition of the poor man or the mean and filthy amenities of the sick room. She herself was bathing his fevered face while his distraught wife ran from pump to fireplace at her bidding. In half an hour or so with the help of what medical assistance I could give, we had the poor fellow comfortable. For days after that I would find her at his bedside on my visits and with the aid of her soups and jellies and solicitous care the man's health gradually improved.

It was on seeing her face the day she arrived to find the fellow up and sitting in the sun outside his door that I resolved to make her my wife.

Our wedding was a simple affair in the church of Deneville. But what a congregation we had. They filled the pews and overflowed into the road - indeed the village square flocked with a merry crowd all in their Sunday best. So great was their number that the Vin d'Honneur soon ran out and the carter had to be sent for another barrel. My wedding gift to my wife was no glittering trinket. No, at her request an avenue of trees was planted along the road from Deneville's little church all the way up the hill to La Mulatière.

-------- -- -------

Pity the man who weds in the belief that he can change his spouse. My dear Elizabeth, so open to my liberal ideas as a fiancée, became tenaciously opposed to them as a wife. I'd thought when she listened with such interest to my views on transmutation that I had a budding scientific mind on my hands. Little did I guess that the truth of the matter was quite the reverse. The Elizabeth who listened with such a patient gaze had vowed internally to bring me back to the straight and narrow path of God. Her mission was to save my soul. Once our 'honeymoon' was over, the truth of the matter became only too clear - each was out to convert the other.

Unfortunately for me, Elizabeth had God on her side. Argue as I might that it was conceivable to have the highest moral values and philanthropy at heart without expecting to be rewarded by everlasting life; I got nowhere. Oh the clicking of beads and the murmuring of lips. My soul was saved so arduously on a daily basis I had little hope of evading the excruciating boredom of heaven. The thing came to a head a few weeks after our marriage. I found Elizabeth in our bedroom supervising the hanging of a crucifix above our bed.

'Elizabeth. For god's sake...' I started.

'Anselme... please,' she motioned towards Fabrice who was precariously balanced on a ladder the wretched thing in his hand.

'Thank you Fabrice you can come down. That will be all,' I said firmly.

When the boy had left I protested in the warmest terms about not having 'a tortured figure' hanging above our marriage bed.

Elizabeth's eyes filled with tears. It seems she had always had 'Our Lord' above her bed, watching over her.

I felt like commenting that the events in that location had hardly being worth observing to date. But I withheld the impulse. My bride was young and with patience I assumed things would improve.

'Come dear,' I said taking her hand. 'I do not object to you devotions, in the appropriate time and place. Find a suitable location, wherever you wish for your crucifix. But please not here.'

She dried her eyes and set her chin with determination staring out of the window fixedly at the barn. I had the mason come and modify the windows. I niche was made and a stoup for holy water was positioned near the doors. Some pails of limewash and industrious scrubbing later, with the purchase of a row of prie-dieux and a couple of cheap plaster statues, the place assumed its ecclesiastical status. The Priest was called and after some waving of an incense burner and muttered mumbo-jumbo the Host assumed residence.

-------- -- -------

Chapter Thirty Eight

Julia 2009

When Anselme Lamulatière died, La Mulatière was not left to his wife but to his two daughters. According to Maitre Bertrand, the same practice remains in France to this day. Anselme's widow Elizabeth would have been allowed to live in the house for her lifetime, but the house legally belonged to the daughters.

'So how did they decide which daughter should have the house?'

'They had to draw Lots for it,' he said in a matter of fact sort of voice.

'Lots! But that's positively medieval!'

I tried to imagine drawing lots for the house with Sarah and Jane. It was unthinkable.

'It's still a common practise today. The party who loses is recompensed with land or money. Louise Lamulatière for instance got all the land on the far side of the valley. She built a new house there. You may have noticed it, built in the neo-gothic style. It's called Chapeau Blanc.'

I wondered if this had caused a rift between the two sisters. It seemed not. According to Jerôme they were buried side by side in a double tomb in Deneville cemetery. I decided to go to have a look for myself.

Deneville cemetery is a typically grim French affair full of hideous shiny black tombstones adorned with garish plastic flowers. At first glance it all looked far too recent to hold the sisters.

But then I came to a second graveyard. This was filled with older tombs, their headstones toppling at drunken angles, their plots unkempt and unadorned. It looked more promising. I worked my way systematically along the clinker paths, reading the inscriptions, stone by stone. I checked through grand pillared family tombs, Rococo urns and humble headstones, noting the names, constantly repeated, of the local families. Here were the names of Deneville's butcher, the hairdresser, and the couple who ran the Tabac. But I could find none with the name Lamulatière.

I came across a sign on the wall inviting people to claim the tombs, otherwise the headstones would be moved to make room for a civic park.

I was distracted from my search by an animated conversation between a stout little man in a tweed jacket and two ladies 'of a certain age'. 'Shocking,' one of them was saying. 'The very idea of disturbing these graves... '

They seemed to know their way around, so after waiting for a suitable pause in their conversation, I asked if they knew where I could find the tomb of the Lamulatière's.

'Why yes. It's just along here. But you couldn't have known because the plaque is missing.'

The younger of the ladies led me to where a double tomb of dark volcanic stone lay cracked and lopsided beneath a broken capital.

She looked at me enquiringly. 'You know the family?'

'I live in their house, you s...'

'La Mulatière! Mother. This is the English lady from La Mulatière. We are delighted to meet you.'

Her mother joined us. 'And so Madame. Are you staying? Are you really going to live in that house all year round?'

I realised they had known who I was all along. In a village the size of Deneville, my English car didn't go unnoticed.

'Well. I haven't really decided yet...'

'But you like the area. The house...'

'Oh yes. After London. It's so beautiful. It's sheer heaven.'

'Ah the Bourbonnais,' the younger woman smiled in agreement. 'How lucky we are.'

'And of course, I knew Mademoiselle Marie,' said her mother. I stared at her. Her hair had been fluffed into a golden beehive, as fine as candyfloss, but her face was a thousand lines. 'I was only a child of course at the time, but I remember her coming to visit my mother.'

'Really? If you had the time. I'd love to hear anything you know about her. I'm writing a book you see.'

'Oh so you're a writer!' the younger woman exclaimed. She was a tall, handsome woman with strong features.

'Trying to be. I'm researching a book. About the people who lived in my house.'

'Come and coffee with us. At Chapeau Blanc. You know it belonged to the same family? That's where we live,' she said spontaneously. She introduced herself as Bernadette Lapalisse, adding: 'Then mother can tell you all she knows.'

I arranged to call in the following day and was taking down their details when the tweed jacketed man joined us. He had a clipboard in his hand and he introduced himself in a jovial and somewhat officious manner as the Eric Charpentier, president of the society which was protecting the tombs from the disgraceful plan of the council to clear the land.

'And the cross of course. We'll have to replace it. That's going to cost a pretty penny,' he said.

The three of them stood staring gloomily at the sisters' tomb. Suddenly I remembered the cross I'd found in the hedge.

'But I have a cross,' I cut it. 'A decorative iron one from about the same period. You're welcome to it. It's in the garden of La Mulatière. I couldn't think what to do with it.'

They greeted this with protestations that they couldn't possibly accept.

'But it would be the right thing to do. The cross must have belonged to the family anyway.' In fact I was glad to get rid of it. So it was agreed that I should deliver it to Chapeau Blanc when I visited the next day.

------- -- -------

When Maitre Bertrand told me about the division by Lots, I was dying to see inside 'Chapeau Blanc'. I'd passed the house several times on the road. It was hidden by a dense bank of trees and I could only get a tantalising glimpse of the roof and a bit of decorative gable. The following afternoon found me driving through the gateway with the iron cross in the boot of the car.

I came across Bernadette in the driveway hacking away at the shrubbery with a pair of garden shears. She instantly adopted the friendly 'tu' mode as she showed me into the house. I liked her relaxed manner - she was more like an English woman than a French one.

Inside, the house was paved with Victorian tiles and the walls decorated with carved woodwork similar in style to my Art Nouveau bedroom. I followed Bernadette into an octagonal salon where a bay window gave a sweeping view over the countryside.

The room had a quaintly French formality about it - heavy oak furniture, a side table displaying hunting bronzes, a few of those low Louis Quinze style chairs - their petitpoint showing its age.

A picture on the wall caught my eye. I went to take a closer look. It was a double portrait of two young men. The one on the right was quite thick-set and unappealing. But the one on the left had a pair of grey eyes that was familiar. The likeness was striking.

'Do you know who these men are?' I asked.

Bernadette came up beside me.

'Two brothers, ancestors of the Lamulatières. Judging by the way they're dressed, they must have lived in your house rather than mine.'

Jean Mulatier and his brother Henri!

I told Bernadette what I'd found out about the brothers, described the find of Jean's portrait and all the other objects I'd been collecting.

'It's as if the house wants to tell me it's story.'

Bernadette laughed. 'If only walls could speak. Thank god they can't, we'd discover no end of scandals.'

As we chatted on, I found my gaze kept returning to those cool grey eyes. That ironic smile of his taunted me.

'Mother will be down soon. But I expect you'd like to look around the house,' said Bernadette. 'It's quite a period piece.'

I followed her up a winding stairway, Bernadatte seemed happy to show me every nook and cranny, she led on at a breathtaking pace, talking non-stop.

'Please don't take any notice of the mess,' she said. 'I don't live here all the time you see. My other house is in St Amand.' She threw open a door into a large light room with a view over woods towards Deneville. I could just make out La Mulatière's pyramidal tower through the trees.

'This was Louise's room. She had it built with those big windows facing her sister's. Before those trees grew up, at night she would have been able to see the light from Marie's bedroom. They were very close you know.'

'What about her husband?'

'Oh he spent most of time in Paris. I don't think there was much love lost there.'

'So there was no bad feeling over Marie getting La Mulatière?'

'No, the trouble came later. When my father inherited this house. He was Louise's godson. Not a blood relative. That didn't go down at all well with the family.'

'No, I suppose not.''

We'd arrived at the top floor. Bernadette opened various doors leading into sloping attic rooms. I was surprised to see incongruous posters of pop stars and footballers pinned on the walls.

'My grandchildren!' Bernadette said. 'Please ignore the mess. But this is their floor. They can do 'their own thing' in it. I let them have free run of the place in the summer.'

I didn't like to comment, but I was sure the other day M. Charpentier had addressed Bernadette as Mademoiselle Lapalisse. I'd obviously got it wrong. She must be a widow or divorced, but there had been no mention of a husband.

'Marie did not like men.' That was what Bernadette's mother told me when eventually Bernadette brought us a tray of tea in the octagonal drawing room.

'Oh? What makes you say that?'

The old lady came out with a story, apocryphal perhaps, and heard no doubt as a child, which had lodged in her memory. She described an occasion when her grandmother had invited Marie to dinner. A young man had been included in the party. Single and eligible. Finding herself seated next him, Marie had been most put out. She had been cross and uncommunicative throughout the meal and complained bitterly afterwards that a 'piège' - a trap - had been set for her.

'I'd love to hear anything else you can remember about her.'

'What do you want to know?'

'Well for a start. What did she look like?'

'Oh she was a very striking woman. Held herself so straight. Quite the aristocrat. Always wore a little white collar at the throat. Not like her sister Louise who lived here - she was quite ordinary. A different sort of person altogether... Marie looked...' the old woman paused with her head on one side giving me a bright bird-like look. 'She looked very like Georges Sand.'

'Georges Sand, the novelist?'

I pictured my predecessor, in darkly masculine clothes, cane in hand. A cigarette perhaps in a slim holder. Arty, Bloomsburyesque, emancipated. She must have been an incongruous sight in Deneville.

'She wrote a book you know,' said Bernadette..

'You shouldn't bother Julia with all that,' said her mother.

'No please tell me about it. What was the book called? Do you have a copy?'

'That was the curious thing,' said Bernadette. 'When Marie died, Louise had all the copies of the book destroyed.'

'Why on earth would she want to do that?'

'Marie was quite a character. Louise was much more conventional. I can only assume there was something in the book that she didn't approve of.'

Chapter Thirty Nine

As is the way with renovations, the deadline that I'd originally set before I would be 'reasonably straight' had stretched from an ambitious June, into a hopeful August, then on to an optimistic October. At last I had to admit the work would take years rather than months.

Weeks had passed and I'd hardly set eyes on Jacques. He seemed to be avoiding me. I had a place by my bathroom window where I could snoop on the farmyard unobserved. It was a pretty depressing view actually, he should do something to tidy the place up.

One morning I stood drying my hair by the window when I noticed there was a mud-spattered *Citroen* parked in the barn. Maybe he'd changed his car. While I stood there, the farm door opened and out came *a woman...*

I slid back into the shadows. She fetched something from the car and then went back into the farmhouse. She was slim with a mass of dark hair – *Kattie.*

The vicious pang of jealousy took me by surprise. It was like a hard lump that burned in my chest. It brought home to me how Jacques must have felt when Oliver arrived on the scene. It was a horrible destructive emotion I wouldn't wish on anyone.

All that day I kept coming back to the window, wondering what was going on. Was she inside? Where was Jacques? At dusk I went up to take another look. The car was still there.

It was still there the following morning.

Over the next few days I tried to avoid looking out of the window. If Kattie had come back that was that. I had to stop this hopeless and self-indulgent pining. I needed to get out more and to find new friends.

A few days later I had a call from Hortense Bertrand. Sunday apparently was the feast of Saint Hubert and she wondered if I wanted to see the hunt being blessed.

'You bless the hunt?'

'Oh yes,' she said in a matter of fact sort of way. 'Thierry of course will be taking part. But I'll be following with the picnic if you'd like to join us.'

Once again I was amazed by the French. Only they could have a patron saint devoted to massacring animals. I tried politely to back out, not wanting to be party to such carnage. But Hortense was insistent, it was to be quite a spectacle and we wouldn't go near the kill. Not that the hunt often killed anything anyway, so reluctantly I accepted.

She picked me up in their Landrover dressed for the part in a neat green loden jacket and green wellies. Her hair was tied back in a black snood and she was, as ever,wearing her pearls.

The ceremony took place at the local kennels. It seemed a popular event. A long stream of cars was parked on the embankment and people in a rough assortment of all-weather wear were making their way down the hill. Hortense sailed past these to the inner courtyard of the kennels where a load of horse boxes were parked. This was where the élite of the day were to be found – the huntsmen. The French hunt in green rather than 'pink' but they more than made up in style for their lack of colour. The men were in long jackets of an 18th Century cut and the women wore neat little hacking jackets and wonderful miniature tricornes complete with a cockade.

Hortense seemed anxious to introduce me to everyone and I was constantly dodging toe-crunching hooves as people lent down from massive horses to shake me by the hand. I recognised the local dentist, and wondered how many crowns and bridges had funded his hunter. There was the fellow who'd serviced my car at the local garage and a couple of older residents I was on nodding terms with, from the bakery. Maitre Bertrand, was in his element, mounted on a fiery looking black hunter, surrounded by a load of Parisiens down for the hunt.

There was a sudden hush as the priest came out in his white surplus. The huntsmen trotted their horses round until they formed a rough half circle. And then the yelping mass of hounds were released and herded into an excited doggy mass behind the horses.

The priest raised his hand for the benediction and as the hunting horns played a strange discordent fanfare a sudden calm fell over the animals. My habitual loathing of bloodsports was suspended for a moment as I realised this was a scene that hadn't changed in centuries. Despite myself, I was caught up in the tide of emotion all around me.

The blessing over, the hounds were frantic to be off, the handlers were constantly having to crack their whips to get them back into line. The excitement of the hounds was infectious. The horses were constantly having to be turned and trotted round to calm them down. Then all of a sudden they were off.

There was a bit of a scramble as the spectators made a dash for their cars, eager to be up front in the convoy. Hortense grabbed me by the arm and having the advantage of being parked in the best spot, we sailed off first in line behind the horses.

'Thank you for bringing me,' I said. 'I wasn't sure if I wanted to come, but I'm glad I did.'

'A,h you English,' she said. 'You have banned hunting, no?

'Not entirely. We still do drag hunting,'

'Hmm,' said Hortense dismissively. 'But it's not the same.'

I fell silent. No it wasn't the same, thank goodness.

The convoy had slowed to a walking pace. Some sort of fuss was going on ahead. A couple of the leading huntsmen were waving their whips and some fellow from the back cantered along the bank to see what was up.

Hortense craned out of her window, letting in a horrible smell of pig manure and then shut it abruptly.

'There's some sort of farm vehicle up ahead,' she said. 'They're trying to get it off the road.'

The convoy came to a complete stop. The horses were getting frisky and the hounds had started baying. I could hear men's voices, raised in dispute.

We sat for a few minutes and then all of a sudden we were off again. The leading huntsmen set off at a canter and Hortense started up the engine.

We soon drew level with a culprit - an ancient muck-spreader perched, two-wheels-up on the embankment. The smell from it was disgusting.

'I imagine, that was intentional,' Hortense said in annoyance. 'These country people. You're doing them a service culling the game. And this is how they repay you.'

I veered round to see who was responsible for the hold-up. It was Jacques. He was leaning up against the side of the spreader with his arms crossed, watching us go by with a sardonic expression on his face. Hortense drove past, her eyes fixed ahead of her. His eyes met mine and his face creased into an ironic smile.

I stared back. How was I meant to react? Wave? Leap out and join him? As ever Jacques made me feel horribly in the wrong.

------- -- -------

Chapter Forty

The following Sunday Jerôme turned up unexpectedly at the front door. He was dressed in his best clothes, it appeared this was a formal visit.

I made him a coffee and asked him to sit down. He drew a paper parcel out of his pocket and laid it on the table.

'I have something for you,' he said. 'I wanted to thank you for all the work you've given me and I wasn't sure how. But I thought you might like this.'

'Thank you. Thank you so much, but there's no need to thank me. It's you who's helping me out.'

'Won't you open it?'

I undid the parcel and found inside a lovely little handmade frame with a tiny sepia photo of La Mulatière with a carriage pulled by a single white horse, standing at the front door.

'It's beautiful, thank you, so much. But I can't possibly accept...'

Jerôme got to his feet brushing away my comment. He pointed at the coachman. 'That's my father driving the carriage.'

'I'll tell you what. I'll make a copy and then we can have one each.'

He seemed satisfied with this but insisted I should have the frame which he'd made himself.

Once he'd gone, I shifted into better light. Surely there was someone in the carriage? But it was virtually impossible to make anything out this size.

The photocopier at the Tabac in Deneville did enlargements. On impulse, I drove into Deneville. The copier worked its magic. Out came the white horse now standing proud and blinkered. The coachman had gained a long whip and a cap with a glossy patent leather peak. Behind him a black umbrella was held up against... the rain? No the sun. The house was in full sunshine, several windows were wide open.

Their carriage stood outside the door, the driver's whip was poised to set off. Just discernable in the shade of the umbrella I could make out not one but two figures. They were children, two little girls, and by the way they were dressed, they could only be Marie and Louise Lamulatière.

The taller one of course would be Marie. I had her exercise book stored away in my little display cabinet. I reached it down and started leafing through its pages and came across a passage that would have today's educationalists apoplectic.

'The family is the primary human condition. And consequently the primary form of society. It is the first and most essential step that man makes in his moral life. Wherever the family does not yet exist as with savages or where it only exists in an unformed manner as with the barbarians, morals are brutal and rough and there is nothing but barbarism and servitude. Women are subjected to a shameful traffic, they are herded up like human livestock in the markets and given the crudest of work. Whereas the men, when they are not occupied in hunting or making war, live a life of leisure. The children who are even worse off than the women are more or less abandoned or are reduced to the condition of slaves and are sold to no matter who is willing to pay for them.'

------- -- -------

Marie-Francoise Lamulatiere 1900

Sometimes I do not understand Papa. Last week, for instance, he asked to see my 'Cahier de Devoirs Mensuelles'. It's my most important book in which I copy out a piece of work for everyone to see. Each month Mademoiselle selects an exercise and I take great care in the copying. A whole morning is set aside and I always have a new pen nib and fresh ink for if I blot or make a mistake I'm not allowed to tear the page out.

This month the étude was 'Orthographe' and Mademoiselle had set me a long text to copy. Imagine my surprise when without any blots or mistakes Father flew into a rage on reading it and asked to speak with Mademoiselle.

I examined my writing to see what could have offended him. The subject was the family and while copying it, I thought it expressed the noblest of sentiments.

When Mademoiselle left father's study her face was flushed and she looked really angry. A few minutes later Father opened the door and called to me with a stern face.

'I hope I have not offended you Papa?'

He put an arm around my shoulders and drew me to him saying. 'Not you my child. Come let's take a look together at these savages and barbarians that Mademoiselle's text has been describing in so vivid a manner.'

He reached down a thick book from the shelves and as he turned the pages he showed me pictures of savages with the most alarming features.

'They are so very ugly,' I remarked.

'Indeed they are not,' said Father. 'Observe their gleaming skin and perfect teeth. Their healthy bodies. See how the mother binds her baby to her back even when she is working. Here are families. Here is love, of mother for child, of man for woman, of brother for sister. Their manner of living may be different from ours but believe me Marie you will see more cruelty and savage practices among those who put their lips to the sacrament at Mass on Sunday than with many of these noble savages.'

'But Mademoiselle says they do not have proper weddings and the men have children with many wives.'

'It is not only among the savages that happens,' Father said almost beneath his breath.

I felt myself blushing deeply for even I have heard the gossip in the village.

'Come I'll have no more of this ignorant moralising. I've told Mademoiselle that in future her texts must be selected with more care for veracity. No doubt, from now on you'll be busying your mind with more important subjects like embroidery and housewifery.'

'Do not joke with me Father. You know me better than that.'

'My dear serious Marie. So what do you want?'

'I want to know about things that matter. Like the prism and light and how it's all made up of different colours and what makes coal burn and...'

'I don't think poor Mademoiselle knows enough about such things herself. She'd only be one page ahead of you in the text.'

'Then I should go away to school, as you promised'

'We still need Mademoiselle for Louise, maybe we will reconsider the matter when she is old enough... In the meantime, we have all the books you could possibly want here on these shelves.'

'But Louise is two years younger than me... That means two more years...'

Father had turned pale. He took a pace or two towards the window and and started coughing again.

'Open the window Marie,' he gasped. 'There's no air in here.'

And there you have it. My departure to boarding school was always postponed. And eventually it was too late. I couldn't go away to school. Not with Father so ill. So when Mademoiselle eventually departed in high dudgeon after one of her 'little disagreements' with Papa, Louise and I were sent as day girls to the convent in Deneville. Whether we learned more there than we would have done with poor Mademoiselle was debatable.

But as Papa said, we had all the books we needed and he always gave me a free range of his library. And so that was our life. Our weekdays spent in the convent. And all other times prisoners in the house. We never entertained. How could we with Father so ill?

I used to sit for hours, upstairs in the room Louise and I had been given as a parlour. After dinner I'd sit reading at the open window until the last rays of sunset died away. Then Marie-Jeanne would come up with a taper to light the new gas lamps. And she'd always give a little jump as those new-fangled things as she called them, lit with a Pop... Pop.

At night I'd often lie awake listening to the sounds outside. The frogs setting up their nightly chorus. The nightingale singing through his repertoire. The soft wings of the owl and the tight flutterings of bats. The crunching of footsteps in the lane as Marie-Jeanne, steps stealthily out while her parents sleep next door behind their firmly closed shutters. She couldn't be much older than me. She has a beau. I've seen them meeting in the lane. I envy her her freedom. She seems entirely happy with her quiet, dull life. She doesn't suffer the fire that is eating me up inside. Of doing nothing. Of having nothing to do. Of being nothing. Of ending my days as ... Nothing.

Chapter Forty One

It was so frustrating knowing Marie had written a book but not being able to get hold of a copy. Logic told me there must be one somewhere. I'd tried Amazon and looked up umpteen websites of antiquarian books. I'd even enquired at the library of the Society d'Emulation but no-one came up with anything by a Marie Lamulatière.

Of course, a woman of her time might well have written under a pseudonym… And then it struck me. M-F Tremailleau. M-F hyphenated not M.F. as in initials. Marie-Françoise! And 'Tremailleau' was a really odd name. I snatched up a scrap of paper and wrote out the two names. I was right! Tremailleau was an anagram of Lamulatière!

I'd been a complete and total idiot. Her book had been in my bookcase staring me in the face all the time. I went straight to the shelf and took out one of the uncut books.

LA FILLE PERDUE
By M-F Tremailleau

Grabbing a knife I started cutting open the pages:

'Excerpt from La Fille Perdue' by M-F Tremailleau

The Sequoia stood dark etched against the hazy blue horizon. The sky was steely grey, across it, trails of vapourous clouds tinted an angry red, sped by. Clouds that were shredded by the wind into shadowy fingers of violet streaked with gleaming silver. Clouds that the mad wind swept into a whirlpool, like currents in a river swollen with floodwater.
The children were shouting at the tops of their voices to make themselves heard, their strident cries competing with the violent gusts of raging wind. In a moment Marie-Jeanne was running barefoot into the neighbouring field gathering her sheep which in their fright had bunched into a stupified huddle. The women watched in silent disapproval as her hair was blown into her eyes, her skirts were flapping and twisting themselves around her

body as she ran.

-------- -- -------

I stared out of my window - the view was eerily similar. *'The Sequoia dark-edged against the hazy blue horizon'* – I was looking at the very same landscape.

I read on hungrily, searching for passages that I could recognise as La Mulatière. But I was disappointed to find that the story soon took me far from France. Her heroine, Marie-Jeanne was no demure country maid. She had an affair with a local landowner and finding herself pregnant, she dressed as a man and worked her way down to Marseille where she boarded a ship for Algeria.

I rang Bernadette that evening.

'Guess what! I've found some copies of Marie's book!'

'No, where?'

'Right under my nose. They were in the attic with a load of old paperbacks. Three copies, all uncut. Would you like one?'

'Most certainly, especially if there's something shocking in it,'

'It's not that shocking. Just about a country girl who had an illegitimate child.'

'Shocking for her time perhaps.'

'I'll bring one over right away.'

Bernadette greeted me at the door with a gift in return. It was a little linen bound book.

'Marie's sketchbook,' she said. 'Mother said she thought you should have it. Keep it with all the other little 'Objets Trouvés you told me about.

------- -- -------

That evening, back at La Mulatière, I sat turning the pages. There were countless delicate pencil drawings, all titled and dated in a neat hand: *The Forum, Rome. The Ponte Vecchio, Florence. A view of the Bay of Naples. An alpine scene in Switzerland.* Fruit no doubt of a 'grand tour'. Nothing special about them. They were very much what you'd expect from a young woman of Marie's time and social class.

But I paused when I came across a watercolour of palm trees set against an oasis. Although unfinished, it was executed with a boldness that made it stand out from the others.

Chapter Forty Two

Marie Lamulatière – 1904

The watercolour stands unfinished propped up against my wash bowl.
I lie staring at it, wondering what I can do to capture the strange effect of
light that so fascinated me. Diffused by the persian blinds the sun sends
slatted stripes across the painting. Dappling it, muddling the pattern of the
slats with the trunks of the palm trees, turning it into a single dazzling
sensation, like that painting I saw in Paris by who was it? That modernist,
Vuillard?

I should take up my brushes now and try to capture the moment, but it
is early afternoon. The midday African heat is almost unbearable. Outside
the brilliance burns into your eyes. Nothing moves. Even the chickens have
taken to their perches beneath the house and the pensione's dog sleeps in a
deep pool of shadow under the pomegranite tree.

The house is silent. Mother, Aunt Florence and Uncle Mathiau have
taken a trip to yet another site. 'So historic', 'What a noble prospect',
'Pray ask the guide, which way is South?' 'Ah there you see my dear.'
'Marie, Marie you must sketch this view, it is so picturesque'.

Their voices ring through my head making it throb again. It wasn't
really such a bad headache but enough to excuse me from yet another
juddering trip across the desert. Yet another pile of unidentifiable rubble. A
doorstep here, a fallen lintel there. Part of a tower still standing. I have
had enough of the picturesque. There are enough pen and ink drawings,
painstakingly executed, by ladies with a penchant to travel. By now these
industrious creatures must have produced enough to paper over the desert.

Louise would laugh at that. But now she's married to Philippe she
won't be travelling with me. No, it will be me and mother and Aunt
Florence and Uncle Mathiau until one by one they all get too decrepit to
climb over their blessed ruins.

I'm thirty-eight. Thirty-eight! Poor Marie. No chance of marrying
now. Who would want her? Unless someone perhaps like Phillippe with his
fat neck and his way of being so obviously galant - the only man among us

poor weak women. Strutting like the coq of the roost.

*Dear Marie. Such a clever girl. So talented. Of course she
frightened all the men off. That's what mother always told me. No it's plain
clothes, flat heeled shoes and a narrow bed for me now.*

*Not that it means we can't feel passion. We single women in our
sensible clothes, feel it as fiercely as any coquette in her low cut dress and
silk stockings. Or see beauty. Oh yes we can see that all right. We who sit
out the dance of life and watch. We have the best view. That young man, for
instance. The son of our hostess. She's certainly not French for all her
pretentions according to Maman. White as she is, you can always tell or so
she said. Look at the son. And I did. And I saw where nature had served
out the amplest of her gifts. The best of both races. The strength, the height,
the strong cheek bones of the French. The smooth olive skin, the white teeth,
the noble bearing of the arab.*

*We'd met in the hallway before dinner and he'd stood politely as
Uncle Matthiau questionned him in a condescending tone that made me
squirm. Standing in the half light, caught on the last stair, yes, I had time
enough to study him in detail. 'Hussan Sir, my name is Hussan. Yes Sir, I
am to serve in the army.' In fact, he'd be off in a day or so. No, he did not
know the Commandante, not personally, as Uncle Matthiau did. He waited
patiently, as Uncle tried and failed to recall the distant connection - some
chap in his club was it? 'Yes Sir, no not in the ranks. I am to be a
capitaine, in the medical corps.' He was a medical student you see. Uncle
Matthiau mercifully seemed to lose interest on hearing this.*

*Our eyes met briefly as I passed by into the dining room, where the
table was laid with its white cloth and best porcelain, ready for us. I tried to
signal a silent apology. But my eyes were met by a twinkle of amusement.
He had met Uncle's type before. Well, of course he had. They were two for
a sou in Oran.*

*We'd met by chance, the following morning in the souk. For several
days Aunt and I had been bargaining for a carpet. A lovely thing. All
russets and bitter chocolate with a pattern of pure scarlet running through.
I'm afraid we'd made an abysmal failure of the process. Aunt had given up
in disgust saying loud enough for carpet seller to hear that these fellows*

were all rogues anyway.

That morning I'd gone without her, accompanied by Amin - the young servant boy from the pensione, for a last attempt to beat down the carpet seller to a reasonable price. The 'old rogue' greeted me with a sly smile and offered me mint tea. Which I accepted, ignoring the echo of Aunt's voice telling me that it was polluted, drugged, in fact most probably poisoned. In total disregard for my health and wellbeing I seated myself on his low divan and sipped the sweet aromatic tea.

Amin was hovering in the doorway fending off the urchins who always followed in a ragged procession wherever we went. We were just getting down to the business of the carpet when a shadow appeared beside him.

Someone was talking jokingly to the boy. I recognised Hussan's voice and rose to my feet. 'Oh please. Monsieur. If you have a moment. Could you help me? I'm trying to buy a carpet and I can't seem to get a straight answer about how much I should pay.'

But of course it would be no problem. More tea was made and a muted conversation started up in their softly spoken dialect. Without me noticing that negotiations had even taken place the carpet was secured at less than half the price I had been prepared to pay.

I watched as it was reverently wrapped in brown paper, hoping that I hadn't done the poor man down. He no doubt had a family to keep. But he was all politeness. The frowns and disgust at the paltry price I had been offering, forgotten. Smiles appeared on the old rogue's face, like sun after rain, now the bargaining was concluded.

Hussan, lifted the carpet over his shoulder and offered to carry it home for me. I was grateful the thing was far too heavy for Amin. He gave the boy a few coins and he ran off in delight with his ragged following of beggars. His playmates.

'Please tell me, what's the secret? How do you bargain with such ease?'

'It helps if you know what the price should be.'

'Of course. But even so, it's so complicated. I seemed to be insulting the man with my offers.'

'Not at all. That is all part of the play-acting. You too, you must act *as if you are incensed by his demands.'*

He then explained the bargaining process of offering and halving until at last a price is reached to which both parties are happy to agree. It all seemed quite logical the way he explained it.

'I suppose it would help if I could speak the language. Your French, by the way, is excellent,' I commented.

'That's perhaps because I am French,' he replied.

I felt myself blush scarlet at the faux-pas. 'I'm sorry. But of course...'

'No please. It is understandable. My father was from Oran. But I was born in France and educated there. That is where I took my diplome, in Paris. But I felt that doctors were needed more here. So I have returned to live here with my Aunt.'

'Oh I thought she was your mother.'

'No she's my father's sister. My mother was French. I never knew her. She died when I was born.'

'I'm sorry.'

We fell silent. As we came within sight of the Pensione I noticed Hussan dropped a step or so behind. 'You go on ahead. I'll follow with the carpet. I'll have it sent up to your room.'

I paused and let him catch me up. 'Thank you so much for your help.'

'It was nothing.' He looked uneasily towards the Pensione.

Maman had emerged in the doorway. She was shading her eyes and staring in our direction. 'Marie? Is that you dear? You shouldn't be out in the sun like that. It's quite hot already,' she said, ignored Hussan totally.

'Oh dear. I'm so sorry...'

'Mademoiselle Marie,' he cut in. 'You must stop being sorry. It is getting a little tedious.'

'I'm sorry .. Oh dear.. Sorry.' He'd made me laugh.

-------- -- -------

He used to seek me out after that. Find me where I was sketching. And we'd chat about Paris. I felt a strange affinity. He reminded me of father somehow. A medical student. But interested in everything. I described to

229

him my own pathetic attempts to help father with his research. I told him about father's unfinished discours and how I'd tried to put the papers together. But the chemistry you see was beyond me. He said if he could, he'd be delighted to help. I could always write, send copies of the relevant pages. It would be nice to have someone to write to him while he was in the army. 'I mean a lady of course,' he'd added. I smiled at the old fashioned way he said it. And I couldn't help feeling... No I was imagining it. But the way he looked at me. I was flattered that he wanted me to write to him of course. He was younger than me. A good seven years I'd say. But I suppose I was nearer his age than anyone else in the village. The boys were all off in the army and the local girls were cloistered away, under house guard, forbidden to meet the eyes yet alone speak to a male outside their immediate family. That's what it was of course. That's what mother would have said. He was simply starved of female companionship and I was there. But still...

-------- -- -------

Hussan would be gone tomorrow. This was his last day. If I was being totally honest with myself, this was the reason I'd stayed back. I wanted somehow to make up. To make up for what? The way my family treated him? The way we'd taken over his homeland? The way he looked at me. As if his soul was trying to speak to me. Through it all. Through the muddle of it all. And he'd be gone tomorrow to the frontier. And I'd never get another chance.

The sun was sinking now. I climbed from the bed and rang for fresh water. The servant girl brought up a jug, scented faintly of rose water and a soft clean linen towel. I ran the water down my neck and over my body, it was sensuous and cool. I wasn't womanly like Louise. I had the thin taut body of my father. I felt supremely conscious of it at that moment. All of my body. I hurriedly buttoned my corset up to my breasts... Which felt sinfully conscious. I had hoped that maybe Hussan might have been around at lunch time so that I could say goodbye then. But of course he would have a lot to do on his last day. But he might be downstairs now.

I finished dressing and gathered up my painting materials. Downstairs the hall was dark and silent. No-one about. I peeped into the proprietress's drawing room. A leather suitcase stood strapped and ready to leave on the floor. His suitcase. Little Amin was lazing on the doorstep but there was no sign of Hussan. Swallowing my disappointment, I called to Amin. I decided to spend the last few hours of the day at the edge of the village, where I'd been working on my watercolour.

For several days now I'd been trying to catch this odd effect of palms set against an oasis. Seen against the hot white of the desert the trunks looked jet black, but where they crossed the dark water my eye told me they were white. And yet they were the same trees. Follow the trunks up with your eye and the colour didn't vary from the roots to the foliage. It was the strangest illusion and almost impossible to capture.

Each day, as instructed, I'd taken Amin with me for protection. He'd sleep to while the time away. Or come and stand behind me watching this odd useless activity. Today his little friends had followed us and I left them playing some game with stones in the sand a little way off.

I set to work, mixing washes in the little dippers. The light was different today, sultry. The brightness of the desert was somehow dimmed, greyish. And although the sun was slipping down towards the horizon the heat was still stifling. There was a heaviness in the air that was quite unlike the other days. Normally, at this time of day, a gentle breeze would send a nervous rustling through the trees bringing with it a welcome coolness off the water.

I wondered where Hussan might be. He would be saying goodbye to his friends no doubt. Perhaps, after all, he would have time to take a last walk around the village before he left. I felt myself flush hotly at the thought of that. Truly, I was making a fool of myself. I hoped he'd be gone by the time I returned to the pensione. Yet I longed to hear the sound of his footsteps approaching.

I paused and glanced over at the boys. They seemed to be arguing with Amin. They kept trying to drag him off with them. He took a few steps towards me and signalled that we should go back to the village. I shook my head. Knowing them, I was going to be tagged along to some uncle or cousin who would try and sell me something: brassware or trinkets or suchlike. It had happened before.

Amin became more insistent. But I was adamant. I still had a lot more work to do on the painting. I wanted to catch this odd effect of the light while it lasted. And it was still possible that Hussan would appear. I was annoyed that the boys should try to interrupt my work.

'Come soon,' I said looking in my purse. As luck would have it I only had a note. Far more than the boy deserved. 'You go,' I gestured to the village. 'I come soon.'

Amin looked at the money in his hand and hesitated. Just at that moment one of the bigger boys came up behind him and grabbed the note. He was off with it before Amin could turn round. Suddenly they were all off in a shouting troupe after the big boy. Amin fastest of all. He'd practically caught the boy when unaccountably he stopped and hesitated at the turn in the road. Then he was gone.

I turned my attention back to the painting. Peace at last. My palm trees had fallen back to a greyish colour as they'd dried. They needed a brighter shade. But my rinsing water had become muddied and I was having real difficulty with the white. I scolded myself for not bringing enough water with me. But there was the oasis not far off. I could refill my jar there.

I left my easel and made my way over the rocky ground towards the oasis. It was much further than it had seemed and off the path the going was difficult. I nearly twisted my ankle on a boulder that shifted beneath me.

As I straightened up I was caught full in the face by a blast of hot air. Sand stung my eyes. The trees were bending in the wind and the oasis had disappeared in a grey mist. I felt cold with fear. That was what Amin had been going on about. A sand storm.

I turned back to my easel and saw it being tossed away like matchwood. The air was filled with a howling and screaming. I staggered against the force of the wind. The bare bit of my neck was stinging with the sand blasted against me.

A stumbled half blown, half falling towards the village. Grit filled my mouth and eyes and any bare skin felt as if I was being flayed alive.

I knew I had to find shelter. But I could hardly see my hand before my eyes. Panic was rising in my throat. I could be buried alive out here. Suddenly through the greyness I dimly discerned a figure ahead of me. A man wrapped in Arab clothing, covered entirely even his face. He was forcing his way against the wind towards me. Within minutes strong hands were gripping me round the waist and I was being half carried, half dragged along. It was some horrible creature from the bazaar, taking advantage of the moment. I tried to scream but no sound came. Everything went dark.

As I came back fully to conciousness I found I was out of the wind. Someone was wiping the sand from my face. The cloth was cool and damp. 'Please speak to me. Mademoiselle Marie.' Flooded with relief, I recognised Hussan's voice.

I tried to rise. 'Oh thank god it's you. Where are we?'

'In the little chapel on the edge of the village. I'm sorry, we must stay here till the storm passes over. Are you injured?'

'No, I don't think so. There's sand in my mouth. I'm thirsty.'

'I've brought water.'

I rinsed my mouth and wiped the grit away with my hand. Then drank a long cool draught. 'How did you know I was here...'

'Amin told me...'

'I feel so stupid. I didn't understand...'

'These storms can be very sudden.'

I realised we were practically shouting. The wind was screaming through the tiles above our heads.

'How long will it last...?'

'I don't know. Maybe all night.'

By the last of the light I could just make out his face outlined against a little arched window. It was a compromising situation. I could see he was embarrassed. 'I could try and make my way back to the village,' he started.

'No. Please stay. I don't want to be left here alone.'

He fell silent. The silence lay between us like an impasse.

And not only the silence. In the silence, there was also mother with her crucifix, a thousand Hail Mary's from the sisters of the convent, all the pious texts of Mademoiselle.

And yet there was something else. A voice in the silence. Father's voice. 'Live Marie. Live for me. Take life with both hands. For its span is so short.' Which brought with it a different set of values. Which every nerve in my body was ready to uphold. For nature has a duty to take the best and make it its own. And nature was quickly backed by the voice of reason. For listen Marie, here is a young man who is about to fight for your country. He may never come back. And poor Marie, life will not present you with this choice again.

'I'm cold. Please come closer,' I whispered.
Despite the howling of the wind he heard me.

-------- -- -------

Julia 2009

I put the sketchbook to one side and went back to Marie's novel.

I turned to the pages that were set in Algeria and read on late into the night. It was a sad tale. One passage in particular really got to me. It was about the birth of Marie-Jeanne's child.

"She lay in a simple room of white-washed plaster, decorated by a rose-coloured frieze, her child in her arms. Outside, the winds rattled the dry palm fronds and breathed heat into the room bringing no comfort to her fevered brow."

Marie-Jeanne gradually faded in Marie's words: '*like a tender flower transported to a foreign land*' and she eventually died.

I couldn't get the passage out of my mind. I could almost see it. A room bathed in light, rough lime-washed walls with that repeat pattern of dusty pink stencil. Long windows opening on to a vaulted gallery. Down below a courtyard garden where waving palms surrounded a white domed chapel. The sound of the hurried footsteps of the nuns in their high coifs as they made their way back and forth across the gravelled paths...

Chapter Forty Three

Marie Lamulatiere 1905

'I lie in a simple room of white-washed plaster, decorated by a rose-coloured frieze, the child in my arms. I watch the filmy net around me as it lifts and falls, lifts and falls on a breeze so impossibly light it seems to be hanging on a breath.

Human flash cannot bear such happiness. Or such sadness. I see everything through a white film. Both actually and metaphorically. As if through... What is that phrase? Yes, a veil of tears. They bring the child to me at intervals to be fed. And I can only marvel at his beauty. Father was wrong you know. I am Mary and this is Mary's child. It's a miracle, you see, Hussan come back to life again. He's raised from the dead. This child is his flesh and blood. I told this to the Reverent Mother and she told me to hush, to sleep. She said they were praying for me. They think I'm going insane. They gave me ether at the birth. They said it would send me to sleep. But it made me see things more clearly. That's what they don't understand.

They brought me a Bible and said the rosary around my bed. I've been reading it. The Annunciation in the gospel of Saint Peter. I saw the painting by Botticelli. The light in that room is just like this room. 'And a sword shall pierce thy side also'. That's what the angel said to Mary. The angel foretold what Mary would suffer. What I must suffer. What it is to have and to lose a child. For I must give him up. I've known that from the beginning. The arrangement has already been made. As soon as I am strong enough to travel he will go to Hussan's aunt at the Pensione.

I have to get up the strength to write to Louise. We have an arrangement. My official letters arrive weekly at La Mulatière. Robust fictions of my daily life in Biskra. The sketching and watercolours, the comings and goings of the Pensione. The others, with the true account of my life are held for her Post Restante at Moulins, under an assumed name of course. This deception is to protect Maman. For as Louise said, the truth would surely kill her.

I wouldn't have burdened Louise with 'my little problem' had she not found me that day, cold as ice, paralysed in my chair, the packet lying open in my lap.

They returned his letters you see. They had been directed on my instruction to Chapeau Blanc. Louise had brought them with her that morning on her daily visit. 'There's a packet for you!' she said with that whimsical smile of hers. 'From Oran. A fat packet.'

I had run down the final stairs and snatched it up. Louise and I exchanged a conspiratorial glance as I took it to my room.

For days afterwards I laboured under the cruel illusion that had I not opened the packet none of it would have been true. Or at any rate as long as the packet was unopened, I would have been immune to the pain.

But I did open it. I examined it first hungrily. Noting curiously, it was not addressed in his handwriting. But then it was as Louise said - a fat packet. I could feel several letters inside. A rush of excitement ran through my body. These must have been collected up, or held back by the censor maybe. At any rate for some official army reason they had been packed together and forwarded to me. Perhaps some penny-pinching military economy.

I turned the envelope over. It bore indeed a return address in official print to the Military H.Q. in Oran.

My shaking fingers slit the envelope open, unevenly, spoiling it. I held back for a second waiting to savour the joy of opening the first letter...

But what was this? These were my own letters returned. Sour bile filled my mouth. He had sent back my letters. He didn't want me. I hadn't understood. Our nationalities, religions, age, colour even... Or another woman maybe, younger, more beautiful...

But there was a further official typed letter with them. I forced my shaking fingers to open it. It bore a military crest.

Mademoiselle,

We regret to inform you that Capitaine Hurak Hussan, hero of the army of garnison, has been killed in an ambush...

It was several days before I could bring myself to finish reading the letter.
Louise had come knocking on the door and when I didn't answer she let
herself in.

One glance told her all was not well. She took the letter from my
hands and then throwing her arms around me she shed the tears that were
held trapped dry in my eyes.

'But you see. It's worse than that, my dear,' I said gently holding her
back

'How could anything be worse? Oh my poor dear Marie.'

'No listen. I must tell you now while I have the strength. You see, I
have to return to Algeria.'

'Oh yes, for the funeral?'

'No. No. Listen, I went to see Doctor Gonville yesterday. He
confirmed what I have been suspecting for some time now.'

'Oh my dearest, your lungs. They're not worse?'

I shook my head and even managed to force a smile. 'For the sake of
Maman, yes. I need to go back to Biskra for my health.'

'Oh Marie... But you've hardly been coughing at all recently...'

'You don't understand... I'm perfectly healthy. Louise listen. I am
bearing his child.'

I could hardly describe the look of horror and disbelief that came into
Louise's face. I think, frankly she might have been less distressed if I'd told
her I was mortally ill. I'd always had a weakness of the lungs like father.

'Oh Marie.'

'I'm sorry to shock you Louise. But it's a fact and it must be faced.'

'But Marie, we can't tell Maman.'

'Of course we can't. That's why I'll have to go away. And soon. Or
it will become all too apparant without me having to tell anyone.'

'How long..?'

'Doctor Lapalisse thinks about three months, maybe four. By my
calculations it must be four months.'

'But surely he'll tell Maman.'

She looked at the door as if she feared Maman could hear our
whispered voices through it.

'He won't. He can't. Doctors are sworn to secrecy.'

Louise had risen and was staring out of the window with her back to me. She said in a faltering voice: 'Marie, listen I have heard of doctors in Paris...'

'Don't...'

'No, but Marie, you cannot have this child. Imagine the scandal...'

'How could you want me to kill his child? And especially now. Besides that is a mortal sin. What would Maman say to that?'

'But what will you do?'

'I will have the child in Biskra. And then he can be adopted. I'll find some good family out there. I can support him you see.'

Him? Yes, I knew the child would be a boy. The same dusky skin. The same dark eyes, like windows to his soul. I shed a few tears at that thought.

It is evening now and the rains have ceased, already the Saharan spring has begun. I sit at the other window overlooking the street, rocking the child in my arms. Down below are the undulating trees of the park. The gas lamps are shining strangely through their leaves. Illuminating the trees with a subtle phosphorescent glow in the calm moonless night.

I'd like to explain to the child staring up at me with his bright knowing eyes. I can't be a mother to him. But I shall see that he will never go without. I will find him a loving family, another mother will take my place. And not a day shall pass when he shall not be remembered in my prayers. For my duty is clear. I have sinned and this is my penitence. Marie, poor Marie, poor good Marie must return to her own country and take up her old life, as if this child had never existed.

-------- -- -------

Chapter Forty Four

Julia 2009

Marie's story seemed to have set a kind of gloom on the house. Winter was drawing in. As the sun grew lower in the sky and the nights lengthened, the house took on a dusky stillness. Down in Deneville the supermarket was selling bright pots of fat-budded chrysanths in preparation for All Souls Day - the day of the dead. I bought a pot of white ones and stood them in the hallway trying to bring touch of brightness back into the house. They were now opening in snowy profusion, much to the clucking disapproval of Jacqueline.

'It's bad luck. Tempting fate,' she said, shaking her duster forcefully out of the window.

'Rubbish. There's no such thing as luck.'

'Huh,' was her only reply.

'Listen. What's that noise?'

There was a strange burbling sound overhead. It was coming closer. I shaded my eyes against the sun and caught my breath. They were strung out - a ragged arrow against the watery sky - hundreds of them, a seemingly endless stream of birds - stretching wider and wider - their wings beating in an effortless rhythm.

'Cranes,' said Jacqueline in her habitual pessimistic tone. 'They know when winter's on the way.'

I went out through the front door to watch and stayed until the last stragglers shrank to specks against the blue. They were heading south, to Africa, to warm marshes, mud oozing juicy prey, sunshine. I wrapped my sweater closer round me.

During the days that followed, long straggling arrows of cranes crossed the sky at regular intervals. It seemed La Mulatière was on the main crane flightpath south. But the birds knew what they were about. The maple at the far end of the lawn had turned from green to peachy pink and the horse chestnuts were shedding their russet leaves.

Now as the cold weather truly got a grip and temperatures dipped below freezing I started to worry about the heating situation.

My stove burned wood at an alarming rate. I tried to eke out my store of decent sized logs. But eventually I was left with a pile of branches too long to fit in the fireplace let alone the wood burning stove.

As the flames in the stove died to a flicker, I shoved in one of the oversized branches, leaving the door open, in the hope that it would burn down to a suitable length. The kitchen soon filled with choking smoke and I dragged the burning branch out into the courtyard where it lay smouldering through the night like an evil red eye in the darkness.

The next day I drove into Deneville and paid a visit to Antoine. He was all smiles as he described the various merits of his rack of gleaming orange chain saws. On his advice I selected one of the smaller models and he gave me a demonstration of how the thing worked. All very simple. Just a matter of giving a good yank on a cable and it responded with a convincingly vicious snarl. 'Goes through wood like butter', said Antoine reaching for his receipt book. Once I'd handed over the cheque he popped the saw in the boot of the car for me, giving the boot a good slap as he closed it and shaking me by the hand.

Back home, I lugged the saw to the woodpile. Thank god I'd taken his advice on the size, I could barely lift it. Probably because it was full of petrol. No doubt it would get lighter as I sawed.

I gave a good tug on the cable. The saw gently hiccougghed. I put it down on the ground and tugged harder. The sound produced this time was more of a purr than growl. Anger added strength to my arm as I tugged with all the force in my body. I was rewarded with a three second 'grrrrrh' which slowly died into silence.

I was about to resort to kicking the damn thing when I heard a movement from behind the hedge. Jacques was standing watching me. I took a deep breath and had another try.

'You're flooding it,' his voice called over.

I yanked again. The chainsaw responded with merely a hiccough. Sweat was running down my face and tears of anger smarted in my eyes.

All of a sudden strong hands took the chainsaw from me. I stood well clear and watched as Jacques shook the thing and twisted a little dial. He gave a nice sharp professional pull and the chainsaw obediently came out with a proper aggressive snarling noise. Within minutes a pile of nice even-sized logs lay at his feet.

'I guess it's a knack,' I said.

'It's got a choke, like a car. Look... here.'

I took half a step forward and looked. A choke was something I remembered from the dim dark history of Dad's cars.

'Do you want the whole pile done?' Jacques asked gruffly.

'I don't know why you should.'

'Nor do I. You make us some coffee, I'll be round in a minute.'

I put the coffee pot on and set out cups and sugar cubes. At last the whine and snarl of the chainsaw stopped and Jacques came to the kitchen door.

'Where do you want the wood stacked? It needs to go somewhere dry.'

'This is really good of you,' I said. 'Especially when you must be so ...busy.'

'Busy?'

'What with your friend staying...and'

'What friend?'

'Oh come off it Jacques. Her car's in your garage.'

'That's my car.'

'But I saw someone...'

'She came back,' he said. 'She came back for those things you saw in the cupboard.'

I stared hard at him and he met my gaze without flinching. So he'd known I'd known about the clothes in the cupboard all along.

'An old friend,' he said gently taking a step towards me. 'It didn't mean anything.' He was intentionally using the same words, I'd used about Oliver.

'So she's not there now?'

'She brought my car back.'

'Why?'

'It had failed its Controle Technique.' I caught a twinkle in his eye. The bastard, he was teasing me.

'And she's not coming back?'

'Julia…'

I guess it was from the strain and and everything but I suddenly burst into tears.

'Come here,' he said putting his arms around me and pulling me close. He whispered in my ear. 'Why don't we start again where we left off?'

I buried my head in his shoulder, crying muffled tears of relief.

'I can't remember where that was.'

'Well I think it was something like this.' He kissed me deeply and meaningfully.

I shook my head. I was laughing with relief now. It was all going to be all right.

'No, I think it was more like this.' I kissed him back.

'No, that's not right. I think you were more sort of horizontal.'

He was backing me out of the room. Suddenly he swept me up in his arms and carried me up the stairs. Up that wonderful sweep of oak stairs and into the bedroom. We fell in a heap on the bed.

Chapter Forty Five

As winter drew on, we shut ourselves away, enjoying the life as a couple that had been denied us for so long. Nobody saw us. Nobody knew. Hidden away as La Mulatière was, no-one was conscious of who was sleeping where. Jerôme had ceased gardening because of the weather and Jacqueline was taking a well-earned break. I avoided telling either Jane or Sarah, as I could imagine their response. What business was it of theirs anyway?

We were great in bed. Better than with Oliver even when things had been going well. Jacques had woken a sensuality in me I'd never known existed. I couldn't get enough of sex. It was as if I'd become addicted.

But I was worried about tying Jacques down to a permanent relationship. He might want children one day. He could easily marry a younger woman - have a family of his own.

One evening, when we were sitting in the cosy gloom of the small dining room lit only by the dancing flames of a roaring fire, I decided to tackle the subject.

'Jacques listen. There's something I think you should know.'

'Uh huh? What's brought this on?'

'The thing is - don't you want children some time?'

'Children? Maybe... some day.'

'I just thought I ought to tell you. I can't...'

'Can't what?'

'Conceive.'

'Can't? Why not?'

'Oh long story - an ectopic pregnancy - then everything went wrong.'

'Do you mind?'

'Terribly. I'd love children. But I have my nieces and nephews.'

'They're a long way away.'

'Yes.'

We were silent for a while.

'But for all I know you have a child already...' I said trying to make my voice sound casual.

'What makes you say that? Tell me.'

'It's just something Jacqueline said..'

'That woman she should keep her gossip to herself.'

'I'm sure she didn't mean any harm. She said she was very fond of you. You were at school together.'

Jacques face had clouded over. 'What exactly did she say?

'She said she thought Kattie was pregnant.'

'Huh,' he snorted. 'She killed my child.'

'Killed it?'

'Aborted it.'

'So you wanted the child?'

'Of course I wanted the child. She was the one who wanted to get rid of it. I tried to reason with her, stop her doing it. I even locked her in for godsake. But she was determined, like a cat on heat. She was going to get rid of that child no matter what.'

'But surely she had the right....

'Julia, you don't understand.'

'No Jacques I do. I want a child more than anything. But not everyone is the same. It has to be a woman's free choice.' A big lump had come into my throat. 'Oh why is life so unfair?'

Jacques had put his arms around me and I could feel his chest heaving. Suddenly I realised this great beast of a man was crying.

'Won't you tell me about it?' I whispered into his neck.

He took a deep breath and composed himself.

'She was beautiful, in a wild way. She had this laugh deep and throaty. She was slender like you. That day. That day I saw you stabbing away at the vegetable garden. For a moment I thought it was Kattie come back.'

'I wondered why you looked at me in that odd way.'

'Thank god it wasn't. She was no good. Bad through and through.'

'No-one's really all bad surely?'

'She tricked me. She said she'd changed her mind about the abortion, that she'd have the child. I believed her. Then one morning I found the car gone and all the money we'd been saving up gone too. I rang round all the clinics in the area and then at last I located her. She was in a small private place in Montluçon. It was too late. They said it "Had all gone well" but they were glad I'd called because they didn't like to let their patients out without someone to keep an eye on them. I said I'd pick her up the next day. I borrowed my father's car and went to the address they'd given. A woman in a white coat opened the door. She said Kattie's 'husband' had come to pick her up an hour ago.'

'Her husband?'

It seemed I was just a romantic interlude. She had gone back to her previous 'copain'. The brutal bastard she'd walked out on when she turned up in Deneville.'

'So that was the end of it?'

'I searched the area, spent days asking around in Moulins, Montluçon, St Amand. I tried the labour exchanges to see if she'd signed on. No-one had ever heard of her. She must have been using a false name. I'd never seen her papers or a driver's licence. In fact I had no idea who she was. At first I thought I saw her everywhere. I'd follow a slender figure along a street and be just about to catch up when she'd turn and I'd find it was some stranger. That's why I went abroad. I wanted to get as far away as I could. I couldn't stand it any longer.'

I slid my hand into his

'I'm sorry,' I said.

'But you've helped Julia,' he said. 'It's the first time I've really felt that Kattie had been… ' he paused searching for a word.

'Exorcised?'

'Exactly.'

Chapter Forty Six

Gradually, I was getting to know all the facets of Jacques. He had a gentle side I hadn't expected. I found him one day fashioning a splint out of a tooth pick and super glue. A baby owlet that had fallen from its nest and broken its leg and he was delicately setting the bone. The little creature joined our menage, suspended in a basket in the kitchen and grew at a staggering pace, fed on as many worms as we could supply from the garden. By the time it had moved on to minced steak, it had started to take its virgin flights.

I experienced the tricky side of him too. An invitation arrived from Maitre Bertrand's wife Hortense, for 'a little dinner' as she put it. After some soul-searching I decided that this might be the ideal way to introduce our relationship to the neighbourhood.

I thought I'd better ring Hortense first to check if it would be all right to bring someone.

'But of course you can,' she said immediately. 'How nice. Do I know him? There will be quite a number of us. I'm doing place cards, so I'll need his name.'

I paused. This was going to be a formal dinner. Not quite what I'd expected.

'Yes, well I mean of course you must know him. It's my neighbour - Jacques Ladier.'

There was the briefest hesitation the other end of the line. Then Hortense continued in a slightly flustered tone: 'Oh right. Of course. I had no idea you knew him so well.'

I felt embarrassed. I could tell from Hortense's tone of voice that here, in feudal France, where attitudes were as backward as turn of the century Britain, I was upsetting her little soirée with what she would consider my 'unsuitable' companion. But bother her. Bother the bourgeoisie. For the first time since coming to France, I felt at odds with the French.

The next problem was Jacques.

'Guess what. We've been invited to dinner,' I said as casually as I could.

'We?' said Jacques. He pointed out that nobody knew we were an item.

'Well, it was me who was invited. But I asked Hortense if I could bring you. And she was really delighted,' I said staring into the sink so he couldn't see my face.

'Anyone else going to be there?'

'Probably. I should think so.'

'A load of those stuffy bourgeois, I suppose?'

'Not necessarily.'

'No Julia, you go. It wouldn't be my kind of thing.'

'I won't go without you,'

'Don't go then.'

'Jacques. We've got to be seen as a couple some time.'

'It's nothing to do with anyone.'

'I know it's not but...'

'Julia you don't understand. Those people... They wouldn't be comfortable with me there. In their eyes I'm just a poor farmer. I haven't got enough land to make me – respectable.'

'God, I don't believe this country! You're so narrow-minded,' I was raising my voice now.

'You don't understand because you're so fucking English,' he flung back at me.

'Well thank god for that. At least I can treat people as people.'

'It must be nice being so broad-minded.'

'But it's you who's being narrow minded.'

'I'm not going and that's the end of it,' he flung over his shoulder as he strode out of the door.

I went straight to the phone and rang Hortense to put her out of her misery. I'd come on my own - Jacques had a previous engagement he hadn't told me about.

------- -- -------

It was a pretty grisly dinner. There was no-one under fifty and the conversation dwelt exclusively on hunting, golf and bridge, to which I could contribute nothing. The dining room was large and formal hung with tapestries and various hunting trophies. As the dishes rotated in solemn order of ascendance, the heads of various decapitated animals surveyed us dismally. I left as early as was politely possible and made my way home.

Jacques was still in a strop and was sleeping at his place that night. I could see his light was still on, shining through the hedge. Slipping on a bathrobe, I climbed through the hedge and went to join him in his bed.

'Good dinner?' he asked.

'You're right. You'd've hated it.'

He threw an arm over me. 'The discreet charm of the bourgeoisie,' he murmured.

I snuggled up to him. 'Sorry.'

'Serves you right,' he said.

------- -- -------

Next day I woke early and lay watching Jacques as he slept. He had one arm slung over the side of the bed. The morning sun was flooding over him turning his dark olive skin a wonderful golden colour. Reminding me of that picture of Samson, who was it by? Raphael? His body spent from toil, stretched out across Delilah.

I found I was smiling. It had happened so slowly. But I realised I loved this man. Not with the anxious, self-doubting possessive love that I'd had for Oliver. Or thought I'd had. No, this was something deeper and a lot less dramatic. It was as if I'd moved out of the shade into deep all-embracing sunlight. I felt bathed in love, buoyed up by it, safe.

He woke and caught me watching him.

'Ummm?'

'You reminded me of a picture.'

'Oh?'

'Umm, of Samson, it's in the National Gallery in London.'

'I hope you're not thinking of cutting my hair off.'

'I might give you a decent shave.'

'And sap my strength? No way.'

'It tickles.'

'Could be to your advantage.'

'Don't be disgusting.'

'Prude.'

'No, I'm not.'

'Come here, English woman and prove it.'

'Beast,' I whispered in his ear.

'Princess,' he whispered back.

------- -- -------

A month or so later the money came through from the sale of my flat. Maitre Bertrand had been hard at work in the meantime working out the legal side for transferring the shares of La Mulatière from my sisters to me. At last he rang to say that I could come to his office and make the final signature.

He got out his bottle of port and poured us two glasses.

'Tchin Tchin. Congratulations.'

'Well now the property is mine at last, I'm going to make a few changes.'

'Oh?'

'You're not going to like this but I've decided to give the meadows to Jacques Ladier.'

'Give them? Why should you do that?'

'He needs them and I don't.'

Maitre Bertrand frowned. 'It'll mean a lot more legal work.'

'I don't care. It's far too much land for me to cope with and he doesn't have enough.'

Maitre Bertrand had fallen silent. He walked to the window and stared out. 'There's something I think you should know.'

'Yes, tell me.'

'Some months after Marie Lamulatière died, the Ladiers made some ridiculous claim that she had left all her property to them, the farm, the land and the house.'

'The house! La Mulatière! How on earth did they get that idea?'

'Old Ladier, Jacques' father, said there was a will and insisted that Mademoiselle had told him about it. Apparently, Marie Lamulatière travelled a lot. She went frequently to Algeria. She stayed at a little pensione owned by his adoptive mother.'

I stared at him in disbelief: 'Jacques' father was adopted?'

'Apparently. I think related in some way to the woman who ran the Pensione. He claimed that Marie Lamulatière was fond of him as a child. There could well have been some truth in it. An attractive child. An old spinster's fancy - who knows...' He paused. 'He claimed the last time she visited Biskra, Marie told him everything she owned would be left to him.'

My head swam dizzyingly. Jacques father was adopted. What if he was Marie's child?

Hoping for reassurance, I said: 'But surely she would have made a proper will if she wanted to leave everything to the Ladiers.'

'That was the odd part about it. My father said he had been urging Marie to make a will for some time but she kept putting him off. Normally, she was very precise about such things - she liked everything legal, cut and dried. But for some reason she shrank from lodging a testament with my father.'

'He would have been a close friend of the family?' I said.

'Yes indeed.'

'And there was something else that has always struck me as strange...'

He paused and got up from his desk and stared out of the window.

'Her sister Louise wanted to settle out of court. Oh they were a stuffy lot. It was to avoid scandal, or so they said. So they gave the Ladiers the farm and not much land, not enough to make a living anyway.'

------- -- -------

Panic set in as I drove home and the full realisation of what he had said dawned on me. If Jacques' father was Marie's son, the whole property should automatically belong to Jacques.

If anyone knew the truth of the matter it was Bernadette. I drove past La Mulatiere and straight on to Chapeau Blanc. Bernadette, as always, gave me a warm welcome. She made us tiny cups of coffee and carried them into the salon.

I got to the subject straight away. 'Bernadette, Maitre Bertrand told me that Marie Lamulatière never made a will. Is this true?'

Bernadette shook her head. 'No will was ever found, Julia. We can't be sure she never made one.'

'He said that when the Ladier's claimed the land, the family settled out of court. Why should they do that?'

Bernadette frowned. 'It was Louise who made the decision. She survived Marie by a good ten years. Her children made a fuss about it of course. But Louise insisted on her deathbed that the Ladiers should have the farm. It's all rather curious but that's all I can tell you.'

------- -- -------

I drove back to La Mulatière with my mind in a turmoil. Louise must have known about the child, she was the one who had the books destroyed. I remembered that vivid description of the convent. It even said where it was – Biskra. Someone could have gone there and looked up their records.

Louise wanted to save the family from scandal but she also felt she had to abide by Marie's wishes before she died. That's why she insisted they give the farm to the Ladier's.

But what if there had been a will? I suddenly remembered what Jerôme had said. He'd found Jacques in the house - *looking for something*. It must have been the will! Perhaps it was still here - hidden somewhere - in the house. I parked in the drive and sat there frozen with indecision.

There was only one thing to do – ask Jacques.

'I've got to ask you something,' I said when we'd finished dinner that night.

'So? Fire away.'

I took a deep breath. 'Jerôme said... I mean, don't take this the wrong way. But he said he found you in the house once looking for something.'

Jacques frowned and his face clouded over.

I felt my blood running cold: 'Jacques, what were you looking for? Jerôme said you'd let yourself into the house. What was it?'

'Oh that. I'm afraid I must've given the old fellow the shock of his life. He virtually accused me of being a burglar. I wasn't going to give him the satisfaction of telling him what I was doing.'

'What were you doing?'

'I was looking for a cat. A poor one-eyed thing. But she was an ace mouser. Thought she must've got locked in somewhere.'

Relief flooded through me. 'You mean that stripey one is your cat? I thought it was a stray. I've been feeding it.'

'No wonder she didn't come back.'

-------- -- -------

As the weeks went by, the thought of a hidden will haunted me. Surely I'd searched everywhere? There wasn't a corner of the building untouched. I comforted myself with this idea and tried to put it to the back of my mind. But it surfaced a few days later.

Jacqueline was back after her break looking for new challenges in her domestic crusade. She set to polishing the panelling in the Art Nouveau room. I was busy on my laptop when she came to find me in my study.

'Do you have a key to the cupboard over the doorway?' she asked.

'What cupboard?' I asked, my blood running cold.

'Well I doubt if you've ever noticed it. I hadn't myself until I was up the ladder. There's a keyhole, so it must be a door.'

I rose from my desk. There must be a niche beside the chimney, like the one where I'd found the portrait. A hidden cupboard I'd never opened...

'I should give it a clean out. Harbouring spiders and no end of other things I should say,' Jacqueline muttered as I followed her into the room.

'You see up there, there's the key-hole,' Jacqueline was pointing up into a gloomy corner.

I climbed the ladder with a thumping heart. She was right, there was a keyhole, so hidden away you would have mistaken it for a knot in the wood.

'There's that bunch of keys that don't fit anywhere. You should try them, you never know,' said Jacqueline.

'Oh I don't know if it's worth the bother.'

'You stay there. I'll fetch them,' said Jacqueline, piling on the agony.

The keys were fetched. As Jacqueline stood watching, hands on hips, I tried them, one by one in the tiny lock. None fitted.

'Well, there you are,' I said to Jacqueline. 'The key's lost, there's nothing more to be done.'

'You never know what's in there,' said Jacqueline with a disapproving sniff. She took over the ladder and gave the panel a good hard polishing.

------- -- -------

Of course I couldn't forget about it. Whenever I entered the room my eye was drawn to the keyhole. A few nights later I dreamed the cupboard door had fallen open leaving a space large enough to crawl through. On the other side I found a passage that led to further rooms. I wandered down it marvelling that there was so much more of the house. I found myself in a banqueting hall with a long tablesset with candellabras and a hundred place settings. This led into a ballroom - its long windows overlooking the park. Why had I never seen those windows from the outside? And why was there a staircase at the far end of the ballroom? I followed the winding stone steps to yet another floor above. Here was a further passage. Narrow, cold and dark. There were doors I didn't dare to open. There was something inside, something hidden, something I knew about but couldn't remember - horrifying, like a body festering. I woke with with Jacques shaking me, trembling and icy - then as full conciousness returned – relief as I realised it was nothing but a dream.

'Hey there you were having a nightmare.' He put his arms around me.

'It's all right. I'm fine now. Go back to sleep.'

Guilt, that's what it was. There was no way I could go on sleeping in that room without knowing what was inside the cupboard.

As soon as I was up I called M. Chabrier, the menuisier.

'By chance I'm working in your area, I'll drop round at lunchtime if you like.'

At twelve sharp his van drew into the drive.

He examined the lock with a torch. 'I don't think the lock's functioning,' he announced. 'I reckon the panel has been screwed into place. I'll have to go down to the van for some tools.'

I watched as he worked with quiet efficiency. The panel soon came loose and he handed it down to me.

'Is there anything inside?' My voice shook.

He swung his torch around. 'Yes, yes there is something.'

He reached inside and came down with a handful of toy soldiers.

'Is that all?'

'Unless you count spiders' webs.'

They were a lovely little things with a hand-painted faces - made of lead judging by the weight of them. One had lost the top of his musket and the paint was worn away from his boots. A couple of others had lost various limbs. No doubt the battle scars of many happy hours of play.

Chapter Forty Seven

Julia 2010

La Mulatière had been built for children. Matthias had six - two boys and four girls. I remembered the sense I'd had of their presence in the house when I'd first come... bare feet on the warm parquet, running from room to room - the garden bright with their piping voices. This house was a paradise for children, there were trees to climb, grass to play on, the pond to fish in. An echo of Bernadette's voice ran through my head. '*The children can 'do their own thing'up here.*'

Bernadette had adopted children or maybe she'd fostered. I hadn't liked to enquire. And she wasn't married. If Bernadette could have children, why shouldn't I?

The idea kept running obsessively round my mind. I rang her and asked if I could come over, I had something particular on which I needed her advice.

I arrived at Chapeau Blanc to find the front door thrown wide open. Spring was in the air. There was some real heat in the sun.

'Julia, welcome. I've made us tea a l'anglaise and we can have it in the garden,' Bernadette's voice called through to me. She came out carrying a tray.

We sat under the dappled shade of a spreading tree. The air smelt sweet and fresh.

'So what was it you wanted to ask me about?'

I felt it best to come straight to the point.

'Most of the work is finished in the house. Bernadette listen, the place is perfect for children. It needs children. You know I can't have my own. But I want to do what you did. I want your advice on how to adopt. I want to find a child or children who need a home...'

Bernadette's face grew serious.

'Oh Julia, I have to stop you there. I hate to disappoint you. But that will be very difficult...'

'Why? Because I'm English. I'm ready to take citizenship -

anything...'

She shook her head. 'No, it's not that.'

'What then?'

She drew a breath. 'It's because you're single - on your own.'

'But you've brought up your children on your own.'

'It's different for me. I work in the social services, I deal with adoption. This gives me special status. Besides it was easier in the past. Now there are so many regulations to protect children...'

'I don't expect it to be easy.'

'It's impossible,' she said firmly. 'I wish it wasn't the case,' she added catching sight of my expression. 'There are so many children who need good homes. But you have to face facts.'

'What if I apply anyway?'

'There's no point. I wish I could do something to help you. But unless you have a man in your life. Or a partner at least. It's impossible.'

'I see.'

Bernadette could sense how disappointed I was. She lent over and patted my hand. 'But you're young, you'll find someone. Maybe there's someone already.'

I stared at Bernadette. I hadn't told her about Jacques. I didn't know how she would take it. I didn't want a repeat of the Hortense Bertrand experience.

'What about fostering - masses of people foster round here?'

'Julia, they're all married or in couples at least.'

She was adamant about it. There was no way I could get round the regulations. We talked of other things but my mind kept going back to the subject.

That evening I Googled adoption societies on the internet. It seemed Bernadette was right. I looked into adopting from the Third World which was even more difficult and took forever. Fostering was the same. Society after society. Catholic, Anglican, Non-denominational, they all came up with the same answer. I needed to have a partner.

Chapter Forty Eight

Julia 2010

As the weeks went by, it seemed idiotic for Jacques and I to be running two separate homes. We ate together, we slept together. In everything but name we were a couple. Gradually thoughts about adopting or fostering reasserted themselves. Now I had a man in my life it was a real possibility. We'd need to make our relationship more official of course. But it all made sense. If Jacques moved in properly, we'd be better off. We could rent out the farmhouse - do it up as a gîte or something. Several times it was on the tip of my tongue to suggest it. But my experience with Oliver had told me not to take the initiative. So I held off, hoping the suggestion would come from him.

Meanwhile, I made enquiries at the fostering section of the Departmental Social Services and tried to arrange an appointment with them. They pointed out that they couldn't even start the discussion unless they had a joint decision with my 'partner' We didn't actually have to be married of course. Jacques had made it pretty clear that he didn't believe in marriage – '*that outmoded bourgeois institution*' as he called it.

The silly thing was, that if we married, everything I owned would automatically become his. Well, ours if you like and there would be no legal costs or anything. The horrible lurking dread I had, that the house, the land, the farm *everything* might really be Jacques' by rights, would wouldgo away. Marriage would solve everything. Why did he have to be so bloody awkward? A marriage certificate was only a piece of paper for godsake.

I fantas, sized about what it would be like if we did marry. How we would uproot the hedge, turn that beastly car of his out of the chapel. For a blissful moment I had a hazy vision of us being married in the chapel – the place all cleaned out and whitewashed, the faded tiles strewn with lavendar filling the place with its aroma as it was crushed underfoot... the congregation seated on straw bales...

------- -- -------

Once the idea had lodged in my mind I couldn't shift it. I thought around it every way imaginable but marriage seemed the ideal solution. I really should pluck up the courage and take the initiative. But one thing was holding me back. I couldn't marry Jacques until I'd come clean about the whole Lamulatière business - about Marie's child. I'd avoided telling him up to now, put it to the back of my mind. After all, it was only a theory. He'd probably laugh it off. But I wouldn't feel right until I'd told him.

A few days later, I decided to have dinner in the courtyard. It was going to be a blissful evening, warm enough to eat outside in the sheltered part of the courtyard. I'd make a meal that was disaster-proof and hope this would provide the right setting for my 'proposal'. But I'd tell him my theory first. When we were both in a relaxed and happy mood hopefully the solution of us getting married might even occur to him.

Jacques arrived late in his work clothes. He took a look at the table. I'd added a vase of the first primroses.

'Ah ha,' he said taking his boots off.

'I thought I'd make a special effort.'

'Oh?'

'Well, it's the first evening it's been really warm.'

'I'd better take a shower first.'

'I'll bring you up a glass of something.'

'A glass of red would be fine.'

We'd reached the cheese before I plucked up the courage to broach the subject.

'So? Why am I being spoiled like this? Out with it?' he asked.

'Jacques, I had another talk with the Social Services today. They want to come and see the house.'

'Ah huh?'

'And I thought... It would be nice if you could be there too.'

He was silent for a moment.

'I mean, I don't really have a chance of fostering on my own. It doesn't help, me being English. But of course, the major problem is that I'm single.'

'You mean, it would be easier if you were married?'

'Yes of course. A lot easier.' Maybe this was going to be less difficult than I thought.

Jacques stared into his wine.

'Got anyone in mind?'

'Maybe.'

'Is this a proposal?'

'Yes, I suppose it is. Of a kind.'

The silence in the air was almost palpable. A couple of swallows wheeled into the courtyard, their cries shrill in the night air. Everything was about to be become perfect.

'Listen Jacques, I'm not asking you to do anything more than sign a piece of paper. We're practically living together anyway... And it would sort out all the muddle with the land.... I was gabbling, in my excitement. 'Look, don't say one more word. I have to show you something first.'

I ran into the kitchen and fetched the family tree. I spread it out on the table.

'What's all this?'

'Listen, you're going to think I'm crazy - but you know I've been doing all this research into the history of the house...'

'What's that got to do with anything?'

'Wait, you'll see...' I pushed the family tree towards him. 'You see here... this woman Marie Lamulatière... she died without children so the property went to her nephews and nieces.'

'Rightly so, since they were her closest relations.'

'Jacques, your father was adopted, wasn't he?'

'Yes, in Algeria...'

'Have you ever seen his birth certificate?'

'Hardly, they were lucky to get out of the place in the clothes they stood up in. There was civil war on.'

'Why do you think the Lamulatières gave your father the farm?'

He shrugged. 'Mademoiselle Lamulatière took a liking to my father when he was a child. She didn't have any of her own.'

I took a deep breath. 'I think she did. An illegitimate child...'

Jacques stared at me as the meaning of what I was saying slowly dawned on him.

'What the old spinster who lived here?'

'She wasn't simply an old spinster. She was a writer. She was highly intelligent, way ahead of her time. She spent a lot of time in Algeria. At the pensione of the woman who adopted your father...'

'How do you know all this?'

'Well, I only know some of it. The fact that she had an illegitimate child is something I guessed from her book...'

'So it's some kind of wild guess..?'

'Well no. I really believe it's true..'

Jacques frowned. His expression had changed. 'How long have you believed this?'

' I don't know, a month, maybe two.'

'And you've never said anything?'

'Well no, as I said earlier, I couldn't be sure.'

'But you suspected it and you didn't say anything?' His voice had changed. He slopped some more wine into his glass.

'Please Jacques don't be like this. This was meant to be a lovely romantic evening. I wanted it to be special... Listen can't you. I believe a terrible wrong was done to your family. I want to put it right...'

'How? How can you put it right.'

I took a deep breath. 'If we got married, everything would come right. You'd have the house and the land. It would all be yours. No complicated legal business, no court case, nothing...'

'Is this what you've had in mind all along?'

'All along..?'

'All the time you've been having me round here. Sleeping with me, fucking me for godsake?

'No, of course not.'

'You mean, it's only just occurred to you''

'Well yes, in a way.'

'So it's a mere whim?'

'Oh for godsake, I can't be wrong both ways!'

'But you can, Julia. Oh yes you can...' I'd never seen him so angry. I'd seen him red with anger. But this time he was icy pale. Silence fell between us. We stood facing each other across the table. Jacques looked down at the family tree. He started folding it very carefully. He spoke now with a chilling calm. 'But if this terrible wrong, as you call it, was done to my family, I wouldn't need to marry you...'

'What do you mean?'

'These days you can prove these things.'

'How?'

'The old girl's still there in the graveyard for godsake. All we have to do is dig her up!'

I shuddered. A DNA test, it hadn't even occurred to me. Of course he was right. But they'd have to exhume Marie's body....

'But that's gruesome. That's horrible. I don't know how you can say such a thing.'

'Of course it would be much 'simpler' and 'nicer' to get married.'

'Stop it Jacques. My god I think you're drunk.'

But Jacques wasn't listening, he was ranting on, as if to himself.

'You come here. You start digging around, inventing stories, living in some sort of fantasy world in your precious stately home. But you're lacking one vital element – a man... Then I come along. And you think. He's healthy, he's strong. He'll do...'

'No! Can't you see, what I'm trying to say. I love you Jacques. I want to make my life with you. And marriage is a way to give back what your family lost.'

'So you think you can buy me, do you?'

'Jesus, talk about being bloody arrogant!' I was angry now.

'Arrogant?' he shouted.

Tears of desperation flooded into my eyes.

'You're not on love with me Julia. You're in love with a romanticised ideal. The house, the gardens, the children. You want it all to be so perfect. Like some eternal romance. But life's not like that...'

'No, life's hard and bigotted and joyless. At least if you want to make it so.' I stormed back at him. 'God how can you be so stupid!'

It was a word that was much stronger in French – meaning thick or backward. He stared at me his eyes blazing but he said nothing.

'No listen, I'm sorry that's not what I meant...'

He suddenly took his full glass and flung it across the table. I watched in shock as it shattered splashing wine on to the paving stones.

For a moment Jacques towered over me. He looked as if he was about to hit me. 'No, I didn't mean... please Jacques'

He swung round from the table. Grabbing his boots he forced his way through the hedge. I heard the slam of his car door. The wheels spun as he accelerated on the gravel.

------- -- -------

I woke next morning feeling utterly miserable. I remembered that word *'stupid.'* What should I do? Phone him and apologise? For what? For telling him I loved him and wanted to marry him? He hadn't believed me. He thought I only wanted him so I could get the children. I wondered how deep the hurt had gone when that woman Kattie walked out on him. I remembered his own description of himself. *'A poor farmer without enough land to make me respectable.'* What he couldn't see was this didn't matter to me. I loved him as he was. Larger than life and flawed and proud. So horribly proud.

I could see now that when I'd made my pathetic 'proposal', he'd been caught off guard. He'd accused me of trying to 'buy' him. Oh why had I brought up the house and the land? I cringed when I remembered the actual words I'd said *'A great wrong was done to your family and I want to put it right.'* No wonder he'd flown into a rage.

How deep did his anger go? As Deputy Mayor he probably had the power to get Marie exhumed. A shiver ran through my body. It was so horrible, like some hideous nightmare from which I couldn't wake up.

------- -- -------

Over the following days Jacques moved back into his house. He avoided

me. And I did the same. I waited until I heard the Espace leave the farm
before I ventured out.

Two days later I came to a stop outside his gate. He'd tacked the 'A
VENDRE' sign back up again.

I watched him miserably from my window. Shunting stuff around
with his tractor Going back inside for his lonely supper. I felt unbearably
wretched. I'd broken what seemed like an ideal relationship, clumsily and
thoughtlessly.

Why did I always have to mess things up? I thought back over those
years when Oliver hadn't wanted to commit himself. And I came to the
conclusion that like Oliver, Jacques simply didn't love me enough.

------- -- -------

I'd started to wonder if I should sell up myself. My love affair with the
house seemed to have gone sour. What was there to keep me here?

Here I was childless, friendless, virtually penniless. Oliver, Mummy,
Sarah and Jane they'd all been right, I was a fool thinking I could make a life
here.

Chapter Forty Nine

Julia 2009

Just as I thought things had hit rock bottom they got worse. I was driving past the cemetery when I spotted a crane and some heavy earth moving machinery. I slowed to a halt. Some men in fluorescent jackets were checking through the graves in a purposeful manner.

I froze. They were moving towards the Lamulatière sisters' tomb. I couldn't watch. I turned on the ignition and I drove as fast as I could to Bernadette's house.

The minute she opened the door she could tell something was wrong.

'Julia, my dear, come in? What can be the matter?'

'Bernadette. I've seen the diggers in the cemetery?'

'Oh that. Oh dear, it seems all our attempts have come to nothing.'

'But they can't. We have to stop them.'

'I agree. But what can we do. It's been voted.'

With that I burst into tears.

'Julia dear, I didn't think you felt so strongly.'

'They mustn't. It's so gruesome.'

'Julia, what are we talking about? They're only moving the tombstones, not digging up the graves.'

'Are you sure?'

'Yes. They're making way for the park. What did you think they were doing?'

'They're not exhuming anyone?'

'Of course not.'

Suddenly I felt I had to tell her everything.

'You know Jacques Ladier, my neighbour?'

She nodded. 'Of course.'

'We've been having an affair.'

She smiled. 'I wondered why you didn't come and see me so often.'

It all came out in a rush now. About Marie's book and the scene in the convent. And how Jacques' father was adopted and might well be

Marie's illegitimate son?'

Bernadette listened patiently. 'It that's only a theory. You have nothing to prove it.'

'But there could be something, don't you see? Jacques flew into a rage when I told him. He threatened to have Marie's body dug up and DNA tested.'

Bernadette patted my hand. 'Oh surely not.'

'Yes. And when I saw the diggers in the graveyard...'

'Julia listen. It must have been something said in anger. No-one's going to dig anyone up. If they did, I'd be the first to know. I'm on Monsieur Charpentier's committee remember?'

'Yes, I suppose so.'

'Exhumation is a very costly and serious business. You have to go through legal procedures. I'm sure Jacques doesn't intend to do anything of the sort.'

'You don't think so?'

'He wouldn't have the money for a start.'

'He would if he inherited the house.'

'Oh Julia, aren't you getting this a little out of proportion?'

'I don't know. I don't know what to think any more.'

'You were having an affair. You looked happy. I noticed the difference. I wondered who the lucky man was.'

'Was it so obvious?'

'Were you happy?'

'I was. I really was. The thing is, I've never felt quite so safe with anyone before. That sounds stupid when you realise what a beastly temper he's got.'

'Was?'

'Well, I've messed it all up now.'

'I've had a lot of experience with people in my line of business. Love has a way of making things come right in the end. And if it doesn't. Well, it wasn't meant to be.'

'That's a tautology.'

'What's a tautology?'

I smiled through my tears. 'A nasty philosophical term for a very comforting piece of advice.'

Chapter Fifty

Julia 2010

What if I did leave? I cast an eye along my little shelf of 'objets trouvé's'. What would I leave behind to show I'd once lived here? My book perhaps? I opened the drawer where I kept the manuscript pages. There were all the stories I'd finished: Matthias, Jean Mulatier, Suzanne, Amisie, Zavier, Anselme, Marie... I lifted out the folder and found "La Fille Perdue" lying underneath.

I stared at it resentfully. This book had a lot to answer for.

-------- -- -------

Later that day I found a message on my landline. I leapt on it hoping it might be Jacques. But it was only Bernadette. She was inviting me to her birthday party the following Saturday: '*With a load of people. Really casual. No presents please. But if you want to contribute, everyone's bringing a dish of something - so I don't have to cook.*'

I felt a cheered by this, at least Bernadette was a friend. It was something to cling to. I toyed with the idea of baking her a birthday cake. But knowing my luck it would probably be uneatable. I considered buying one from the patisserie. But the baker's cakes were all replendantly French and professional-looking, I could hardly pass one of these off as made by me.

By Saturday afternoon I was feeling a bit desperate when I noticed the cherries in the orchard were reaching the ultimate point of ripeness. They were big and black and juicy, just the thing to fill a basket for dessert.

I took the old ladder with the splayed feet from the barn and climbed up into the tree. It was one of those long warm evenings typical of the time of year. Above, the sky was a brilliant blue, the air was bright with birdsong. I thought pensively that this would have been one of life's magical moments, sitting high up in the branches, gathering fruit from my very own tree. That's if it hadn't been for the view out across Jacques farmyard, reminding me of what I'd lost.

Then I noticed something. The estate agent's sign had gone. A hard lump came in my throat. Jacques must have found a buyer.

It got worse. I saw Jacques come out of the farm and get into his car dressed in clean clothes for once. He was going out. Perhaps he'd found someone new. Someone younger, prettier who wasn't trying to tie him down with a load of foster children.

I climbed down from the tree. Bother Jacques, blast and confound him for spoiling my evening. I was going to pull myself together and enjoy myself in spite of him. I snapped off a big sheaf of cherry leaves and wound them round the basket in a kind of garland. Then I went inside and had a bath and washed my hair and made a real effort with my make-up. I was checking my reflection in the mirror when there was a ring on the front doorbell.

I went down and opened it and did a double-take. Jacques stood there looking oddly formal. He'd had a haircut and his habitual designer stubble had disappeared. I'd never seen him so clean shaven.

What on earth was he doing here?

'You're looking very smart.'

'I felt it was time for a change.' His eyes searched mine, but he didn't take a step closer.

'Look I'm about to go out. It's a friend's birthday. Bernadette's.'

'I'm coming with you,' he said.

'Oh?'

'If I may?'

'Of course. It's just casual. I'm sure she won't mind.'

'Shall we go then?'

Dumbfounded, I went and got my basket and followed him to the car. He opened the door for me. I climbed in. As he was about to close the door I held it open. 'Does this mean I'm forgiven?'

'For?'

'For asking you to marry me, I suppose?'

'Most women would have waited to be asked first,' he said closing the door firmly. My mind was racing. What was going on? We drove in silence through Deneville. Things I wanted to say kept surfacing in my mind. But I stopped each in its tracks. I'd learned my lesson. I'd let him make the first move. A glance at his face didn't give anything away. He turned the car in through the gates of Chapeau Blanc.

There was a row of nice clean respectable cars parked in front of the house. Jacques lined up the dented and manure-spattered Espace alongside them and came round to my side and opened the door for me.

Bernadette was standing on her front steps, greeting a bunch of guests who had arrived shortly before us. They turned at the sound and even possibly the smell of the Espace, obviously intrigued to see who would get out.

As soon as she caught sight of me, Bernadette hurried down the steps and kissed me on both cheeks, murmuring admiring comments about my basket of cherries.

'I've brought Jacques, I hope that's all right,' I said.

'But of course. I'm so pleased you could come,' replied Bernadette with real warmth.

I watched as Jacques shook hands with her. And then in turn was introduced to the guests on the steps. He followed Bernadette as she walked across the room and we were introduced to each of the people inside. Jacques was all politeness, he was on his best behaviour.

I took Bernadette aside. 'I hope you don't mind. He kind of insisted on coming.'

'But Julia. I invited him,' said Bernadette.

'I didn't know you knew him.'

'Only professionally. I tried to help him with a personal problem.' She squeezed my arm conspiratorially: 'He's a fine man, Julia.'

I searched Bernadette's face. 'What kind of problem?'

'My lips are sealed. Professional secrecy,' she said.

I looked across the room to where Jacques was talking in a relaxed manner with a fellow of a certain age dressed in a formal grey suit. This was Jacques - the man who couldn't stand the bourgeoisie, remember? But tonight he was making small talk, blending himself in for godsake. I watched suspiciously as he hovered by the fireplace. He was standing beneath the picture of the two brothers. One of whom I was certain was my chevalier - Jean Mulatier de la Grolière.

And then suddenly it hit me like a bolt out of the blue. Jacques' eyes were a different colour but there was something in the shape of his chin, the slight tilt of the mouth as he smiled. Jean Mulatier de la Grolière. If my supposition was right Jacques would be his direct descendant - on the wrong side of the blanket of course. Jacques Ladier, the great socialist - how galling it would be for him to discover he was actually one of the bourgeoisie himself. I suppressed the impulse to gloat, but a smile surfaced anyway.

Jacques came over to me. 'What's so funny?'

'I've just realised who you remind me of.'

'Oh? Who?'

'I'm not sure if you'll like this.'

'Why not?'

'Because you can't stand the bourgeoisie.'

'I never said that.'

'You made it pretty obvious. Until tonight that is.'

'Bernadette invited me.'

'I didn't know you knew her.'

'We met professionally.'

'Professionally... Why? What about?'

Jacques glanced out of the window. 'Is that a lime tree out there, or a sycamore?'

'I've no idea, why?'

'Let's take a closer look.'

I followed him outside. He was behaving in a very odd fashion.

It was a lime tree. It's boughs untrained swept almost to the ground. Underneath, we were surrounded by a living canopy of green. At one point a branch bent invitingly, providing a kind of seat. Jacques drew me down beside him.

' I went to ask her...' he paused and took my hand and leaned very close. 'What I would have to do to adopt a child.'

I stared at him in disbelief. 'And?'

The slightest breeze sighed through the lime.

'She advised me to find a good woman and marry her.'

Chapter Fifty One

Julia – 2019 - ten years later

There had been a winter gale of almost tornado force. The sequoia had finally met its end. The topmost branches had been rent from the trunk. We'd hired a professional woodcutter to fell it.

I climbed the creamy spiral stairs into the attic. I'd come to close the shutters, those shutters that still had Marie and Louise's names on them, I wouldn't allow Jacques to paint over them. I couldn't hear their voices any more. Or any of the past inhabitants, for that matter. It was as though they'd retired into the shadows or discreetly slipped away. But they were all there in my book. Oliver had published in the end. He'd actually been quite complimentary. He called it a new 'genre' - 'From Fact to Fiction', some such nonsense.

These days the house was filled with different sounds: laughter, shouts and quarrels, pop music, dogs barking - the raucous noise of living people. Today it was the moan and whine of the chainsaw that permeated it.

The death of the tree had been inevitable. We'd watched its slow decline as it turned from healthy green to russet. The dryness spread inwards from the tips of the branches, leaving ragged skeletons that showered us with needles whenever we passed underneath. As the woodman said kindly - its time had come.

The chainsaw had ceased for a blessed moment and I found the fellow leaning in through the attic door.

'Don't you want to see it come down? We're just about through. It'll be quite a spectacle.'

I shook my head, 'No, you go ahead.'

But I heard it fall. There was a gargantuan groan, followed by a thud that shook the house. It was done.

I found it hard to go out in the park for the next few days as they worked at dismembering its great body. The woodman warned us that we'd have to wait for a still day to burn it. When that day came the flames rose higher than La Mulatière. The resinous sap went off like pistol shots. The fire burned for three full days. At night the flames lit up the entire park.

By the end of the week all that was left was the great oval expanse of stump which had recorded every summer and every winter, each rainfall and frost, every drought and every deluge, in its rings - going back to that providential year of 1758 when the house was built.

The stump remained at the far end of the garden, flat and permanent, shaped like a great wooden 'O'. It became, in turn, a circus rink... a stage... a picnic place... a bandstand... a fort... a spaceship or a pirate's galleon - whatever took the children's fancy. Michel, Hussain, Marie-Louise, Corinne, Bernadette, Carlos, Mireille... So many children grew up at La Mulatière.

If you've enjoyed this book, you might like:

'How to Knit an Opera' by Chloë Rayban

ISBN 978-1-326-08622-0

Available in paperback from: www.lulu.com

It is the story of Opera Loki - the opera company Chloe and her husband set up at their home La Mulatière - which now has a thriving season in chateaux in France, as well as in London and other UK venues.

Printed in Great Britain
by Amazon